YOU ARE NOT ALONE IN THIS

NICHELLE KOVACHEFF

Trade Paperback ISBN 978 1 7387403 2 1
eBook ISBN 978 1 7387403 3 8

ONE

Grace is hunched over, balancing a textbook and a notebook on her knees with a pen in her hand. Against the frigid metal bench, her bum has gone numb.

There's a group of parents sitting together a bit farther down in the community hockey arena. They erupt in a series of outcries: "That's bullshit!" "Come on, Ref!" "You have got to be kidding me!" Grace tries to block them out to concentrate. She goes through the muscles in the human leg, the tendons and ligaments. Picturing them in her mind. As the line changes, Alex comes out onto the ice, and Grace looks up to watch him.

A young scout from the competitive league is there too, sitting apart from the parents. He cups his hands together and blows into them, annoyed that he forgot his gloves, and then continues to doodle next to the few notes he's jotted down for the Sunday night games. All in all, the weekend hasn't been a total bust. You never know with these smaller towns. He has four solid names and two maybes. But if he's honest with himself, he probably wouldn't be able to tell the kids apart if he saw them on the ice right now. Not a good sign. He'll watch for ten more minutes, make sure he's seen every kid play, then get into his nice warm—

A kid—average size, a bit scrawny perhaps—steals the puck off a defender and starts to take it down the ice. He glances to his left and right, looking for someone to pass to, but no one is there. No one can keep up with him. He pulls his stick back to shoot but then shifts his weight and flicks it right over the goalie's shoulder.

Hol-y shit.

A few of the parents glance at the scout, and he can see it in their eyes. They're saying, *Yeah,* that *kid.* He realizes his mouth is open and closes it.

Grace is waiting for Alex in the hallway outside the locker room. She shuts her eyes and leans against the wall, resting on the bulge of her backpack. Textbooks and homework assignments that she'll have to type up on the school library computer tomorrow. There is Gatorade, dry ice, and sweat in the air, blades on ice, chatter, and laughter. She attempts to stifle a yawn, lifting the back of her hand to her mouth. It's been a long weekend.

The scout comes out of the bathroom, and the parents descend on him, but there is only one person he wants to speak with.

"Excuse me, sir," one of the moms says as they approach him.

"Could you spare a second?" a dad cuts across her.

Grace opens her eyes, bracing herself.

"Yeah, absolutely," the scout says. "But before we talk, is anyone here with Alex Saint?"

Grace doesn't move, not one inch, but one of the parents nods at her.

"Hello, miss." The scout approaches her and notes that she can't be more than sixteen or seventeen. She glances at him like she's trying to figure out the quickest way to get rid of him. Must be a sister, he decides, in the teenage angst phase where she doesn't like to interact with people or be helpful in any way.

"Hi," she says, standing up straight. She's medium height, with dark wavy hair and tired brown eyes. Beneath the reticence and annoyance, she's quite pretty.

The scout cocks his head. "Do you know how good that boy is?"

"Yes," she says. "He's very good."

"I'm not the first one," he says.

The girl shakes her head. Most parents beg to have their kids go up a level. It's them he needs to speak with. "Are your parents here? Picking you guys up, by any chance?"

She ignores this question entirely, except for a slight huff of exasperation.

Grace is relieved when Alex exits the dressing room, always the first kid out. He never keeps her waiting. His dark curly hair is matted down from his helmet, and his cheeks are rosy. Grace shifts her backpack and takes one of his secondhand bags, slinging it over her shoulder. Much to Grace's dismay, the scout follows them outside into the bitterly cold parking lot.

The snow cuts through the beams from the streetlights. Large, thick flakes that cling to her face and dissolve. Grace stops and turns to look at the scout, careful to balance the bags on each shoulder. Alex continues to the stop. She knows that this man, just a few years older than her, is doing his job. Watching nine-year-olds play hockey, finding ones to funnel into the competitive league, and Alex is too obvious a player not to pursue. But she doesn't have the time or the energy to deal with him right now. How to explain that they simply cannot afford it. The competitive league fees, the new equipment he would need, the tournament hotels. But above all, the time they would need to commit. Instead, she says, "I'm sorry, I can't talk. We're gonna miss our bus."

"That kid—I've never seen someone his age with talent like that. Those hands, his skating ability. He doesn't belong here." He gestures to the arena. "Can't you see that? He must be bored out of his mind."

That strikes a chord with Grace.

"Call me." He hands her his card.

Grace and Alex sit at the front of the bus with his bags at their feet. It's too dark and blustery to make out any shapes through the window.

"What do you think?" she asks. "You want to go up a couple of levels?"

Alex shrugs. "It would be pretty expensive."

"What if money wasn't a factor?"

He picks at the strap of his bag. "Money is always a factor."

"Al."

"I love to play."

"The kids will be bigger, faster. It'll be a contact league."

Alex glances at her. "I'm pretty fast too."

She grins. "I know you are." She tries to sound casual, not pained, as she says, "If you want this, I'll do my best to make it happen."

Two

Ten Years Later

It's a brisk autumn morning as Grace Lawrence walks the well-known path to work. The leaves on the trees are golden around the edges, and those at her feet emit a satisfying crunch when she steps on them. In the lobby of Oakwood, a high-end nursing home, she greets the receptionist, a middle-aged woman who has an uncanny ability to remember the names of all the residents, staff, and many family members.

"Did you walk here?" Donna asks, peering over her computer.

"I did. Beautiful day."

"Good for you."

There's the fading scent of polish on the wood floors. She clips her name tag onto the pocket of her purple scrubs and walks past the elevators to the stairs.

Tony is sitting up in bed, wearing silk pajamas, the gold ones his son brought him back from China. His wiry gray hair sticks out at all angles. On Grace's arrival, he reaches for his thick-rimmed glasses.

"Good morning," Grace says.

He lowers the bar on his bed.

"Hold on a sec," she says. "I want to check a couple of things first."

"Grace."

She follows his finger to the calendar next to his wide-screen TV. "Is Tony Junior coming today? Well then, we shall have to get you spiffed up." She reaches into his closet for a pressed shirt and a pair of pants, then helps him into his wheelchair and glides him into the bathroom.

Half an hour later, Tony is dressed, his damp hair is combed over, and his nails are clipped back. She helps him into his plaid armchair, and he takes her hand. "Thank you, Grace," he says, and she smiles back at him.

Through the crack in the door, she catches a glimpse of Riley Carlsen, her coworker and friend, flustered and striding down the hall. Grace goes out to her. "Hey, everything all right?"

Riley whips around but doesn't stop moving. "Carl's gone." She holds up Carl's sensor bracelets.

"Shit," Grace says. She follows Riley into the stairwell, and they descend the four floors, going through the door and into the lobby.

Will, a police officer in his late twenties, is standing at the reception desk with Carl, who is confused and agitated. He has dementia and technically shouldn't even be at Oakwood, but his family are generous donors.

"Oh, thank God," Riley says under her breath. She turns to Will. "We really appreciate you bringing him back again. I honestly have no idea how he gets out of these things." She puts the sensor bracelets back on Carl, tightening them around his wrists.

Will cups the back of his neck and turns toward Grace. "I hate to tell you this, but the boss says—and this is off the record—if he goes missing again, we're not searching for him. Does he have someone in his family who could?"

"They don't really like him," Grace says in a low voice so that Donna can't hear her. Not to mention the fact that they're also incredibly difficult to deal with.

Will is distracted, glancing shyly at Riley, who is now crouched down beside an elderly woman in a wheelchair. Her short blonde hair is wild today.

"There are a few of us nurses going out for drinks this Friday. Would you like to join us?" Grace asks Will.

"Oh, I don't know. I've got—where are you going?"

"It's the bar with the red neon... the one that's kind of dark inside..."

"Moby Dick's," Riley says, standing.

"Oh, okay." Will nods. "Yeah. Maybe."

Riley and Grace are slowly climbing the stairs with Carl between them. He is a sinewy man, stubborn in his movements and strong when agitated.

"You realize you have to come out with us now, right?" Riley says. Grace looks across Carl at her. "To Moby Dick's."

Grace is taken aback. "I didn't invite him for me. I thought, you know, for you."

"Me?"

"Every time Carl disappears, Will brings him back," Grace says. "He's your patient; it's not a coincidence."

Riley glances at Grace with an expression she can't read. "I know that you don't go out much." That was generous. Grace never went out. "But you can't just invite someone and then not go. We'll go together; it'll be fun."

Grace makes a noncommittal noise. What has she gotten herself into?

Back on the fourth floor, the television in Harry's room is booming, and Grace swoops in, trying to keep her composure. His hearing aids are on his bedside table, and she picks them up. "Harry," she says loudly. "You need to wear these. You can't listen to this—"

"Here's an update on what's going on in the hockey world," a voice at top volume says. Clips of Alex come onto the screen, and Grace freezes. He's skating with children at a charity event, standing with his teammates around the Stanley Cup, bowing his head as the gold medal is placed around his neck at the Olympics. Then there's the famous clip, the one where he makes a miraculous pass to his teammate who scores and wins the Stanley Cup final in overtime. It's a close-up in slow motion. He's about to whip off his helmet when Grace lunges for the remote to change the channel.

Before she can, the image switches to a broadcaster sitting at her desk. "Many were shocked when Alex Saint was accused of sexual assault. There will be a press conference today at five p.m. to address the allegation—"

A shot of adrenaline goes through Grace as she drops the remote and backs out of the room. Heat rises to the surface of her body, and she breaks into a sweat as she makes her way down the hall. Sexual assault. *Alex.* It didn't make any sense. He couldn't have. It isn't possible. He just . . . couldn't have.

She tries to calm herself as she quietly enters Annie's room, shutting the door gently behind her. Annie is sleeping, her hearing aids on her bedside table. Grace picks up Annie's phone and takes it with her into the adjoining private bath.

She usually enjoys having to call Daniel, but not today. Today, for the first time in years, she is nervous.

Daniel is sitting at a large oak desk with freshly cut flowers on the glass coffee table in front of him. A long gray couch runs along the far wall. He has the smallest office of any partner at the firm, and he prefers it that way. He doesn't like too much space, to get too comfortable.

He's on the phone, talking to another lawyer. With his elbow on the desk, he presses his fingertips to his forehead. "Are you saying that you cannot or you will not?" he asks, wanting to get to the point. His phone buzzes, and he glances at it. "Okay, great. I'll have the paperwork drawn up. Yep. Sounds good. Goodbye." He switches calls. "Nan?" There's silence. It could've been an accidental dial. Wouldn't be the first time.

"No, it's me, Grace."

"Oh," he says. Then, "How are you?"

A young timid office helper knocks on Daniel's door, and he waves her in. Eager to please, she is still trying to finesse her timing. Daniel points to a place on his desk and nods his thanks.

"I'm fine," Grace says, but her voice is tight. "Do you follow hockey?"

"It's not my sport of choice."

"Did you hear about the incident with Alex Saint?"

"I follow the news."

"Right. Would you be able to give him legal counsel?"

Daniel sits back in his chair. Give Alex Saint legal counsel? One of the best players in the NHL. If he hadn't known Grace's disposition better, he might've thought this was some kind of a joke. He chooses his next words carefully. "The team must have lawyers, no? Wouldn't he be set up with one of them? This isn't exactly my area of expertise." He wants to know more. Why this is so important to her. Every time he has tried to venture into topics involving her personal life, or more specifically her past, she has deflected or given him surface-level answers.

"I'm not sure if the team has lawyers for this sort of thing or how all this legal stuff works," she says. "But from what I hear, you're very good at your job, and I was hoping that maybe you could look into this."

"Grace, I really appreciate everything you do for Annie—"

"I'm not trying to leverage you, Daniel." There's a strain in Grace's voice he's never heard before. "It won't change how I care for your grandmother. I'll pay you for your work, but if you don't want to do it, that's fine."

His brow furrows. Then he asks the only question that really matters to him. "How do you know this kid?"

Grace is sitting on the edge of the bathtub, trying to keep her voice even and not let the desperation slip through. "We"—she squeezes her eyes shut—"lived in a home together when we were kids." There's a long pause, and in that moment she regrets having called him. This was a mistake. It's why she didn't ask people for help.

"Get me his contact info. I'll see what I can do," he says.

"Thank you. I—thank you." She hangs up.

She pulls her cell phone out of her pocket and searches through her contacts for a number she hasn't used in almost a decade. One she's not even sure is still in service. Her thumb hovers between the call icon and the text icon. Remembering who she's dealing with, a woman who is as direct as she is efficient, she taps out a text.

Hi Sarah, it's Grace. Would you mind sending me Alex's cell phone number?

Grace holds the phone in her palm and tries to think of a plan B, another way to get his contact information if Sarah's number has changed. Her phone lights up before she even has time to worry.

Hi Grace. It's nice to hear from you. Hope you're well. I'll forward you his contact information.

Thank you, Sarah. I appreciate that.

Grace sends the number to Daniel and comes out of the bathroom. Annie snorts awake and slides her hearing aids in.

"Were you on the phone?" It's not an accusation. Grace has spoken to Daniel on the phone many times over the years. Explaining drugs, medication changes, hearing aid options, and culinary upgrades Annie could get. He and his siblings were by far the easiest people she had ever dealt with.

"Yeah, Daniel was checking in." Grace puts Annie's phone back on the bedside table.

"He's coming to visit me this weekend."

"Is he?"

"I'd really like for you to meet him, Grace. You'd like him."

"I'm sure I would." Grace opens the blinds, careful not to knock over the family photos and the plants on the sill, and then helps Annie sit up. She counts out her pills and passes Annie's water glass to her. "What time will he be here on Friday?" she asks. She definitely wants to avoid seeing him. The chance of meeting him always makes her nervous, but the possibility has become more and more likely as Annie's mobility decreases. Her grandchildren no longer take her for weekend getaways like they used to. Instead, they visit with her here at the home.

Annie points to the calendar on her bedside table. "What does that say?"

Grace leans in. "Five." Relief. "I'm afraid I'll miss him. I'm done at four."

Three days later Annie is sitting up in her bed with her reading glasses partway down her nose and a pen in her hand. The newspaper's crossword is folded over in front of her, and she holds the phone to her ear with her other hand.

"No, it's not Caesar; it's shorter," Annie says. She must be speaking with Eric or Daniel. Grace hopes it's Eric, wanting to delay the inevitable. "Morning, Grace. Hmm? My grandson wants to talk to you." She holds the phone out.

Dang.

Grace takes the phone from her and goes over to the window, trying to breathe normally.

"Hello," she says, bracing herself.

The sleeves of Daniel's light-blue collared shirt are rolled up his forearms. He has a newspaper splayed out over his desk with the crossword in front of him. "I spoke to Alex for a while," he says. "I don't think he did it."

Grace shuts her eyes, relieved that he believes that too. "It's not in his nature." Then she forces herself to ask, "How was he?"

"He was stressed, but we had a good chat, and I laid out the different courses of action he can take going forward." He pauses. "He asked how you were doing. I hadn't realized you guys haven't spoken in a while other than some notes you used to send him."

Grace feels slightly nauseous, and she has to fight to get the words out. "I appreciate you doing that, Daniel," she says. "Let me know what I owe you. I'll e-transfer you the money or send it however you want it."

"My going rate would pay for a family vacation."

"Well, I don't go on vacation."

"I'm not going to charge you, Grace."

"Please, Daniel. I don't want Alex to have to pay for this, not with everything he must be going through. You have to charge *me*."

"I'm not charging either of you."

That didn't make any sense. "What?"

Daniel's assistant, Nora, comes to stand in the doorway, signaling him. "I gotta go. Oh, and tell Nan, twelve down is Nero." He hangs up before she can argue anymore.

Grace puts Annie's phone back on her bedside table. "He had to go, but he said to tell you twelve down is—"

"Nero," Annie says. "Done that section." Grace moves behind Annie, but she tenses, her frail hands clutching the small desk in front of her. "I don't want to go to the dining room."

"Annie, you can't stay in here all day. Tony will be there. You like talking to him."

"Judy put me next to Carl yesterday."

"I'm not going to put you next to Carl."

Nora packs Daniel's laptop and chargers into his smaller travel bag, then stands next to his wheelie suitcase while he unrolls his sleeves and puts his suit jacket on.

Blessed with good genetics and the inability to sit still for long periods of time, he had the lean, muscled body of someone who was constantly in motion but never worked out. His skin was fair, and he had electric blue eyes paired with dark hair that was cut short but that curled a bit if allowed to grow.

It took some time for her to understand the many nuances of Daniel Hurley. The way he tackled mammoth tasks head-on. Every morning he greeting her with a smile, the kind that reached the eyes, unlike most other partners. He was appreciative, thanking her for even small tasks. He shielded her from angry clients, redirecting their aggression when they yelled at her. If she ever had a question or concern, he was approachable and made time for her, and soon she started to thrive in her role. Senior partners had offered her pay raises and memberships at their clubs in an attempt to get her to work for them, but that didn't entice her. She knew their personalities too well. After long hours at the firm, she had seen them at their best but most importantly at their worst. And Daniel never crossed the line. He was never inappropriate or pushy.

At the staff Christmas parties and galas, he never overindulged, never became glassy eyed, irritating, or outlandish like the many others who used these nights to let loose. He was adept at engaging others in topics that interested them and then politely slipping from that conversation and onto the next. He could easily converse with almost anyone, and it took her a while to realize that although he was quite candid, he gave little of himself away. Appearing calm and casual on the surface, there was a constant current that pulled at him.

It was the first time that she overhead him talking to his sister, Beth, that she discovered there was another side to Daniel. The charm he exuded around the office was a layer. Something that could be shed. With his family he was open, genuine, kind, and frustrated. These were the people he truly cared about. These were the ones who he dug into. She could tell if he was talking to one of them the moment she walked into his office by the way he eased back in his chair and focused his attention on the call. The way his eyes would set.

A couple of years ago as she walked in, she heard a woman's voice as he was saying goodbye.

"How's Beth?" she had said conversationally.

"That was my nan's nurse, actually."

Daniel scans his desk one last time.

"I've emailed you the flight details, and your wallet's in here." Nora taps the side pouch of the small bag. "I'm glad you're taking the weekend off."

"Everyone takes the weekend off."

"That usually means that they don't come into the office, that they don't work."

The young timid office helper comes into the room and passes Daniel a file. He slides it into the smaller bag with his laptop.

"What is that?" Nora points accusingly at the file.

"I have one meeting, scheduled tonight."

Nora shakes her head as the woman leaves the room. "Daniel, I cleared your calendar for the weekend, the whole weekend, including Friday. I literally had to move a mountain to do it."

"And I appreciate that. But face-to-face goes a long way."

"Kiliman-fucking-jaro." Nora didn't speak to any of the other partners in this way, but she also didn't like the other partners nearly as much. She didn't want him to burn out. Not that it seemed possible. But three days earlier, Daniel had suddenly left the office, only to arrive back that very morning. She'd had to reschedule his meetings into next week, which was already jam-packed.

"I'm saving the company money," he says. "I won't have to fly out again."

Nora studies him, her eyes narrow. There's something he isn't telling her. He's always been discreet, but he also trusted her. It must've been something big and urgent that he'd had to leave for. Something *very* confidential.

It suddenly dawns on her—interviews. Why else would he not have told her?

"Have a good weekend," he says. "I'll see you Monday."

THREE

Nine Years Earlier

Grace unlocks the front door of May's house. Her backpack is pulling on her shoulders, and one of her textbooks is sticking into her spine. The bottom has thinned, and Grace hopes it can get her through to the summer when she can pick up more shifts at the diner.

She sees the faint glow of the TV from the living room.

The house was once well kept and cared for but has since fallen into disrepair. Little things like the light bulbs going out, a kitchen cabinet panel off-kilter, the dishwasher stuck on the drying cycle, the vacuum cleaner with no suction, the toilet on the main floor constantly running so they had to close the pipe to that bathroom. Little things that added up, putting more on Grace's plate than she could handle. Now she does her best to keep it neat and tidy, especially when the social workers come for their checks, and hopes they won't have to use the bathroom.

She takes her boots off and sets her backpack on the floor but leaves her coat on. Going into the kitchen, she warms up some leftover Kraft dinner and hot dogs. Thankfully, it's something May doesn't like to eat, so she always knows it will be there. May is only fifty-eight but moves around the house like she's eighty-eight, making seizing, aching sounds as she goes from room to room or sits back in her armchair to settle into her TV shows for the evening.

Grace is halfway through her dinner when May shuffles into the kitchen. She must want something. A little favor to ask of Grace.

"I left you the Kraft dinner," May says as if it's a thoughtful gesture. She puts a box of hair dye on the table and slides it toward Grace.

As May stands in front of her, all Grace can think of is the fifty dollars May gave her for the week. Fifty. No amount of coupon cutting and grocery store hopping could cover them.

May receives $4,000 each month from the government for Grace and Alex. Grace becomes physically ill thinking of how May wastes the money and all the things she could do with it. The food, clothes, books, and hockey equipment she could buy. If she was able to manage it, she would easily have enough left over to put away for school. But for now, all she can focus on is the basics. Food, toothpaste, shampoo, bus tokens. All for fifty dollars.

Grace's chest tightens. "I'll do it tomorrow," she says without looking up at this woman, for whom the words *manipulation* and *deceit* wouldn't even begin to describe. The only reason she touches May's hair is for the check-ins with the social workers. Even as the house falls into disarray, May continues to pride herself on her appearance, wearing pastel-colored tops and matching bottoms. She is soft-spoken and has a practiced smile when the social workers ask their questions, coming across as kind and maternal. During these visits, Grace does her best to battle the tension that seizes her body when she enters May's house, forcing herself to smile and nod along.

May leaves the package on the table. "Tomorrow then."

"May," Grace says, lifting her eyes. "I need more money."

May pauses in the doorway, her back to Grace. "I've given you enough."

Grace has already cut every corner there is. "Fifty dollars is not—"

"It's plenty," May says and shuffles back to her chair in front of the TV.

Grace massages her temple with the pads of her fingers and realizes that she's holding her breath. She's finding more and more that she has to remind herself to breathe when she's in this house. And to breathe evenly or she gets these pangs through her ribs.

She forces down the last of the Kraft dinner and leaves to meet Alex at the arena.

On the first day of grade twelve, Grace's English class is arranged into two horseshoes. A bigger outer one and a smaller one. She takes a seat in the middle of the smaller one, facing the blackboard. She's wearing a tie-dyed T-shirt that she made at day camp two years ago and has the light glow of a summer's tan. With her dark hair scrunchied up in a high ponytail, she sits with her arms crossed in front of her, leaned back in her chair, ready to get through this day.

Jackson Martin walks into class just after the bell with his bag slung over his shoulder and makes his way to the only seat left. The one next to Grace. Their English teacher is at the blackboard writing out a list of books for them to choose from for their end-of-semester reports, and the kids around Grace are chatting. Jackson is part of the twenty or so popular kids in her grade, some of whom call her Greasy Grace, so when he sits down next to her and pulls out his binder, she does not acknowledge him.

"Hey." He snaps the rings of his binder open and threads the holes of their course syllabus through it. "You have a good summer?"

"It was fine," she says, her arms still crossed, staring straight ahead.

"I'm Jackson, by the way. Jackson—"

"I know who you are, Jackson Martin." The intensity with which she says this surprises her, but it's ridiculous that he would introduce himself. Everyone knows who he is. Then she realizes that maybe he doesn't know who she is. "I'm Grace—"

"Grace Lawrence," he says with a nod. "I saw you playing tennis with your brother a few times this summer. You can see the courts from my backyard." Grace knows the houses. They're large custom-built homes with beautiful gardens and pools with cabanas and patio setups. When she doesn't respond, he presses on. "You guys were pretty good. I almost came out to join you."

She looks at him then. His brown hair is ruffled like he's just gotten out of bed, and one side of his collared T-shirt is up. He's lean, and at just over six feet, he's the shortest player on their school volleyball team. There is a warmth in his eyes that is disarming.

Mr. Connors, the volleyball coach and biology teacher, comes into the class. He nods at their English teacher as he heads into the center of the horseshoe toward them. "Jackson, you got your forms?" he says.

"Sorry, Coach. Meant to bring them by your office," Jackson says, rooting around in his bag.

"Good summer, Grace?" Mr. Connors asks.

She gives him a small smile. "Yeah."

She had taken grade twelve biology in grade eleven, wanting to space out her course load knowing that the universities would weigh her math and science classes more heavily when deciding. At this rate, she knew she was going to get into nursing school. Her grades had always been pretty good. But it was the scholarships she was after now. If she was able to get through this semester with a ninety average, she would be eligible for an $8,000 scholarship to the school she wanted. The one closest to May's house.

Near the end of the semester, Mr. Connors had been walking up and down the rows of desks when he paused behind Grace. She had the university brochure out in front of her, reading it, instead of learning about the different types of diabetes like she was supposed to, with her target number circled. Embarrassed, she slid the brochure from her desk and onto her lap. Mr. Connors continued walking.

When she wrote the final exam on a Monday morning, she had just come off working two doubles at the diner. She hadn't reviewed her notes properly, and she knew with a sinking feeling in her stomach that although she would do fine, it was no ninety. Coming to pick her exam up a week later, she joined the group of students crowded around Mr. Connors's desk as he passed them out. Finally, Grace came forward, her head bowed. Mr. Connors handed it to her, rolling it inward to keep the mark private. As Grace walked out of the class, she opened the paper, just a tiny bit, to glance at the top corner, her chest tight.

There was a 90 circled in black.

She turned back to look at Mr. Connors. He just nodded at her and then passed a rolled exam to the next student.

"Here you go." Jackson gives his form to Mr. Connors, who takes it and leaves.

After a moment Grace says, "We were thinking of playing again on Thursday night, around six thirty."

"Yeah? I'll see if my sister, Lettie, is free, and maybe we could do doubles," he says. "If it's a nice night, bring your swimsuits. I'll turn the heat up in the pool."

"Your parents won't mind?" Grace asks. She couldn't even imagine inviting someone to her house so nonchalantly.

"My parents?" he says. "Why would they care?"

"Grace Lawrence," their English teacher says, scanning her clipboard from the front of the class, her speckled glasses perched near the tip of her nose. "You can't sign up as a single for the book report. You need a partner."

Grace looks to the sides of the horseshoe, but everyone lowers their eyes to their desks.

Jackson throws up a finger. "Sign me up with Grace." As their teacher writes on the clipboard, he whispers, "You better pull your weight, Lawrence."

She glances at him with indignation, but it's immediately doused by his grin, which crinkles slightly around his eyes. She grins too, finally lowering her crossed arms.

After that day she never hears Greasy Grace uttered in the hallways of her high school again.

It's an unseasonably warm fall, and they're basking in the sun of their last weekend together by the pool. Alex's hockey and Jackson's volleyball games start up next weekend, but for now Alex and Lettie are straddling inflatable logs, trying to knock each other off with giant pool noodles.

Grace pulls herself over the ledge of the pool and lays back on the sun-drenched concrete, her feet dangling in the water. Shutting her eyes, she lets herself be enveloped by the cocoon of warmth, the voices drifting over her. A shadow covers her face, and she cups her hand over her eyes as she turns her head.

"You want to come with me to Brooke's tonight?" Jackson asks, standing next to her. "There are a bunch of people going."

Grace cringes and shakes her head. Jackson lets out a sigh, his hands on his hips, his shoulders dropping. Grace pushes herself up and joins him on the lounge chairs. His bathing suit bottoms are a rainbow of colors. This is a different Jackson from the one at school. They'd spent so much time together over the past few weeks that she'd started to notice little things about him. Parts of him that endeared him to her. Like how he rubbed his bicep when he was nervous or how he teased his sister but never put her down. She didn't realize how fulfilling it was to have a friend until she met Jackson. How much someone's mere presence in her life could bring her so much joy.

"May I ask, why do you hang out with them? You don't seem to enjoy it all that much," she says.

He shrugs. "We've always been around each other. Our families are all interconnected. Our parents work together or are on boards together. Most of us went to the same preschool."

"Do you enjoy it, though?"

"I enjoy aspects of it. Why don't you come? *You* might enjoy yourself."

"I'm sorry, Jackson, but Brooke's always been a bitch to me."

He rests his head back against the lounge chair. "All right. Fair enough."

"Grace! Alex!" Jackson's mom yells from inside the house, giving her a start.

Grace straightens, perching herself on the end of her chair. "Yeah?" she calls back.

"Chicken burger or hamburger?"

Alex's noodle goes still. He's watching Grace, waiting for her response. "Um, neither. We should be heading out, actually." She gets to her feet.

Alex slips off his log and swims to the side of the pool.

"Are you a vegetarian?" his mom calls, standing at the screen now.

"No!" Grace yells back, rolling her towel and shoving it into her bag. There's a smile pulling at the corner of Jackson's lips as he gazes up at her from his recliner. "What?" Grace says.

"Why are you so panicky?" Jackson says, reaching above him and wrapping his arms over the top of the lounger.

"I'm not panicky. I'm just . . . we just don't want to overstay our welcome."

"Is that what this is about?" He turns his head toward the house and addresses his mother. "Grace will have a chicken burger, and Alex will have a hamburger."

Last week, Jackson, Lettie, and Alex had stopped by the diner to eat with Grace while she was on break. And he had remembered their order.

Grace puts her T-shirt on over her swimsuit. "Where are you going?" Jackson asks as she's buttoning her shorts.

"To help your mom," she says.

Alex drags his towel over his arms and legs and follows Grace into the house. Jackson's mother is pulling food from the fridge, putting condiments, tomatoes, lettuce, and cheese on the granite island.

"I can set the table," Grace says, opening one drawer and then another to find the utensils.

Alex slides the cutting board toward him. "You want me to slice the tomato and cheese?" he asks.

Jackson's mother stares at him for a moment, then says, "That would be wonderful. Thank you." And to Grace, "We'll eat outside."

Lettie comes into the kitchen, taking the napkins and glasses from her mom's hands, and Jackson grabs the plate of burgers.

"Well, I'll be," his mother mutters under her breath as Jackson opens the screen door with his foot.

Grace sets a pitcher of lemonade down next to the condiments on the table and joins Jackson by the barbecue.

"So you've officially become my mom's favorite," he says.

She gives him a sidelong glance, and he playfully nudges her with his shoulder.

After dinner, ice-cream sundaes, and a few rounds of cards, Jackson goes upstairs and changes into a collared shirt and khakis.

"You sure you don't want to come?" he says to Grace.

She nods. "Thanks so much for dinner."

She and Alex get their bikes from the side of the house. The neighborhood streets are quiet. The sky is pink and the clouds are fluffy. It's that time of night when everything is still and beautiful.

"That was fun," Alex says, biking up alongside her.

"It was. They're a nice family."

"Yeah," he says. Then, "Why didn't you go with Jackson to that girl's house?"

"They're not really my crowd. The girls are all made up and not the easiest to talk to, and some of the guys are part Neanderthal. Either way, this outfit wouldn't have cut it."

As they approach their house, Grace's stomach drops. Over the past few weeks, she's had a lot of fun, but she hasn't kept up with her chores. Even in this light, their lawn looks terrible. Overgrown and weedy. Their reel mower is so rusty, she doubts it will get through the grass, but if she's going to try it, now is the perfect time, just as it's getting dark so that none of the neighbors can see. They swing their legs over their bikes and tuck them up against the wall of the garage.

Alex turns to her. "I don't think Jackson would've given a crap what you wore. He likes you for you."

She pauses with her hand resting on the handlebar of the mower as Alex grabs a bucket and the weeder. Now that was a statement that stuck with her.

Four

Eight Years Earlier

The buzzer sounds, reverberating against the walls of the arena, signaling the end of the hockey game. Outside the dressing room, parents wait for their sons, dissecting the game in animated conversation.

Sarah is flipping through her notes, running her manicured nail down the column of names, her tennis bracelet hanging from her wrist. With glossy blonde hair and a keen sense of organization, her finger stops. She scans the hockey parents until her eyes fall on Grace, who is, as usual, standing alone against the wall reading a tome.

Sarah walks up to her. "Hi there."

Grace glances at her, shifting her textbook. "Hi."

"I'm Sarah Bedard, Ethan's mom. I noticed that you weren't at the hotel last night."

"We're staying at the motel down the street."

"Wouldn't it be easier for you guys to be at the hotel?" Sarah says. "And easier for the bus pickups."

"I have the bus schedule. We won't hold you up." Grace shuts her textbook, the weight of it causing an audible snap, as the boys start to come out of the changing room.

"No, I didn't mean—I did the fundraising for this team," Sarah persists. "We have money set aside for you . . . because of your situation."

"That's very kind of you," Grace says, jostling her book into her bag. "But we don't need it."

"It's already there, though, and there's a room for you guys at the hotel. All paid for." If it had been anyone else, Sarah would have given up, ended the conversation in silent exasperation, but she had seen these kids getting onto public buses late at night, checking into sketchy motels while the team had driven on, comfortable in their coach bus seats. She had questioned the commissioner, many times, until she found out a bit more about them. They lived with a foster mother, and Grace had aged into the young adult program, having just started university. By the state of Grace's clothes and the slab of a laptop she did her homework on, Sarah wondered what kind of foster mother they lived with. She had never seen the woman, but surely, if the government didn't provide enough money, the *woman* could at least buy Grace a new pair of shoes or a proper winter coat with a zipper that actually worked.

When Sarah announced that she was building them into her team fundraising budget, she had been prepared to take flak for it, but no one said a peep. Alex was by far the best player on their team, and everyone knew it. In fact, it was the easiest fundraising she had ever done, a face to their cause. They raised the money in record time. What was she going to do now, tell the hockey parents that this stubborn girl was refusing to accept all their hard work?

"All paid for?" Grace says, straightening.

"Yes. All of your rooms are for the out-of-town tournaments this season."

"You didn't tell the Foster Home Services about this, did you?" Grace's eyes alight with panic.

"No," Sarah says. "No, this was all done through the hockey organization."

Grace lets out a breath. "Oh. Okay." Then, "I appreciate that. Thank you."

Grace and Alex stack his duffel bags in the entrance hallway of their room and lean his sticks up in the corner. There are two double beds, a large TV, and a minibar. Grace does the first thing she always does in a new room—lifts the mattress to check for bedbugs.

There's a knock at the door, and Alex, being closer, peers through the peephole. "It's Sarah," he says quietly over his shoulder.

Grace nods, and he opens the door.

"Hi there," Sarah says from the doorway. She's in high-waisted black pants and a beige cashmere top and is holding a light-pink tote at her side. "There are some parents playing cards in the lobby. Would you like to join us?"

"Thank you," Grace says, taken aback. "But I've got homework."

"The boys are starting up stick hockey in the hall," she says to Alex. "We have the whole wing."

Alex glances at Grace, and she gives him an upward nod. He takes a room key, and Sarah moves aside, stepping into the room as he leaves.

"What're you studying?" she says, gesturing at Grace's bulging backpack.

"I'm in nursing school."

"Oh, have you thought about exploring the social sciences? I've heard they're up and coming."

"I can't really afford to explore."

Sarah recalibrates, realizing it was a silly comment. "A good friend of mine is a nurse. She was in emerge for a while but found it to be a bit much. There's a high burnout rate, especially in the bigger cities. Understaffed and overworked. She's just started working at a high-end nursing home and loves it. If you wanted, I could set up a chat."

"Really?" Grace is waiting for more, a catch.

"Yeah, absolutely."

"That'd be great."

"All right. Well, I'll leave you to it," Sarah says but then pauses in the doorway. "I'm not supposed to tell anyone but half the parents know already. There are a few scouts coming tomorrow, so the boys might be going a bit harder than usual."

"That's good to know, thank you."

Alex comes back into the room with damp hair and pink cheeks. He takes his shoes off and puts them neatly next to Grace's.

"Hey." Grace finishes the last line of notes she's been making. "You have fun?" She snaps the caps back onto her highlighters.

"Yeah." Alex flops down on the bed next to hers and turns the TV on low.

"Sarah was saying there are some scouts coming tomorrow, so you be careful out there."

"I'm always careful."

"I know you are," she says. "Look, forget I said anything. Just play how you want to play."

"Lettie's here for a dance competition."

Grace sits up. "Where'd you see her?"

"In the lobby with Jackson just now. He asked what room we're in."

"Did you tell him?"

He glances at her with a grin. "Yeah. And Lettie told me they're in two twenty."

Grace puts her shoes on, and Alex turns off the TV. "Can I come?"

"Of course," she says.

She opens the door just as Jackson is about to knock, his fist raised. Lettie is at his side, her sleek golden hair pulled back in a ponytail.

"Great minds," Jackson says as Grace pulls him into a hug.

The last time they were together, they had won a doubles Ping-Pong tournament at their local community center. Five hundred dollars each. Alex got new skates, and she bought herself a used laptop.

"Hey, Lettie," Grace says. Lettie smiles back at her and Alex.

They go down to the lobby, which is mostly empty now. Lettie has brought a deck of cards and deals out a game of crazy eights for her and Alex. Grace sits with Jackson; their time is too precious for a game. Every day they used to sit side by side at school. Oh, how she missed it, and even though his university was only an hour away, it could have been the moon for all she saw of him now. Both of their schedules pulled them apart. She craved the coming summer when he would be back at home. The one like the summer before.

He had gotten her a job at the golf course where he worked, the nicest members-only golf course in town, and the tips had been great. Way better than the diner. The smart black uniform she put on every morning meant that she blended in. She could wear the same thing over and over without it being scrutinized and mocked. The team of people she worked with were friendly and helpful. They had one another's backs, and Grace came into their fold.

Grace and Jackson had both requested Mondays and Tuesdays off. They were easy enough days to get, and because they were in different departments, both were granted. On these days, Jackson would drive the four of them to the beach or they would have barbecues in his backyard. His parents buzzed around asking Grace and Alex how they were. Would they like to stay for dinner? Watch a movie? Play a board game?

It took her a while to realize, mostly with a nudge from Alex, that Jackson didn't think of her as a foster kid who needed to be tiptoed around or cast sympathetic glances at the most random times. He was kind to her, but he also pushed her. He saw her reticence and her nerves, and he knew she was capable of more. He saw *her*. Not the same sweater she would wear for days on end, her unwashed hair, or her fading belt. It was because of him that she had entered the Ping-Pong tournament and learned how to drive on back roads on the way home from the beach.

Jackson never commented on the fact that Grace wore only one bathing suit or alternated between two dresses for the entire summer.

In fact, he didn't even seem to notice. His mother did, though. One day she said to Grace, "I don't know what I was thinking when I bought this bathing suit. Totally the wrong size and final sale. Maybe it would fit you?"

It fit her perfectly, and it was the highest-quality bathing suit Grace had ever owned.

"How have you been?" Grace asks as they sit in two armchairs with a small table between them.

"I'm good. I'm—I hate school," he says, lowering his eyes. She has never heard him like this. The tone of his voice, the seriousness in it. He's rubbing his bicep.

"What part of it don't you like?"

"Any of it. The classes, the people. I'm in a dorm with a dozen kids from our high school. I thought when you went to university, you were supposed to meet new people, do new things," he says. "But they all requested to be together, and I got lumped into it."

"I thought you didn't mind those guys?"

"Yeah, some of them, but seeing them all day, every day, it's too much."

Grace angles her body so that her back is against the arm of the chair and she's fully facing him. "If you could do anything right now, what would you do?"

"Anything?" His eyes lock on something in the distance, and there's the old sparkle of excitement in them. "I'd go out west. Hike, explore, ski in the winter. See where life took me. Who knows, maybe apply to a university out there."

In a year when she needs more than ever something to look forward to, she forces herself to say, "Why don't you?"

"I brought this up to my dad at their golf club when we were having dinner, and you know what he said to me? *Do you like your lifestyle, the fancy cars and the nice house? It's because your mother and I have worked hard.* Like if I want something else, then *I'm* not working hard or I'm going down the wrong path because it's not theirs. Who says that to their kid? All they want is for me to be a doctor or an accountant or some fancy fucking title they can tell all their friends. If I do anything different, they'll say I'm wasting their money."

"You could apply for government money. Pay your own way. Make your own decisions if that's what you want."

"My parents make too much. They wouldn't give me a dime."

"You have only one life, Jackson. You might make some mistakes and have regrets but at least they'll be yours. If you don't do what you want, you'll always wonder what if, and you'll live with that resentment. You have a safety net in them. They'll support you even if things don't work out. You know they will."

He glances down, embarrassed. "I'm sorry," he says. "I'm going on about all this stuff, and you've got much bigger things—"

"No," she says. "You're welcome to talk to me about this. I'm glad you are."

"So you don't think it's a terrible idea? Dropping out?"

"You know what you could do," she says, thinking through the logistics of his plan. "Wait until the end of the semester so that your parents can't be mad at you for dropping out. Keep your marks up, then if you want to switch universities down the road, you can. Go out west for the summer, and if you like it, stay." The last part is hard for her to say. The happiness that was last summer was one of the things getting her through this year and dealing with May.

"I don't know if I'll make it," he says.

"February, March, April," she says, throwing up her fingers. "Three months. And most of April is exams. That's all you need."

"Three months." He nods slowly. "I could do that."

"You absolutely could. And keep those marks up. Just in case."

"Thanks, Grace," he says, planting his hands on his thighs. "I think my parents are still up. I'll go talk to them. Just tell them about the going out west bit for the summer. Sort the rest out later."

She gives him an encouraging nod and watches as he leaves the lobby.

In the morning one of the dads from their team comes out of his room with his son's equipment. Grace is carrying her and Alex's overnight bags while Alex takes his hockey bags down to the bus. The dad stops when he spots Grace. He stands so that he's partially blocking her path and holds a grin on his face as she approaches.

"Hey, Grace, right?" he says.

"Yeah." Grace glances at the space between him and the wall, wondering if she can slip through without touching him.

"Man, that kid, he's amazing. I tell my kid, *you watch him, you learn from him*. Hey, maybe you could tell the coach that Alex wants to be on his line. Let him know Alex thinks it would be better for his game."

"Um." She tries to get by him, but he moves so that he's fully blocking her.

"What do you think?" he says.

"I don't know," she mumbles, shifting one of the bags as it pulls on her shoulder.

"Why not? My son is pretty good. You see him out there? Number thirty-seven."

Grace didn't even know there was a thirty-seven on the team. Someone a few doors down comes out of their room. Laughter and voices fill the hallway, but the sound just makes Grace's stomach squirm.

The father of number thirty-seven finally moves so that she can pass.

The game is tied. The parents on both teams are becoming more and more vocal, and some are becoming irate, yelling at the referee and at the coach. Grace, who is sitting apart from the parents, hasn't been able to read her textbook since five minutes into the first period when she realized something was wrong. Gary, the coach, hasn't played Alex once.

The scouts weren't hard to miss. They sat apart from the parents and one another with their clipboards, tracking the movements of the players, jotting things down. The first period ends with a resonating buzz. The parents stand and filter out into the warmer area. Grace doesn't move.

The scout who had gotten Alex into this league comes toward her along the row of seats, carrying a tray with two steaming bowls of chili. "You're not a vegetarian, are you?" he asks her.

"No." She reaches for her purse.

"Don't worry about it." He carefully passes her one of the bowls and a spoon. "One of the perks of being a scout—you get free food." He sits so that there's a chair between them. "What are you onto now?" He nods at the textbook sticking out of her bag.

"Nursing school." She's conscious of the parents in the gallery behind her, watching her eating with a scout.

"Nice one," he says and scoops a spoonful into his mouth. "So is Alex injured or has he pulled something?"

She shakes her head and gingerly dips her spoon into the bowl. She doesn't know why, but she has found it difficult to eat recently. She's hungry and wants to eat, but the actual act feels unnatural and doing it in front of others even more so.

"Then why isn't the coach playing him?"

She glances at him, unable to hide the concern in her face. "'Cause you guys are here," she says.

He stares at her in disbelief. "He doesn't want to lose him." He shakes his head. "Selfish bastard."

Sarah strides over to them with the determined, no-nonsense intensity of a woman who has been able to push her whole life without any real consequences. "Hi," she says briskly to the scout and then to Grace. "Just had a word with Gary. I told him if he doesn't play Alex, this will be the last game he ever coaches."

Grace's eyes widen as Sarah walks away.

The scout lets out a low whistle in appreciation. "Well, I like her."

FIVE

It's 3:50 p.m. on Friday afternoon. The Friday that Grace accidently committed herself to going out with some nurses to Moby Dick's. She's dreading the evening ahead, trying to think up any reasonable excuse to get out of it but knows that there are none. Riley would know. She'll just have to do her best to get through it. She heads down the hall to the lunchroom to grab her empty container but comes to a halt when she hears a voice that she recognizes instantly.

"Hey, Riley. Do you know if Grace is still here?" The words are deep, rich, and confident. The execution is casual, but Grace knows that there is nothing casual about this man arriving to the home over an hour early. Without realizing it, she has walked into and is now staring at the broad back of Daniel Hurley. *Shit.* Shit, shit, shit.

Riley, who is wheeling the blood pressure machine down the hall, catches Grace discreetly shake her head just behind Daniel. She doesn't miss a beat. "She's gone home for the day, I'm afraid."

He shifts his weight, disappointed. "I was hoping to catch her. Is she in on the weekend by any chance?"

Grace turns. She knows that the cleaning staff throw out the contents of the fridge every Friday, but she can't risk it. At the elevator she presses the down button.

During the short wait, Daniel pulls up alongside her, causing a nervous flutter in her stomach and a rush of adrenaline. Angling away from him, she unclips her name tag and slips it into her pants pocket. Heat rises through her body, and it takes everything she has not to fidget.

When the elevator arrives, he follows her on and, standing a couple of feet away, glances at her. His eyes flicker back to her face and linger for a brief moment. She doesn't know if it's because of the redness that has taken hold of her or the fact that many of the residents have commented over the years that they think she is quite pretty. Something she's never gotten used to after being called Greasy Grace for most of high school. Though she wonders now if that was more to do with the state of her lifestyle. Either way, she stares straight ahead and prays he doesn't try to start conversation.

After what might just be the longest thirteen seconds of her life, the elevator doors open, and she is filled with relief as Daniel waits for her to get off first.

As she strides through the parking lot, she glances up and mutters, "Thank God."

Standing on the stoop of Riley's townhouse, Grace double-checks the number before knocking. Riley opens the door and looks positively chic in a leather miniskirt and a royal blue tank top. Her blonde hair is in beachy waves.

"Hey," Riley says while adjusting an earring but then falters. "What are you wearing?"

Grace glances down at her black pants, black cashmere sweater, and flats. Her hair is in a French braid. "What do you mean?"

"You look like a librarian who's about to attend a funeral."

On the rare occasions Grace has been social, usually for a fellow nurse's retirement party or a milestone birthday, it has been to avoid questions like these: How could she possibly miss an event when given so much notice? Was something wrong with her? Had she contracted some serious illness and, if so, how much longer would she be able to work at Oakwood?

These questions are the reason she forces herself to attend the get-togethers, casually slipping into them and usually ending up enjoying them, which never fails to surprise her. Before an event Grace stares at her closet for a long time, trying to find that fine line between blending in and not sticking out in any way at all with a limited supply of clothes to choose from. Most of her formal tops have been bought just for these parties.

It seems that tonight she has missed the mark completely, but to be fair she has never been inside a bar. Only walked by them, peering through the windows to look at those inside. And she doesn't usually notice how the people dress; it's the interactions that catch her eye.

Grace is about to tell Riley that this was a mistake and that she'll see her at work on Monday when Riley ushers her inside.

Riley's house is cozy and welcoming, with warm lighting and wood floors. Not at all like Grace's house, whose stark white walls were meant to be painted, as the real estate agent said, in any homey color that spoke to Grace. But Grace has never done it. She has never felt comfortable in her house and has no desire to change that.

Stepping into Riley's home, she slips off her shoes and takes it in, this extension of her friend, who's made this space very much her own. There's abstract art and sketches of nudes on the walls, a vase of light-pink roses on the kitchen table. A record player sits in the corner next to a shelf of books, bestsellers and classics, and there's a large map with pins in it. The furniture in the living room is midcentury modern with a blue velvet couch and quaint armchairs. Makeup, nail polish, and a large purse are scattered across the wooden coffee table.

"Okay," Riley calls from her bedroom. "I've got some stuff that could work." Grace goes into Riley's room, which is large with herringbone oak floors and an adjoining walk-in closet. There's a wall of photos. Riley with her family and friends at Christmas parties, in cafés, in front of the Eiffel Tower, Big Ben, Machu Picchu, the Sydney Opera house. "What about this?" Riley says, pulling Grace's attention away from the photos. She holds up a high-necked metallic purple tank top. "And this belt and . . . what's your shoe size?"

"Seven."

Riley tosses the shoes she had just picked up back into the closet, and Grace changes into the tank top and slides the belt through her pant loops. Riley passes her a leather jacket, and after putting it on, Grace turns to face her.

"Well, this looks good," Riley says. "What about a little makeup?"

"No, I'm all right."

"Just a tiny bit of color." She puts some lipstick on her. "And can you take your hair out." Grace releases her hair from the braid, and Riley runs her fingers through it a couple of times. "Perfect."

Daniel's tailored suit is illuminated by the blue light of the aquarium, where exotic fish bob along the length of the wall behind him.

Knowing that Daniel will be picking up the tab, Doug has spent the evening ordering expensive bottles of wine while Sheila, in a sharply cut striped blazer, takes an extravagant amount of time deciding on each course. As client meetings go, this one is shaping up well but is incredibly tedious.

Daniel is doing his best to feign enjoyment throughout this whole interaction. He nods, and smiles as they talk, adding in quips and anecdotes here and there. Sheila's stories have no end of detail, and she rolls one into the next without taking a breath. She does pause for Daniel to agree on a point she's made or to set him with an intense gaze as if daring him to challenge her. Every so often she taps him on the arm, and he has to force his tensing shoulders down.

When Sheila does glance at the menu, Doug takes the chance to redirect the conversation to something that seems light and casual but that has undertones of being critical and cynical. Daniel adds in the odd comment, careful not to agree with Doug or put him down either. He knows he has the ability to seem effortlessly charming, which is why these people are so candid with him, eager to please and show off a bit.

But inside he is cringing, wanting nothing more than for this night to end.

The server is standing over them, once again, waiting for Sheila to deliberate over which dessert will pair best with the wine Doug has just chosen.

"Would you mind giving us a minute?" Daniel says to the server for the third time that evening. He hates keeping them waiting while Sheila seems oblivious, as if they are the only table the man is waiting on.

"You're not in a rush, I hope," Sheila says. She's in her midforties, and her eyelash extensions lift coyly toward Daniel as she takes her eyes off the menu.

"No, take your time," Daniel says. How could he be? It's only entering the third hour.

"How long do you think it will be before the company goes public?" Doug asks.

"I would say six, eight months tops." Daniel reaches for his napkin and starts to fold it over and then again.

"Have you invested in them?" Sheila says, eying his hands.

"I have." He releases the napkin. "But that being said, my portfolio is quite diverse." Someone catches Daniel's eye at a nearby table. "Excuse me a moment."

Daniel approaches Scott, a young man who works at his firm. Daniel had seen him on the plane but didn't want to bother him. Here at the restaurant, he knows that saying hello is the right thing to do and will make Scott look good in front of his friends. Scott's table is made up of a dozen or so well-dressed men and women in their midtwenties.

"Scott," Daniel says. "How are you?"

Scott stands to shake Daniel's hand. "Good. I flew in for my brothers' birthdays." Scott nods at two identical young men at the table.

"Double celebration."

Scott chuckles nervously. "Exactly."

"Well, you have a great night."

Daniel goes back to his table, and one of Scott's brothers says, "Who was that?"

"My boss—one of my bosses. He's a partner at the firm."

"Pretty young to be a partner."

"Yeah, I think he's in his early thirties."

"Damn, Scott, he's cute," one of the women says. "Is he single?"

"Yeah, he is, and he's nice, but he's pretty intense, one of those guys who's always on."

A server brings a tray of tequila shots to the table. "Compliments of the gentleman," he says, nodding at Daniel, who raises his glass to them.

Daniel pays the bill, and their coats are brought to them.

"Any plans while you're in town?" Sheila asks as they make their way to the exit. This is the first personal question she has asked Daniel all night.

"I'm visiting my grandmother," he says.

"Is she in a home here?"

"Yeah, she's in Oakwood."

"How'd you get her in there?" Doug asks. "My great-aunt was on the waiting list for seven years. We move her in, and she dies seven days later. Huge hassle."

Sheila nods understandingly.

"We must have gotten lucky."

Doug scoffs. "Yeah."

Outside, Daniel opens the cab door for Sheila. "Have a good night," he says.

"Thank you, Daniel," she says, touching his arm as she slides inside. "You're such a gentleman. Let us know next time you're in town."

He nods and shuts the door, then straightens and turns. Doug is staring at him with excitement in his eyes. Like their night is just about to begin. Daniel forces himself to remain inscrutable, pushing down any annoyance that might betray him. Doug takes a couple of steps toward him, his thumbs through the front loops of his belt like a cowboy, as if this is the moment he has been waiting for.

"I know a great place we could go," Doug says. "The women are top-notch, divine."

"That sounds fun," Daniel says, but he has never liked strip clubs, and the few times he has had to go, he's found them agonizing. "But I want to be fresh for my nan in the morning."

"Just a drink then," Doug says.

"Next time I'm in town."

"Fuck it. Just one drink."

Daniel knows men like him. It's never just one.

Grace slides into the booth next to Riley in a dimly lit, medium-size bar, buzzing with activity. She has just lost royally at a game of darts, and she's really enjoying herself.

"Grace is from there," one of the nurses says. "What did you think of it?"

"It was a good town to grow up in," Grace says.

"What was the night life like?"

"Yeah, Grace would be an expert on the night life," another nurse jokes.

"I haven't really been back much since I left." Grace hadn't been back at all, but she couldn't say that because then they might ask questions. "I'd be more apt to know about the community hockey arenas and bus schedules."

"Hockey arenas?" Riley says. "What were you doing in hockey arenas?"

She glances at Riley. "Al played hockey." Then adds for the others, "My brother."

"I didn't know you had a brother," one of the nurses says. "I have a brother in Oz, but we never see him. At first it seemed all cool and exotic, but now my parents are really worried he'll never come home."

Grace leans into Riley. "I think I'm going to head out."

"I'm glad you came." Riley presses the side of her head against Grace's and lowers her voice. "Will didn't come."

"It could be for a million reasons," Grace says, letting her head rest for a moment against Riley's. "Okay, I'll see you Monday." Grace slides her purse strap onto her shoulder. She uses the bathroom before she leaves, and as she washes her hands, she can't help but be pleased by her appearance. The leather jacket is flattering on her, her shoulder-length brown hair is lightly tousled from the braid, and the metallic tank top contrasts nicely against her olive skin. With a smile, she dries her hands.

At the bar Grace waits for the bartender to serve the man next to her. He is quick and efficient, his tattoos a blur as he mixes the drinks.

"What can I do for you?" he says, approaching Grace.

"I'm at table seven," she says. "I'd like to pay for three vodka crans, a shot of tequila, and a plate of nachos, please."

The man sitting a few seats down from her recognizes the voice instantly. Bright and rich. Warm yet reserved. It has captivated him for years. As he turns his head, he's taken aback. It's the very same woman from the elevator. Glancing over his shoulder, he spots Riley and shakes his head with a grin. Lowering his drink, he stands.

"Sure thing. I'll grab the machine," the bartender says to Grace.

"Thanks." Grace pulls out her Visa. She can feel someone come up beside her, quite close to her. She smells the faint scent of their after-shave. She glances at the man, and there's a dropping sensation through her stomach. She's been caught. She knows it the moment she meets Daniel's eyes, the way they stare at her so intensely. He knows exactly who she is.

"Ready to go." The bartender passes Grace the machine. She enters a tip and taps her card before passing it back. "Want a copy of the receipt?" He rips it off.

"No, thanks," Grace says.

Daniel is about to speak when an overweight man comes up

behind him, letting out a belch. He's ruddy faced, and his forehead is glistening with sweat. "Dan, Dan, Dan the man," he slurs. "Let's have another."

Daniel's nostrils flare slightly. A flicker of exasperation crosses his face, and in that moment Grace knows that he's extremely agitated and wants nothing more to do with this man.

In a flash, without even thinking, Grace's face breaks into a smile. She doesn't know if it's the drinks she's just had or the high she's still on from laughing and chatting with her co-workers but right now, she is bold and confident. Totally unlike her usual self, who would have withdrawn into her shell and left immediately.

"Oh my God," she says putting on a voice. Higher and singsongy. "Daniel Hurley. It is just so good to see you. How have you been?" She raises her eyebrows a little, hoping that he'll go with it.

Daniel hesitates, but only for a second. "Great. Yeah, I'm great."

She places her hand on his arm. "I cannot believe that we've run into each other." Now that she's looking at him, right at him and not stealing an awkward glance, she realizes just how handsome he is. Tall with electric blue eyes and dark hair, his forearm is muscular beneath her hand. To see Daniel in a situation like this emboldens her, knowing that she can help him. And she notices too how strangely comfortable she is next to him. "I know I shouldn't be saying this, but do you want to come back to my place? Just this once, for old time's sake or . . ." She trails off and glances at Doug.

"Fuck, man, I'm not going to stop you," Doug says, staring almost hungrily at Grace. "Not a day in my life would I stop you."

"You're such a doll," Grace says.

Daniel gestures to the bartender and throws down two fifty-dollar bills. "So great to see you, Doug," Daniel says, shaking his hand. "I'm glad we could close the deal."

"Let's have just one more before you guys go. The three of us," Doug says, putting his hand firmly on Daniel's shoulder. There's something controlling in the way that he does it, and Grace doesn't like it. Not one bit.

"I love your watch," she says to Doug.

"Young lady, you have impeccable taste." Doug removes his grip and brings his hand down to show her. "I got it while I was in Spain. My wife and I—"

"That's fascinating," she says, the remnants of her singsongy voice gone. She edges her way between him and Daniel. "Well, you have a great night, Doug." With that, she takes Daniel's hand, and they leave the bar.

Outside in the cool night air, Grace lets Daniel's hand go and pauses to zip up her jacket. Unable to stop herself, she says, "What are you doing here with an asshole like that?"

"He's one of our biggest clients," Daniel says with a pained expression on his face. "Thankfully not one I have to meet with regularly. It was either this or a strip club."

"Charming," she says and notes how odd and normal this is. To be having such an easy conversation with someone she has avoided meeting for years. Someone who had crept into her life without her quite realizing it.

In the early days, before she'd gotten a good handle on the nuances of her job, she thought that she needed to be in constant motion. To work through her breaks and tighten up her lunches. To prove to the others that she was meant to be there.

One day she whipped into Annie's room to grab something, and Annie held out her phone.

"Is it Daniel? I don't have time," Grace said. "Can I call him back?"

"He said it's very important."

Grace took the phone from her. In those days Annie was still fairly mobile, and she left the room to go on a "little walk down the hallway."

"Hello?"

"I need you to do something for me."

"Okay."

"See the chair in the corner of Annie's room."

"The floral one or the other one?"

"The other one—the green plaid—"

"Okay, yeah."

"Would you mind sitting in it and letting me know how it's holding up?"

Grace sat. "It's fine. It's holding up fine."

"Are you sure? Have you settled into it?"

She sat right back and, easing into it, her body relaxed. Then she grinned, realizing what he was doing. "What did Annie say?"

"It was Beth, actually. She called me yesterday after her visit. Said you guys had a nice chat in between you running around."

"We did." There was a long silence, and Grace let herself be engulfed by it, closing her eyes. Everything slowed down, and in that moment the noises in the hallway faded away. "Are you still there?"

"I'm still here."

Daniel is staring at her now, and she takes a step back, lowering her gaze. "It's nice to meet you. In person."

"Wait a sec, Grace. Is there somewhere we could go? Grab a drink, have a chat."

She notices then that Will is pacing a few yards away. "Will," she calls over to him. He turns, and she recognizes the slight terror in his face, the hesitation in his gait. It's the fear of the unfamiliar, the uncertain. She knows the feeling all too well.

"Grace," Will says. "I was just . . . I didn't know if . . . if you guys were still in there or if I was too late." He's clutching his hat. He's been pacing awhile.

"They're still in there," Grace says. "Riley was looking forward to seeing you."

"Was she?"

"Yeah. There's a spot open next to her."

"Okay, cool. Thanks, Grace." A look of determination comes over Will, and he enters the bar.

Grace glances at Daniel. "I'm not really much of a drinker, but there's a late-night pie place down the street," she suggests.

"I love pie," Daniel says.

Grace places her order at the counter, and Daniel says, "I'll take the same," in a way that makes Grace wonder if he would've said that no matter what she had ordered. Then they both try to pay for the other.

"Let me," he says. "I owe you one."

"No, I owe *you* one," Grace counters. "A much bigger one."

He starts to argue, but she taps her card, and he says, "Thank you. Thank you very much."

As the woman pulls the pie from behind the glass, Daniel turns to take the place in. The 1950s diner-style tables and chairs, the eclectic plates and teacups, none of which match but that all fit perfectly together. Ones you might find in your grandmother's china cupboard.

The woman flicks a large dollop of whipped cream onto Grace's slice and then pauses, her hand hovering over Daniel's. He nods, and she drops a generous helping on his as well. They thank her and head to a small table with their plates and mugs.

Daniel rests his suit jacket over the back of his chair and takes a bite. For the first time all day, his shoulders relax as he sits back. "Oh man, that's good."

Grace grins. "I know, right?"

"You come here often?"

"I've been a few times over the years—for date night."

She notices the smallest flicker in his eye. "You're seeing someone?"

"Oh no." She glances down, embarrassed. "That's what Riley calls it when we hang out sometimes—date night."

"Ah. Gotcha."

"You have the tiniest bit of an accent. I can hear it more in person than on the phone."

"From living in South Africa when I was a kid." He takes a sip of his tea. "Not many people pick it up."

"Did you like living there?"

"Yeah, parts of it were great, but there were periods of time when we couldn't go far from the house, and with the political unrest, some things could be tricky to navigate."

"Your grandma said she really missed you guys when you were over there. She was happy when you came home."

He puts his fork down. "Why didn't you say hi earlier, on the elevator."

"I'm kind of shy sometimes, and you surprised me. I was expecting this short, festively plump—"

"Jesus, is that how I come across on the phone?"

"No, that's how your grandmother describes you."

"Yeah, that was me until I was like thirteen."

"And it's around the same time that the photos she has of you guys stop. You should really bring her some updated ones."

He chuckles softly. "I've never even looked at those photos."

"You should check them out; there are some real gems in there."

"Wait a second." He sets his eyes on hers. "Is there one where we're in the—"

"Yep."

"How long has that one been up?"

"Since the beginning."

"Christ almighty."

Grace laughs, and Daniel glances down at the table, seemingly pleased to have made her laugh. But then he crosses his arms over his chest and leans back in his chair. "Well, now I feel like this isn't fair. You've seen all these photos of me as a kid, and you've gotten off scot-free."

"I don't have photos of my childhood."

"Bullshit. You've gotta have a least one. Something saved to your phone or some hideous yearbook photo."

Oh, there had been lots of hideous yearbook photos, ones Grace never wanted to see again. She hesitates and then reaches for her wallet. "I do have one. I'm not sure where it was taken. A school maybe." She thumbs out a photo of her in a floral dress sitting in a little pink chair, holding a teddy bear. She's probably five or six.

She watches him closely as he takes it and holds it carefully around the edges. He stares at it for a minute before he looks up at her. "You were freaking adorable."

She can't help but grin.

As he passes the photo back to her, there's a shift in him. "Alex told me a bit about your life when you guys were together. He said you did a lot for him, made a lot of sacrifices, like how you skipped your prom to take him to a tournament—"

"Skipping my prom wasn't a sacrifice. I couldn't afford to go anyway," she says offhandedly.

"Not just that. Studying on the go, trying to make ends meet, the stress you were under constantly." He says these things matter-of-factly, regarding her without apprehension or dismay, which makes her uncomfortable. She would rather he just pity her so that she could dislike him for it.

"No one forced me to go to his games," she says. "It was a choice I made."

"Like how you're choosing not to speak to him now," he says.

These words cut through Grace. The honesty laid bare. "You don't know what I went through," she says.

"You're right, I don't. But I can see on your face that you're still going through it."

Her whole body becomes warm, and a surge of emotion erupts through her, right into her throat. She stands and her chest heaves slightly. "Look, leaving him was the hardest thing I've ever done. It almost killed me, and it haunts me every day but not for one second do I regret it." There are tears brimming to the surface, but she won't cry. Not in front of him.

Daniel stays seated. There is such kindness in his eyes that it hurts. Why is he so calm? So unmovable. She wants to push him. "I'm not saying you should," he says gently. "But there is this void in his life, and it messes with him. Knowing that you're out there and not being able to talk to you."

She fights to keep her voice steady. "What if it's anger that fills that void?"

"I can promise you it's not. He's a good kid, and he loves you."

Those last three words, paired with his even gaze, make her feel exposed, naked even. No one has ever made her feel like this before. She has always been able to guard herself.

This is too much for her.

Grace leaves the café, and Daniel follows her onto the street. A cold front has come in, and the temperature has dropped. The night has gone from cool to freezing.

"Are you getting an Uber?" he asks, his breath rising above him.

"No, I don't have Uber." She turns to face him, suddenly agitated, her arms crossed over her chest. "Is that why you said no charge? 'Cause you feel sorry for us? Or you feel sorry for me?"

Daniel doesn't answer, and Grace shakes her head.

"Where do you live?" he says.

"It's just a twenty-minute walk."

"It's two in the morning. You can't walk home alone. Put your address in here." He holds his phone out. "A car will pick you up and take you to your house."

"What about you?"

"My hotel's right there." He nods down the street.

He seems adamant, so she takes the phone, puts her address in, and then passes it back to him. "You don't have to wait with me," she says, angling away from him.

He doesn't move. They stand in silence for a few minutes until the car pulls up.

Six

Eight Years Earlier

The dean of the nursing school is sitting across from Grace, surveying her over her fingertips, pressed together like the steeple of a church. Grace is so annoyed that she's not nervous, but she is trying to keep her composure.

"Why does it say 'Needs Improvement' in so many categories?" Grace asks, holding her term results.

"That would be because you need improvement."

"Yes, I understand that, but in what? I aced all the tests. I did well on my practicums."

"All of them?"

"What did I mess up?"

"The nurse's corner. Many times."

"I have 'Needs Improvement' because I didn't make a *bed* properly?"

"Some say sloppy bed, sloppy mind."

Who the fuck says that? "Could there be any other reason?"

"You mean the fact that you're a product of the foster care system and will soon be caring for members of our vulnerable and frail society? No, we wouldn't judge you for that."

Grace comes home to angry mail spread across the kitchen table. Unpaid bills, warnings of credits being overextended, final notices. May would have left them there for Grace to see. To deal with while she's at the casino. A painful wave of frustration overwhelms Grace, and she grips the top of the chair to hold herself together. To stop the tears. She scoops the letters into a pile and takes them upstairs to her room. She doesn't want Alex to see them. Shutting the door behind her, she bites down on her fist, sick to her stomach.

She needs something to distract herself. She takes the duvet off her bed, pulls the sheet tight at the corner, and folds it under. One side, then the other. Crinkled. She does it again. Pulling tighter, sweeping her hand under. It's better but still crinkled.

She clutches her ribs as a sharp pang pierces through her. *You're fine. You're fine.* Her body grows warm like an ember about to ignite, and now there are tears. Her breath quickens and becomes shallow. The pang intensifies, and she presses down harder on her ribs, trying to catch her breath. Why is she crying? *You're fine, goddammit.*

Afterward, as she lies on her bedroom floor, totally drained and trying to breathe normally, she stares up at the ceiling. Something needs to change. Something soon. Or this crack running down her is going to split wide open.

Grace is waiting on a park bench when Sarah approaches in a gray pencil skirt and a white sleeveless blouse. Sarah pauses before she sits, checking that the bench is clean, and then puts her white Kate Spade tote on her lap. Once settled, she angles in toward Grace.

"Thank you for meeting me," Grace says.

"Of course. What's going on?"

Grace doesn't have time to beat around the bush, so she launches into it. "The woman we live with has a gambling addiction. Alex doesn't know. Well, he does, but not the extent of it. It's getting worse, and I'm not able to take legal guardianship of him. I'm having these episodes, and they're getting worse."

"Episodes?"

"It's like there's something wrong with me, and I can't stop them," she says quickly. "I can't keep going on like this."

"Grace, there are people who can—"

"No, no. Please just listen to me because I don't have much time. Some of the hockey parents are crazy, and I'm afraid that if he goes into the system, they'll descend on him. But you are sensible and kind. Is there any chance you would take Alex under your guardianship until he turns eighteen? If he continues on like this, he'll probably be billeted to a family in a few years anyway. He's easy to be around, and he's neat and he can cook a bit."

"I wish I could. I do. But my husband and I have just separated. I have a lot going on right now."

"Okay, okay. Don't worry about it." Grace stands. "Alex and I really appreciate everything you've done for us."

Sarah stands too. "I'll ask around. I'm sure there's a nice family out there who would love to have such a talented kid."

"No," Grace says. "I don't want them to take him because of what he can do on the ice. All I want is for him to be in a safe and comfortable environment where, if he decided to give up hockey tomorrow, he wouldn't be pushed to play."

Sarah's brisk and focused demeanor had gotten her through life and especially the past decade. A stay-at-home mom of one who desperately needed a purpose. The president of the Parent Teacher Association, the head of the hockey fundraising committee, the lead organizer of every neighborhood drive. She thrived on a busy schedule, filling in any gaps whenever they came up. She was never *enough*. Never fulfilled. Always moving. Her husband had married a go-getter and realized only too late that she would never settle into things. She would never be satisfied. She always wanted more. Another task. Another thing to complete and to do it well.

She is now staring into the face of a young woman who is desperate. Who is advocating on behalf of another person when she herself is left adrift. And Sarah is turning her back on her. This was not the sort of woman she was. If she said no now, all the tasks she took such pride in would mean nothing because when someone truly needed her and she could do something that actually mattered, she had said no.

She slides her tennis bracelet along her wrist and finally looks at Grace. Really looks at her. Grace's red-lined eyes are puffy, and her hand is shaking slightly. This young woman, a kid really, is running on fumes. The things that Sarah had chosen not to see when she first arrived fill her with an overwhelming shame and guilt. "I'm a selfish woman," she says, thinking of the two large inheritances she has just received from her father's sisters who died months apart.

"It's all right," Grace says. "It's a big ask."

"Yeah, it is. And I have a big fucking house, and I'm going to be seeing my son every other week. I'll take Alex. He's a good kid. I'll have to talk to Ethan about it, but he's always liked Alex, and he's a good kid too."

"Are you serious?" Grace says in disbelief, a huge weight lifting off her. One she didn't realize was pressing down on her with such force.

"Yeah," she says. "Oh, and I'll make that call for you. The nursing home I was telling you about, the moment you're done school. I know you've taken classes through the summers to finish sooner."

"I really appreciate that," Grace says. "I've got all the paperwork ready. I'm assuming you've had police checks before, having helped out with kids. You just need to register as a foster parent, and with your background, it should be pretty simple."

"When are you thinking?"

"As soon as possible. I'm . . . I'm exhausted. And not the kind that needs a good night's sleep." An unexpected tear falls down her cheek, and Grace wipes it away, embarrassed. "Would you mind not telling Alex about the nursing home or where I'm going? I need to figure out my life, and I'm afraid that I'll drag him down with me if I stay in his."

"If that's what you want, Grace," Sarah says. "But he adores you."

"I need this, Sarah."

"Okay." Sarah leans in to hug Grace, but she sways backward. She's not used to hugging others, having rarely been hugged herself. "You have my number," Sarah says, unaffected by Grace's lack of affection. She understands now much better than she did before. "You let me know, and I'll make the call."

Grace and Alex have spent the past couple of hours packing—their whole lives into a few duffel bags. "Al, is there anything else you can think of? Once we're gone, we won't be able to come back."

Alex zips up the large duffel bag Sarah lent them. "This is it."

Lights illuminate the room as a car pulls into the driveway. They shoulder their bags and head down the stairs. May comes into the house and doesn't acknowledge them, probably thinking that they're headed to another hockey tournament. Grace doubts that she would've noticed the luxury SUV parked just down the street. Alex slips by her and turns over his shoulder, giving Grace a reassuring nod.

May goes to sit in the living room and turns the TV on. She must have eaten at the casino. Grace stands in the doorway.

"What is it, Grace?" May says, already in her TV trance.

"You've made my life very difficult, and it doesn't seem to have fazed you one bit."

May flinches in irritation. She's wearing her beaded turquoise necklace. The one she'd gotten a few years earlier on a cruise they took to the Caribbean. It had been Grace and Alex's first time on a plane. May invited a church friend to come as their fourth. As far as Grace knew, they hadn't spoken since. Grace and Alex had loved it. The freedom of roaming the boat on their own, the all-you-can-eat buffets with pizza, pasta, and soft ice cream, the rock climbing and Ping-Pong tables. At the ports they would disembark to wander around the towns, swim in the ocean, and read under palm trees. May would get off the boat for short stints to shop on the main street.

A few weeks after the trip, their cupboards, which were usually bursting with food, had thinned out. Grace didn't think much of it when May didn't take them back-to-school shopping for the first time ever or to buy them new boots, jackets, mitts, and hats in November. It was when Alex needed money for a class field trip and she said to him, "Just ask the teacher for the money. They have funds for special situations" that Grace realized they had a problem. A big problem. She knew how much money May received every month for each of them.

On the way home from school, Grace stopped at the diner and applied for a job so that Alex wouldn't have to ask his teacher. And May took note. The things she would do for that boy.

Letters started to come in the mail, and May would call her friends, her breath wispy with excitement. She had *free* tickets. To shows, lobster dinners, spa treatments, overnight stays. Nothing is ever free. They were all at the casino.

On Grace's eighteenth birthday, she took the bus to the casino. She had seen the flyers. Of young women in short black dresses and men in suits, laughing at a table with a group of people around them and a pile of chips in front of them. But inside it was a dark, sad, windowless place where people stood like zombies. It wasn't hard to find May, standing in the soft glow of light coming off her machine. Grace grew woozy at the sight—the woman's hands never stopped moving. Pushing coin after coin into the slot and pulling the lever. She had never really liked May. But in that moment, she hated her. Just hated her.

"I've contacted Foster Home Services and told them everything," Grace says. "About all the money you took from us and dumped into those slots." May unglues her eyes from the screen. Grace has finally gotten her attention, but she doesn't relish it. This woman has caused her so much frustration, so much grief. When Grace leaves this house, she will put this behind her and won't think about May again. "There will be no more checks."

May turns, her body contorted in the chair and stares up at Grace, panic in her eyes. "But . . . but you'll be separated."

Grace just stares back at her with tired eyes.

"The payment that's supposed to go into my account today," May says. "That'll be there, right?"

Grace shakes her head.

"I-I can't afford—"

"To have a gambling addiction? No, I wouldn't think most people could. I would wish you luck, but I don't. So goodbye."

Grace hoists the strap of her bag onto her shoulder, turns, and leaves May's house forever.

Alex is standing next to Grace, and Sarah is waiting nearby as people load onto the coach bus. This is the only part of the plan that Grace didn't think much about. She could never picture herself saying goodbye to Alex.

"Why can't I come with you?" Alex says suddenly.

His question throws Grace's already frayed emotional state off-kilter—to the point where she's teetering on the edge. She had already explained this all to him. To avoid this.

"Sarah's got a good setup for you," Grace says again. He would want for nothing. Sarah had made that clear to her. She'd also tried to give Grace money, but she'd refused it. Sarah had already done so much. "She has a lovely home with lots of space, and I'm going to be starting out from scratch."

"I don't need space."

"You'll be able to stay in the hockey system here. You're on a great team—"

"I don't care about the hockey."

"Oh Al, you love hockey."

"Not if it means I can't go with you."

She can't look at him because her voice will break. "I wish I could take you, but I just need some time. For me. To get my shit together."

"And then you'll come back?"

The bus turns on, lighting up, the engine humming.

"And then you'll come back, right?" he says again, his voice urgent.

"I love you," she says, pulling him into a quick hug.

She steps onto the ledge, her legs wobbly, and waves through the window as he drives away. The tears fall the moment Alex is out of view.

Grace is sitting in the Oakwood nursing home lobby, so nervous that she hasn't so much as glanced at the other five women. She's clutching her résumé, the sides of it crinkled from her grip, her palms coated in a film of sweat. *You're going to be fine, you're going to be fine, you're going to be fine.*

A stout redheaded nurse comes toward them. "Hello, ladies. My name is Judy. I'm going to be bringing you in two by two for the interviews. Grace and Riley, if you'd like to come with me."

Grace and Riley follow Judy into her office. She plops down at her desk and holds her hand out for their résumés. Lifting her glasses onto her short spiky hair, she gestures for them to sit.

"I'm going to be frank with you," she says, flipping through the pages. "The reason you're in here together is because you've both been referred to Oakwood by people whose opinions I value highly. There will be a three-month probation period, and—" She pauses as she looks at Grace's practicum results. "Why does it say 'Needs Improvement' in so many categories?" She peers up at Grace.

Grace swallows. Her heart is beating so hard against her chest that she has to grip the sides of her chair, trying to fight the intensity of it. "Because I didn't do the nurse's corner properly—many times."

"You're shitting me."

"No, I'm not shitting you."

"Well, that's a first. Okay, you'll have some paperwork and things you'll need to sign, but come in tomorrow for that. And when you walk out of here, don't look happy."

Riley shakes Judy's hand. Grace is in shock but wipes her hand on her pant leg before taking Judy's hand as well. Nothing in Grace's life has ever been this easy.

Grace and Riley walk through the nursing home lobby, past the other candidates, and through the sliding doors. Outside in the fresh air, Grace's heartbeat slows. She has done it. She has a job. She will make decent money and get benefits.

"I can't believe my dad did that," Riley says.

"What?"

"He's a doctor, a fertility expert. He must have called in for me."

"That's nice of him, no?"

"I would've liked to have gotten the job myself. I have a good résumé," Riley says. "You want to grab a bite to eat?"

Grace twitches like she's coming out of a trance. She stops and turns. Riley's standing in front of her so casually, her hip jutted out, like they've just exited a movie theater and they're talking about where to get ice cream. Not like that was one of the biggest moments in Grace's life. She's in a coral dress with a cerulean purse slung over her shoulder and gladiator sandals. As Riley scoops a strand of short blonde hair behind her ear, Grace takes a step back. The casual warmth that Riley is directing at her causes her to swallow thickly. It catches her so completely off guard that Grace just stares at Riley for much longer than is socially acceptable.

"There's a burger place that just opened up, and I've been dying to try it," Riley continues, then adds helpfully, "and they have vegetarian options." Like that's the reason it's taken Grace so long to respond.

Grace can barely afford a can of beans, even with the twelve fifty-dollar bills that Sarah had secretly slipped into the side of her duffel bag. "Maybe another time," Grace says. "See you tomorrow."

As Grace starts to cut through the parking lot to the bus stop, Riley calls, "You want a ride?"

"I'm good, thanks!" Grace yells back.

SEVEN

The nursing home lobby is decorated for Christmas with a girthy tree strung with gold lights, a table of gingerbread houses made with the help of grandchildren, and stockings lining the mantel above the fireplace. Poinsettias everywhere.

Having trudged to work through the swirling snow, Grace stomps her feet a few times on the entrance mat. Rosy cheeked, she shakes the flakes from her hair.

She hangs her bag on the hook in the staff lunchroom, puts her dinner in the fridge—she's on the midday shift—and switches her boots out for her running shoes.

"Grace!" Annie says as Grace opens the door to her room.

"Annie!" Grace says right back. She feels the joy in the room instantly and can hear the energy in Annie's voice. Annie, who would usually have finished the crossword by now, is leaned over it with Eric, who is in a chair next to the bed. Beth is writing out Annie's Christmas cards on her other side.

"You look like you've come through a blizzard," Annie says.

"It was a gentle blizzard. Very refreshing."

Although all the Hurley siblings are tall and lean, Eric and Beth have naturally tanned skin and windswept golden blond hair, like something out of a Hawaiian resort brochure. Many of the nurses, not just on their floor but on the other floors too, have commented on what a good-looking family they are.

Eric smiles at Grace and moves to get out her way. He's wearing a red sweater with a Christmas tree on it.

Beth waves the card she's just finished to let the ink dry and then slides it into an envelope. Annie's shoes are by the bed. "Did you go for a walk?" Grace asks.

"Did two laps around the building," Annie says proudly.

"Could barely keep up with her," Eric says, perching on the edge of Annie's walker while Grace counts out her pills.

Grace passes Annie a glass of water and glances at the clock. "Annie usually rests her eyes around now for about an hour," Grace says.

"Not when my family is here," Annie says.

"No, you should rest, Nan," Beth says. "We'll go grab some lunch."

Grace shuts the blinds, reaching over a stack of neatly wrapped presents. She pauses to admire a large bouquet of pale pink and orange flowers.

"Aren't those nice?" Annie says.

"They're lovely," Grace says.

"They're for you," Daniel says.

His voice startles her. Annie had told Grace he was arriving later that week.

"Daniel was able to fly in early," Annie says. "Such a lovely surprise."

He's in the corner, closing his laptop, and is wearing a Christmas sweater too. His is green with a gold reindeer.

"They're a small token of thanks," Eric says. "It's a great comfort for us to know that you're here with Nan and keeping us up to date with things."

"That's very kind," Grace says, but she leaves the room without taking them.

Daniel follows her into the hall. "Hey," he says.

Grace does a quick check to make sure that they're alone. "Did you buy any of her other nurses flowers?" she asks, her voice low. The Hurleys have selected the highest care ratio a resident can have, and there are three other nurses assigned to Annie. She reads the answer in his eyes. "I'm sorry. I can't take them."

"I wasn't thinking," Daniel says.

"It was a really nice gesture, though," Grace says. She struggles for a moment, wondering if she should say something about leaving so abruptly the last time she saw him—a tinge of embarrassment coming over her. But if she's honest with herself, she probably wouldn't have done anything differently. Her eyes fall on the gold reindeer, and she fights a smile.

"What?" he says.

"That sweater. I—"

"Eric made me wear it."

"—love it."

"Oh." He glances down at it like it's the first time he's seen it.

Beth and Eric come into the hall, and Beth turns the lights off to Annie's room. Eric passes Daniel his coat.

"Riley told me about a café off main street I want to try," Beth says.

"That's perfect. Something quick so I can finish up a few things," Daniel says, pulling his mitts out of his pockets.

"We're not rushing lunch," Eric says, opening the door to the stairwell.

"I've got a couple of calls to make this aft," Daniel says.

"Then you can make them this aft, *after* lunch—" The door shuts behind them.

At seven o'clock Grace goes into the lunchroom to grab the remnants of her pesto pasta salad. Carmen is putting her snack in the fridge. She's on the evening shift, taking over for Grace.

"Did you guys see what the Hurleys got you?" Ellie nods at the back table.

There are four large bouquets on it, each one a bit different, and

Grace spots the one she had been admiring earlier with her name on it.

"For us?" Carmen says. "I didn't even think they knew my name." Carmen is the newest member of their team. She picks hers up to admire it.

"Sweet of them, isn't it?" Ellie says to Grace.

"Those are gorgeous," Riley says, admiring Grace's flowers as she comes out of the staff bathroom. She's changed out of her scrubs and is wearing a black dress under a caramel colored coat.

"You look nice," Grace says.

"Dinner with some uni friends," Riley says. "I know I ask you every year, but I'm just throwing it out there again. Christmas Eve, my parent's house. People come and go. It's super chill. If you want to bring something, my mom loves chardonnay. If you're wondering what to wear, something like this is perfect." She waves a hand down her outfit.

Music comes toward them from the common room. Glancing at each other, they swivel around and stride down the hallway. Riley opens the door, and music engulfs them. "Reach Out I'll Be There" is coming from a speaker nestled in the lights strung along the windowsill. The residents have gathered, sitting in their wheelchairs and perched on their walkers. Eric is dancing gingerly with Annie.

"Eric," Grace starts.

"It's all right, Grace," Tony says. "Let's just listen to a couple of songs." He's watching Eric and Annie, tapping his foot to the beat. Even Harry is smiling.

Eric lowers Annie back into her chair and offers Grace a hand. Reluctant, she shakes her head, clamming up. Unfazed, he does a spin and keeps dancing. Riley puts her things on a chair and joins him to the delighted cheer of the people gathered together. There is such ease to their movements as they dance together but not together. Their dancing and smiles are infectious.

Grace starts moving her shoulders back and forth to the beat of the music. Placing her coat and bag on Riley's, she joins them. Eric is lip-syncing and pretending to pull an invisible rope attached to Grace in time with the chorus of "reach out," which makes Grace laugh.

Daniel comes into the room and leans against the coffee counter, watching them.

"That was fun," Grace says as the song ends.

"One more," Eric says.

Grace shakes her head, and Riley says, "Come on, what have you got to rush off to?"

Absolutely nothing.

Yazoo's "Only You" comes on. It's too slow to dance to, and Grace backs out of the triangle. Eric offers a hand to Riley. Effortlessly, Riley steps into him, and he twirls her in a lazy circle, like they've done it a million times. It's beautiful to watch.

Daniel comes to stand alongside Grace and tilts his head toward them.

"No," Grace says, suddenly self-conscious. "I'm not a dancer. Not like that."

"Neither am I," he says.

He takes her hand gently, and as he slides his palm over hers, it feels natural and warm against her skin. He's moving so slowly that she could pull away from him or shake her head, but she doesn't. As he comes to stand in front of her, she doesn't know what to do, where to put her hands or how to stand, but it doesn't seem to matter.

They are swaying smoothly to the music, and as he lowers his head toward hers, her body folds into his. She puts her hands on his arms and feels his muscles move beneath the fabric of his shirt. His hands are just above her waist. She shuts her eyes and for a moment forgets about all the other people in the room. Just her body and his, warm and steady in front of her. She is surprised by how comfortable she is with him. She's never felt like this before, being so close to someone else. When the music ends, she pulls away as if coming out of a dream.

He grins at her, and she stares back at him.

"Have a great weekend, everyone," Riley says with a theatrical twirl and then bows before grabbing her things.

In the stairwell Riley says, "Eric's a great dancer."

"So are you," Grace says.

Riley grins at her in a way Grace can't read.

"What?" Grace says.

"Nothing."

A sudden bang jolts Grace out of her sleep. In a foggy daze, disoriented, she lifts her head from the pillow. The banging persists, urgent and loud. She rises quickly, her feet soft thuds on the stairs as she descends them in her cotton striped pajamas and is instantly lit up by flashing red lights filling her living room. She swings the front door open to find a man in a firefighter uniform on her porch about to bang against the door again. "Hello, miss." He takes a step back and gestures to his right. "There's a fire at your neighbor's house, so we're going to need you to evacuate from the premises until we make sure it's under control."

Grace leans forward to peer at Mary's house but doesn't see any smoke, just more flashing lights. "Can I get a couple of things?"

He glances over his shoulder at another firefighter who is attaching a hose to a fire hydrant. Grace turns before he can answer and grabs her purse, her bag with her nurse's uniform, and a sweater off her armchair.

"Okay, okay," he says. "I gotta get you outta here. Just you, right?"

"Yeah." She slips her feet into her boots. "Do you know how long it'll be?"

"Could be a while. Might want to bunk in with a friend tonight," he says.

The first two hotels she goes to are full. There's a dental convention in town. What they could be convening about, she has no idea. The second concierge kindly calls a few hotels for Grace. They're all full. Even the motel on the edge of town.

"Want me to try the Forester?" she asks.

It's by far the most expensive, but Grace nods. There are a few rooms available there she tells Grace, her hand covering the mouthpiece.

"Thanks," Grace says, appreciating the effort this woman has put in for her.

Grace drives slowly down the main street as people meander out of bars and restaurants. The car clock shines 1:04 a.m., but it feels much later. A gush of cold air engulfs her as she once again parks and steps from the car.

The lobby of the Forester is intimidatingly stylish, with a massive chandelier hanging from the dome ceiling high above her and a white marble floor with a black swirl spiraling toward her. Grace steels herself before walking toward the imposing front desk made of dark mahogany and to one of the women standing behind it. As Grace approaches, the woman surveys her from behind thick eyelashes that flicker up and down. The vibrant red cable-knit sweater that Grace had quickly grabbed doesn't do much to cover her blue and white pajamas.

After a succession of rapid typing bursts, the woman's manicured nails hover over the keyboard. "We're all booked up, I'm afraid," she says.

"You don't have *any* rooms?"

"We do have a couple of suites, but they're quite expensive."

"Right, okay."

"Anything else I can help you with?" Her voice goes up an octave.

"Nope."

She's been in worse situations. She can sleep in the back of her car. She's thinking about where she'll park it when Eric comes through the revolving door. Then Beth and Daniel. They're in midconversation and Grace ducks her head, hoping to slip by them unnoticed. But the lobby is fairly empty and her sweater is fairly bright.

"Grace," Eric says jovially. "What're you doing here?" Daniel and Beth go quiet as they take in her pajamas and red sweater. She runs her hand over her hair in an effort to pat it down and appear more presentable. "Are you all right?" Eric's tone changes, concern creasing his brows.

"Yeah. There was a fire at the house next to mine, so I had to evacuate for the evening."

"Shit, that's terrible," Eric says.

"The firefighters seemed to have it under control, and I couldn't see any flames." This doesn't alleviate the worry in their faces, so she adds, "I think it was just a precautionary measure."

"Are you staying here then?" Beth asks.

"No, I'm . . . not." She doesn't look at Daniel, whose eyes she has felt on her throughout this entire interaction. He'll probably know that if she's here, she will have tried every other hotel in town. She hoists the strap of her bag farther up her shoulder and tries to act casual as she says, "Well, I'll see you guys tomorrow."

"Wait, where are you going?" Eric says. "You can stay with Daniel or me. Beth's crashing on my pullout, but there should be enough room."

"I've got a pullout as well," Daniel says. The way he suggests it, like it's no big deal, almost makes it sound like a normal, sensible option.

"That's kind of you, but I'll figure something out," she says, starting to cut through them.

"Figure what out?" Eric says. "It's one in the morning. What're you going to do, sleep in your car?"

Grace glances down, now in between the three of them.

"No way, I was joking," Eric says. "Come on, that's ridiculous, not to mention unsafe. You could freeze to death."

"Grace," Beth says, taking the bag from Grace's shoulder. "You've been through enough tonight."

Grace turns to face Daniel. "You won't mind?"

He holds her gaze. "Not at all."

Daniel opens the door to his room, and Grace takes her bag back from Beth.

"Good night, guys," Beth says.

Daniel flicks the lights on, which illuminate a large sitting area with ivory couches, wood furnishings, and a marble fireplace. There are floor-to-ceiling windows overlooking the city and a deep balcony through a sliding door. "I'm just going to . . ." Grace nods at the bathroom.

When she comes out, Daniel plants his hands on his waist and glances at her. "Turns out I was wrong; it's not a pullout."

"No problem. I'll sleep on the couch."

"It's not all that soft," he says, pressing down on the cushion to show her. "The bed is huge. We can share it." He shrugs. "Whatever you want."

He goes into the bathroom, and she walks to the bed. It is massive. She runs her hand over the duvet. It's quite plush. She takes off her sweater and pulls back the cover to lay down. In the quiet dim, she feels the adrenaline coursing through her limbs. She hadn't allowed herself to acknowledge it, burying it deep within her, but now it's rising to the surface. It's been a long time since she's felt like this. The burning embers of survival. She needs to calm her mind if she is going to sleep.

Daniel comes out of the bathroom, turns the lights off, and approaches the bed. From what she can make out through the shadows, he's in shorts and a white sleeveless top. He lays down on the far side of the bed.

"Thank you," she says. "I really appreciate this."

"It's no problem at all, Grace," he says. Then, after a moment, "Riley didn't pick up?"

"Riley? I didn't call her." Grace liked Riley a lot. She would trust her with almost anything. But to call her for something like this, in the middle of the night, would be nuts.

Daniel puts his hand behind his head. "You two seem so close," he says.

"We work together," Grace says by way of explanation.

"I've got work friends, people I respect and enjoy hanging out with, but they're not like you and Riley."

"What do you mean?"

"You guys are just so easy together. So in sync."

She turns her head and takes in his silhouette. The side of his smooth face, his muscular shoulder and arm resting on top of the duvet. He's open. Relaxed in a way she's never seen before. "Do you think I'm weird?" The question is out of her mouth in an instant. Without thought. She clutches the comforter, silently chastising herself.

"No," he says without hesitation. "I think you've been through some stuff."

"So that forgives my oddness?"

He glances at her. "That's not what I meant. Honestly, I have trouble getting a bead on you. I notice sometimes at the nursing home that you avoid me."

"You make me nervous," she says.

"What? Why?" Shock lines his voice.

"At first it was because you're so intense but also calm at the same time. I couldn't get a read on you. When I would call with updates on Annie, I thought you were annoyed or angry with me. But then I realized that you were quiet and brief because you wanted to know what was going on, no matter how busy you were. And that's another thing —you're a workaholic, just like me. But you have this compassionate side where you care for the people in your life who matter most to you."

"So do you, Grace. Don't think I don't see it, because I do. With Riley and Annie and others in the home. And with Alex, it's on a whole different level—"

"Daniel," she says with as much warning in her voice as she can muster.

"—yet you keep him at arm's length, if you could even call it that."

"This," she says, anger curdling within her. "This is why I avoid you. Because you push. And you pry. It's why I've scheduled appointments and days off when I knew you were coming to visit."

"Are you serious?"

"Yeah," she says weakly. "Now that Annie never leaves the home, it's friggin' hard."

She can see his eyes searching in the darkness. "But you're less nervous now that you've met me? Now that we've talked?" he asks, his tone hopeful.

She shakes her head, and her breaths become shallow. He waits patiently, not rushing the words from her. "Daniel, I'm so fucked up." Her voice breaks, and she's thankful for the darkness. She would never be able to say this in the light. "I don't allow anyone to get close to me because I have such guilt. And every time I feel happy, I try to push it down. To push it away."

"Because of Alex?"

"Yeah. Because I abandoned him. I couldn't deal with it all. I was suffocating in that house. And I left it all behind. I left him." Her thoughts flicker to her hands clutching the railing behind her, and she shuts her mind to it.

"Grace." He shifts, and she balls her hand into a fist, worried that he might try to touch her. He doesn't. "You're stronger now than you were then."

She scoffs.

"You are. You didn't have the support that you needed. That you deserved. You were young and vulnerable, trying to keep it together for the two of you, living with a selfish addict. But you've risen from it. You're not reliant on others anymore. You're self-sufficient and independent."

If she was so self-sufficient and independent, why did she fear and avoid such basic interactions? She has already said too much. She needs to end this conversation.

"Good night, Daniel," she says.

After a moment he says, "Good night, Grace."

Grace pops a bagel down in the toaster.

"You want some tea?" Riley asks, coming into the lunchroom.

"That'd be great, thanks. Bagel?"

"Yeah. You all right? You look tired." Riley pulls two mugs from the cupboard.

Grace had spent the night trying not to toss and turn, then tiptoed out of the room and changed in her car. Grace nods but then says, "There was a fire at my neighbors last night, so I had to leave my house."

"Jesus. Where'd you go?"

"I tried a couple of hotels and then ended up at the Forester."

"*The Forester?* Why didn't you call me?"

"It was one a.m."

"So?" Riley pours some milk into Grace's tea and slides it down the counter to her.

"So then you'd be tired too. I wasn't going to bug you for that," Grace says, taking a crunching bite out of her bagel.

"Bug me? Grace, I wouldn't have given a shit."

The director of the nursing home, Janine, comes into the doorway of the lunchroom. "Grace, a word in my office, please," she says.

Riley glances at Grace as she puts her bagel down and follows Janine down the hall.

Janine sits but doesn't invite Grace to, so she stays standing, a large desk between them. "I'm surprised at you, Grace," Janine says, easing back in her chair. "You're a smart girl, so you must know how entirely inappropriate this is."

"I'm sorry, I'm not following," Grace says.

"It's a conflict of interest, simple as that. As this is a privately funded home, we must keep a high level of standard to ensure a fair environment for everyone. Without favoritism. We can't take advantage of our residents' families, however convenient the situation might be for you," she says.

Convenient the situation? What was she talking about?

"I'm going to send you home and mark this in your file. You can decide whether it will count as a vacation day or as unpaid leave. Take some time to think about your actions, ones that I hope end now."

Had Daniel told someone that Grace asked him to help her with Alex? A warmth gathers in her chest as she tries not to panic but then she realizes that it didn't make sense. He was a lawyer. Part of the job description was being confidential, but more than that she didn't believe he would say something to out her. He was too subtle, too good at what he did. "What actions?" Grace asks.

"Your relationship with Daniel Hurley."

"My . . . what?" Grace says, at a loss for words.

"I'm going to be honest with you. I know you were a nepotism hire and that has never sat well with me. Anyone skipping the line to get ahead. Taking advantage of the system put in place."

This hits a nerve with Grace. Usually adept at letting things roll off her back, she can't let this go. "I spent my first three years here working every holiday and long weekend." She worked her ass off. Yes, it had been to pay off her debts, to send Alex money every few months, and to save for a house, but every nurse had appreciated her taking their holiday shifts.

Janine clasps her hands together on the desk. "You don't have a family, and you don't travel. It's not a huge inconvenience for you to work and get paid time and a half, is it?" Grace's whole body goes rigid, igniting with anger. So many thoughts dash through her mind, but she can't say any of them because then she'll be in real trouble. "Many of your fellow nurses are much quicker than you are, much more efficient in their duties."

Grace took her time with each resident. Knew their wants, needs, preferences, and what made them anxious. She had gotten to know each of them as people, even the ones she didn't like. While some of the other nurses were more concerned with giving them more pills and vitamins, Grace wanted them to have balanced diets and exercise, activities and hobbies to look forward to.

"We'll keep this conversation between us but know that this is a warning," Janine says. "If things continue with Daniel, be prepared to find employment elsewhere."

"I'm not with Daniel." She hates herself for saying it, but it's the truth, and Grace wants to defend herself from being accused of something she simply hasn't done.

"Lying is not an attractive feature. I overheard Eric telling Annie that you stayed in his hotel room last night."

"Did you happen to overhear why?"

"No, I'm not one for gossip."

"There was a fire at my—"

"I'm busy, Grace," she says pointedly. "I don't have time for your stories. As illuminating as they might be." She angles toward her computer screen.

Grace comes into the hall so annoyed by the conversation she's just had that she isn't tired anymore.

"What's going on?" Riley has finished her tea and bagel. She's been waiting for Grace to come back.

"Janine thinks that I'm sleeping with Daniel and that I'm taking advantage of the nurse-resident relationship."

"Sleeping with Daniel?"

"It was his hotel room I stayed in last night, and Eric told Annie. Oh, and I'm a nepotism hire who doesn't deserve to be here as I'm shit at my job because I take too long to do everything. So now I have to go home and have a good hard think about my actions."

"That's insane. The only reason the other nurses on this floor can do their jobs so smoothly is because of all the stuff you do. It's because of you that the residents are in such good moods. Do you know Tony won't let any other nurse pick out his clothes for him? He asked Carmen the other day if she was color-blind for suggesting an outfit you'd dressed him in the week before."

Grace lifts her strap onto her shoulder. "Thank you. I appreciate you."

"It's true," Riley says fiercely and then lowers her voice. "But also, you stayed in Daniel's room last night? How was that?"

"It was out of necessity," Grace says. "I left before he woke up this morning." She couldn't believe the things she'd admitted to him. She had all but run from the room, mortified, and prayed that he wouldn't wake up.

"And all this time you've been trying to avoid him," Riley says.

Grace groans. "Is it that obvious?" She reaches for her coat.

"No, you're *very* subtle." Riley grins at Grace. "Don't worry, it's just because I know you." Grace loves Riley's smile, the way her hazel eyes warm and brighten. When she's stressed it puts her at ease. They head to the stairwell door slowly, keeping their voices low. "That night at the bar, when you rescued Daniel from that big guy, I knew it was the start of something."

Grace hadn't realized that Riley had witnessed that interaction. "What do you mean?"

"The way you were with him and his tentative glances at you while you spoke. Unlike you," she says this tenderly, "I don't avoid Daniel. I've seen him many times over the years, picking Annie up and taking her to dinner, driving her to Beth's house for the weekend. I've never seen him look at someone the way he looked at you that night."

"With confusion?" Because he was trying to feel out the situation, not knowing where Grace was going with it. It made total sense that he was tentative, unaware, and unsure.

"Smitten. He was totally smitten."

"It was really dark in there. You might've misread—"

"I know what I saw."

Grace lets her hand rest on the door handle behind her. "What about you?" She'd wanted to ask Riley about that night but didn't want to pry. This seems like a good segue. "Have you talked to Will at all since then?"

"No." Riley makes a face. "He walked me home, and we had a really nice chat, but when we got to my house, I took a step in and he took a step back. He seemed kind of nervous and then he waved at me. Like literally waved." Riley impersonates it. "I was so surprised by it, I just said good night. I didn't even get his number."

There are voices in the hall coming toward them. Grace opens the stairwell door. "Oh, Harry just got new hearing aids. I was going to help him set them up today."

"I'm on it," Riley says, squeezing Grace's arm. "I'll see you."

In the early afternoon, Daniel comes into the hallway as Riley is wheeling Tony down to the community room.

"Hey, Riley. Do you have a minute?"

"Give me one sec," Riley says. She sets Tony up at Annie's table and gets them a deck of cards. Then she nods at Daniel to follow her to the servery off the hall. "What's up?"

"Do you know where Grace is? I thought she was working today."

Riley tells him about the conversation with Janine.

Daniel shakes his head. "Eric shouldn't have said anything."

"It's not his fault," she says quietly. "Janine's always had a stick up her ass, and she's never liked Grace. She's a coldhearted bitch who's never been able to see the bigger picture. I was a nepotism hire, but you think she gave a shit about that? No. Because my dad is a medical specialist, and if you don't think she's called in favors there then . . ."

"Did Grace say anything else about last night?"

"You mean about her neighbor's house potentially burning down?"

He plants his hands on his hips and lowers his head. "I couldn't believe it. Eric and Beth had to convince her to stay with me. She was going to sleep in her car. And now this woman is punishing her." He takes an angry breath, and his nostrils flare slightly.

"Don't say anything," Riley says. "She wouldn't want you to."

"She doesn't accept help readily."

"No, she does not," Riley says. Then, "Has she shared any of her past with you?"

"Like about her life in the foster home? A little bit."

"I can't even imagine. The shit she went through."

EIGHT

Six Years Earlier

After Grace's first week of work, a wave of exhaustion unlike any she has ever known drapes over her. Gripping her mind. Crippling her. Filling her with doubt. The motel room she is staying in is heavy with heat and humidity. She turns on the air-conditioning unit, and it rattles to life. Her skin is damp and cool to the touch. She absolutely cannot afford to get sick.

Perched on the edge of her bed, the voices of the construction workers come through the walls, loud with drink. Smoke seeps through the cracks of her door and the vents. She feels nauseous when she thinks of Alex and squeezes her hands against the sides of her temples, trying to block out the thoughts. He'll be fine. He'll be well fed and given proper clothing. Sarah is a good person. Grace made the right decision. *Everything will be fine.*

But sometimes when she's alone, she can't block out the one thought coursing through her. That there is only one person in the whole world who loves her unconditionally and she has just left him.

Now this is her life. Living out of a motel room. Eating out of cans and bunches and bunches of bananas. She has worked so hard for *this*? To be surrounded by strange voices that have her twitching awake in the middle of the night. Washing her clothes in the sink. Staring at the walls, not wanting to use too much energy, because then she'd need to eat, and her credit card is already maxed out. Yesterday when she had gone to the grocery store, she had suffered the sinking humiliation of having to leave her few items on the conveyer belt.

The voices go quiet in the early hours of the morning, but the smell of smoke lingers, and she cannot fall asleep for the life of her. She has never been this low. Light-headed, she stands and pulls her running shoes on.

There is a man jogging through the forest on a path well known to him. It's a warm, humid morning, and a light breeze ripples against his damp T-shirt. He runs here to clear his head, to reset and recharge. It's the darkest time of day, just before the sun rises, and so he's wearing a headlamp. It's his favorite time to run, when the fewest people are out and he can lose himself in his thoughts. He makes his way toward the lake and stops to tie his shoe, breathing in the fresh earth and feeling for a moment his heart beating against his chest.

He walks along the railing as he climbs the hill to the lookout and then checks his watch at the midway point. He'll have to turn around now if he's going to have time to make his lunch and shower before work.

His eyes fall to a figure below him. A woman passes under a streetlight to the stairs, the more direct route to the lookout. Something about the way she takes the bottom steps unsettles him. Her legs are wobbly yet determined. He gives his earbuds a small yank, and they dangle around his shoulders. He quickens his pace, bounding up the hill.

The railing is cool under Grace's touch, a reprieve she may have noticed if she was of another mindset. She climbs the bars of the lookout barrier and lowers herself onto the other side, with only her heels biting the ledge. Below her is darkness, but she knows that it is far enough that the impact of the water will be enough. At this height it will be like hitting cement.

Numb and completely devoid. Drained of all energy. She shuts her eyes, leans forward, and lets her hands go.

With a jolting start, she opens her eyes. Her whole body is tilted forward, but something is holding her back. Dark hands clutching her wrists.

"Hey, hey. What're you doing?" a man's voice says from behind her.

"What does it look like?" she says weakly. She tries to tug her hands free, but the man's grip is firm. "Please let me go."

"Just listen to me for a sec," the man says. He's breathing hard. "Have you ever seen the sun rise over the lake?"

"What?" Her voice is small. Barely a whisper. "No."

"Seriously?" He's trying to buy time, and they both know it. "Would you do something for me? Watch it as it breaks the horizon. And then if you want me to, I'll let you go. Okay? I'll let you go."

"Okay," she says. She doesn't have the energy to fight. She knows that something is truly wrong with her because her heart isn't racing. In this moment she is calm, and that is the most terrifying thing of all.

Slowly he eases her back toward him so that she's up against the railing.

The air turns to gray and then a rich blue before becoming a radiant pink as the sun peeks over the horizon. Columns of light slice through the clouds. As the beauty of it cascades over her, a tear falls down her cheek. Her whole body relaxes, and she shuts her eyes to its glow, her guard lowered. The man wraps his arms tightly around her, bear hugging her, and in one swift movement pulls her back over the railing.

Angry, she turns and pushes him hard against his chest. He holds his hands up. "Look, whatever you've got going on right now, it's not worth ending your life over." She shakes her head. There is no way he can understand what she's going through, the exhaustion and despair. "What you feel right now, you might not feel this way tomorrow or the day after that," he says, a pleading note in his voice.

"I can't even afford a loaf of bread," she says.

"You're going to kill yourself over some bread?" His voice is hoarse.

"No, not . . ." She trails off. Her hands are shaking, and she doesn't know if it's from the adrenaline or the hunger. He digs into his back pocket and pulls out three twenty-dollar bills. All the cash that he has in his wallet and holds it out to her. Her throat is thick as she speaks. "I don't want your money."

He bends to set the bills on a large rock, placing another small rock on top of them so that they don't blow away. "I'm going to leave this right here," he says. "And if you want to come back tomorrow and jump, I won't stop you. But today is not the day." He stands up straight and turns to face her. "Today is not the day."

In the years that followed, that morning would remain a blur for her because she wouldn't allow herself to think how she was about to end her life and how sixty dollars changed everything. That money bridged the gap. It was how she got through to her first paycheck. Queen of coupons, she made it. But it wasn't the money that gave her the will to live. It was the voice, the pleading desperation from a stranger. The hands on her wrists and the man who lifted her back over the ledge.

Just a few hours later, Grace is at work, going about her day like she wasn't about to end her life that very morning. She washes the remnants of her beef and potato stew from her Tupperware container. She had emptied it from a can earlier that morning so that it wouldn't look like she was eating two-dollar stew that she could barely swallow. The skin beneath her eyes is searing red streaks, and dark circles have taken hold of them. She will need to work harder at sleeping better. She descends the stairs. One foot in front of the other, pushing the door to the lobby open.

"Hey." Riley jumps up from the armchair where she is sitting.

"Hi," Grace says, slowing to a stop and wondering why Riley is still there.

"I was just waiting to walk out with you."

"To the parking lot?"

"Yeah," Riley says brightly and holds out a Christmas-themed tin. "My mom made some blueberry scones last night. I'm not a huge fan of scones, but these ones are pretty good."

"Thanks." Grace takes it from her. "I'll bring the tin back tomorrow."

"Don't worry about it. We've got lots."

They walk the fifty or so feet to the point where Riley goes left to her car and Grace goes right to the bus stop.

"Have a good night, Grace."

"You too." As Grace turns away, she feels a bit lighter.

A week later, Grace is counting out Annie's morning pills and vitamins. Annie isn't her usual patient—Grace is filling in for one of her regular nurses who's on holiday—and she hasn't warmed to Grace.

"What're all these for?" Grace says mostly to herself as she lifts a few of the bottles to study them. The tray is full of them, jammed together. Large containers of vitamins and vials of prescription medications and over-the-counter drugs.

"For my bone density, iron, blood pressure . . ." Annie waves a hand in the air like her answer is all-encompassing.

"Right. I just don't think you need all of them." Grace starts to sort them into rows based on what's necessary, what might actually help Annie, and what she could do without.

The cell phone on Annie's bedside table lights up. Her finger shakes as she tries to swipe it open. After three attempts Grace leans over and does it for her. "Hello?" Annie says like she's asking a question and if she doesn't like the answer, then she'll hang up. "Daniel? Can you talk to someone here for me? They want to make changes." Annie holds the phone out.

"You want me to talk to him?" Grace says, realizing that she must be the *they* Annie is referring to. Judy is the point of contact for the Hurleys, and Grace hopes she isn't overstepping by taking this call.

Annie just waves the phone at her like *isn't that obvious.*

Grace takes it. "Hello," she says.

"You're not Judy."

"No, I'm . . . my name is Grace," she says. "I'm filling in for one of Annie's regular nurses. You're Annie's grandson, right?"

"I am, yes. What can I do for you?"

"I was looking at all these vitamins and medications your grandma's on, and I was thinking that maybe we could scale back on some of them."

"Are you saying that Judy is overmedicating her?"

"No!" Grace exclaims. "Just that with some daily exercises and a change to her meal plan that she might not need all of them. Especially some of these vitamins."

"So you're saying that my nan isn't getting enough exercise there?"

Lord, he's intense. This wasn't getting off to a great start, but at the moment, as far as Grace knows, Annie isn't getting any. "She could be a bit more active."

"How would you go about organizing this?"

"I would add strengthening exercises into her weekly schedule and a walk or two down the hallways and take her out to the garden on nicer days. I'd be with her the whole time or nearby. And we could go over the meal choices with her to make sure she's getting the proper supplements in her diet. I'd keep an eye on her and reintroduce any meds or vitamins as she needed them."

"That sounds like a good plan," he says. "You need anything from us, you let me know, Grace."

"Um, well, Judy's your point of contact, so she'll be the one letting you know after I draw up the plan."

"Is there a way to change that?"

"Yeah, it's totally flexible. We can make adjustments at any time."

"No, I mean the point of contact."

"Oh, that's not something . . . I'm new here, so I don't know how all that works exactly. I'm not on Annie's regular team. As I said, I'm a fill-in."

"Right. Okay. Thank you," he says and hangs up.

The next day when Grace comes into work, Judy calls her into her office. Being the head nurse, she's in charge of everyone's patient assignments. Judy gestures for Grace to sit and then moves the stack of binders and folders so that she can see her across the desk. "We had a call from Daniel Hurley yesterday. He said that you wanted to make some changes to Annie's schedule and medications."

Shit. Perhaps she should've just kept her mouth shut.

"What did you suggest to him?"

"It was more to do with her diet and the vitamins she's taking. She's still as sharp as ever, but she's becoming frail."

"I've asked her to join the strengthening classes in the community room and to go on the group walks, but she refuses. So I stopped."

"I think Annie is a bit stubborn and shyer than she lets on. She might not be comfortable doing the exercises in the community room or walking with the others if she can't keep up. That's why I thought I could do a bit with her every day. Just the two of us."

"I see," Judy says, studying Grace.

"I'm sorry, Judy. I'll call Daniel and tell him I was off base and shouldn't have suggested these things."

"I don't have a problem with these changes, Grace," Judy says. "I just want you to understand what they entail."

"Oh. I see."

"He wants you as the point of contact for the family from now on," she says. "So we're going to add her to your patient assignments." When Grace doesn't answer, she adds, "Okay?"

"Yeah," Grace says. "If that's all right with you?"

"Of course it's all right." Judy nods and goes back to her paperwork. "You'll keep me updated on how she's doing?"

"I will. Thanks, Judy."

NINE

"Bonjour," Riley says in greeting to Daniel as she and Grace come into the lobby. He's on his way out, wearing a black pea coat and holding his gloves. Grace hasn't spoken to him since the night in the hotel room, and she glances at him shyly.

"Bonjour," Daniel says with an amused tilt of his head and then swinging around. "There's a gala at the hotel I'm staying at on New Year's Eve. Would you two like to join my siblings and me?"

"Are we talking about the Forester here?" Riley says.

"I am, yeah."

"They've been sold out since October."

"I have access to six tickets through my firm. If I don't claim them by tonight, they're going to give them away."

"Who would be our sixth?" Riley says.

"Will?" Grace offers, and Daniel's eyes alight on hers.

"So you're interested?" he says.

"Will?" Riley repeats.

They hadn't seen him since that night at Moby Dick's, and as far as Grace knew, he hadn't made any contact with Riley.

"Yeah," Grace says, trying to sound casual. "I could call him at the station, see if he wants to come."

"Perfect," Daniel says, and he pushes himself through the revolving door.

As Grace and Riley climb the stairs, Riley says, "You've always had a soft spot for him."

"Who?"

"Will," Riley says, rolling her eyes. "You know this is going to be super fancy, like floor-length dress fancy." Catching the dread that fills Grace's face, she adds, "Don't worry. We'll go shopping together. It'll be fun."

Grace is in the Forester's lobby bathroom wondering why she didn't take Riley up on her offer to go together. At the time it seemed so impractical. Driving somewhere to drive somewhere else. But now that she's alone in the bathroom, in a floor-length lilac gown that is nicer than anything she has ever worn, she realizes she has made a mistake.

She had told the cab driver to let her out early so that she could at least walk the last little bit. He probably thought she was nuts. But her nerves had gotten the better of her, and he had the heat on high. After paying him she had literally leaped from the car and narrowly avoided a pile of slush. The cool air rippled against her warm skin, dousing it like an ember, the movement of her limbs helping to calm her.

She grips the sink, her chest constricting, and stares into the mirror at the marble fountain behind her. She tries to focus on the water cascading down its tiers and the smell of the cinnamon soap. She breathes in. Filling her stomach like a balloon. Music and laughter drift through the walls, and she wishes she was light and effortless like Riley. God, she would kill to be like that. To have a day when she wasn't petrified of doing something different, something new. Something that should be exciting and fun but that seemed so daunting. Fuck. She needs to get out of here.

She's approaching the coat check desk when a voice calls her name. Grace freezes like a thief caught and turns. Beth is cutting through the lobby toward her in a canary yellow dress that is vibrant against her glowing skin. Her shiny blonde hair is pulled into a high, elegant bun. She weaves her arm through Grace's. "I'm so glad you could come tonight," she says, leading Grace toward the dining room. "We're at table thirteen."

Grace slows as she enters the ballroom to take it all in. Her eyes travel up toward the crystal chandeliers and gold balloons then down to the gold plates and delicately embroidered napkins lined with gold trim. There are round bouquets of roses at each table, and everyone around them is gorgeously dressed.

Eric stands as they approach the table with the number thirteen propped in the middle. He's in a shiny black suit with a pink tie, and his blond hair is slicked back. "Daniel will be down in a minute. He had to finish a couple of things." He says this tightly, and Grace can tell it was a bone of contention.

"Our brother," Beth says. "Always working."

"Even on days when the rest of the world is not," Eric says.

"I was wondering who to pay for my ticket. I didn't see anyone when I came in," Grace says.

Daniel comes into the room then, adjusting a cuff link. He's in a perfectly tailored black suit. With his smooth face and dark hair, he looks like he could be in a magazine ad. Without glancing at their table, he heads to the baskets set up for the silent auction to raise money for the local hospital. Grace weaves around the tables toward him.

"Daniel," she calls.

At her voice he stops and turns in one swift movement.

She gives him a small smile. "Hi," she says drawing closer. God, he's attractive.

"Grace, you're so . . ." His voice trails off, and his gaze lingers on her face and then travels down her dress. Is Daniel Hurley at a loss for words? She didn't think it possible.

"Fancy?" she offers.

He swallows.

"Were you checking out the baskets?"

"The what?" he says like he has no idea there's a table full of elaborately decorated baskets along the entire wall behind him.

His mind must still be on work. He's definitely distracted by something, and it's hindering him from thinking properly. She should just let him be. Give him a few minutes so that he can unwind and regroup. "Never mind. I'll stop bugging you. I'll see you at our table."

She starts to turn, but he takes her by the wrist and then lets her go. His eyes close briefly as if composing himself. "You're not bugging me, Grace." His voice is deep, pitched low.

"Would you care for a glass of champagne?" A man in a white tux holds a tray of glass flutes out to them.

"No, thank you," Grace says.

"I'm all right, thanks," Daniel says.

As the man offers a drink to the people next to them, Grace says, "I brought cash."

"Cash?"

"For my ticket."

"Oh, don't worry about that," he says, sounding more like his usual self. When she opens her mouth to argue, he leans in. "Please. Let me do this."

"Guys!" Riley says, joining them with Will, who is looking quite dapper in his slightly too large suit. His face lifts to the ceiling in much the same way Grace's must have as he takes in the room. "Doesn't this just give you all the New Year's Eve feels?" As Riley hugs Daniel, Grace is envious of how easy she is with her greeting.

"Hi, I'm Will." Will steps forward and shakes Daniel's hand. "Is it you I pay?"

"Don't worry about it."

Riley clutches Grace's arm. "Lord help us." Grace follows Riley's gaze to the five-tiered chocolate fountain on the other side of the room.

As they make their way over, Grace leans in to Riley. "Did you try to pay Daniel?"

"Not you too," Riley says.

"What?"

"I'm going to say the same thing I just said to Will. He wants to pay for it, and he has the money, so let him. Trust me. I grew up around people who have money. I know when to push in and when to leave it. This is a time to leave it." They each take a stick with strawberries on it and hold it under the cascading chocolate. "This is heaven."

"It's on your face," Grace says, wiping chocolate off Riley's cheek.

"It's on *your* face!" Riley laughs. "Hold on, let's get a picture. Let me grab that woman."

Grace is still wiping her mouth when Riley comes back and wraps her arm around Grace. "You got it," Riley says and they smile.

"Grace?" The woman holding Riley's phone lowers it.

Grace freezes.

"Holy shit," Brooke says. "You look *totally* normal now. How have you been?"

"Fine," Grace says, feeling as though she has just been placed in a vise and wants nothing more than to break free.

Riley takes her phone back.

"That's great. That's so great. A bunch of us from high school were at a wedding last night, so we decided to tag this on too. Stop by our table later, and we'll have a chat and catch up, okay? Table six."

As Brooke walks away, Riley leans into Grace. "You okay?"

Grace nods.

"You went to high school together?"

"Yeah."

"She wasn't the nicest, I take it?"

Grace shakes her head.

"Forget her," Riley says as they head back to their table.

As Grace sits between Daniel and Will, and Riley between Will and Beth, a server places a large silver plate with oysters and lemon slices in the middle of the table. Beth squeezes some lemon on one and lifts the shell to her mouth, gracefully tilting it and sucking it back. Eric, Daniel, and Riley do the same. Grace and Will share a skeptical glance, and she's glad to know she's not the only one who's never tried oysters.

"I will if you do," Grace says to Will.

"I'm in."

They each take one, squeeze some lemon onto it, and toast each other with the shells. Before she can think too much about what she's eating or the texture of it, she sucks it back.

"You don't like it?" Daniel says after she swallows.

"No, it's actually quite good," she says.

Near the end of the meal, a server places a cup of green tea in front of Grace. "Thanks," she says over her shoulder. They've had so much to eat that she's full to the gunnels and everyone except Eric and Will, who seem to have bottomless appetites, are picking away at their chocolate lava cakes. Riley's deep in discussion with Beth, and Eric is explaining something to Daniel.

Grace swallows thickly. She needs to do this before she overthinks it and chickens out yet again. She has wanted to say something since the first time Will brought Carl back to their lobby three years ago, but she has never been brave enough. She lightly clutches her forearms and sets her elbows on the table, leaning toward Will. "Hey," she says.

Will shifts in his seat.

"I . . ." she starts, her voice small. "I've always wanted to thank you. Not just for pulling me back over the railing but also and especially for not telling anyone." Will glances at her, a pained expression on his face, and she can see that as hard as it is for her to say this, it's just as hard for him to hear it. But he acknowledges her words with a tight nod. "You were the person I needed in that moment, and I'm very grateful to you."

"It was nothing, Grace," he says quickly.

She looks at him. "It was everything." She sits back in her seat, relieved, and reaches for her tea. It's then that she realizes that Daniel is no longer talking to Eric. He's gone still, and her face grows warm.

"Grace!" Eric cuts across Daniel. "Would you like to dance with me?"

"I would, Eric, but I'm not much of a dancer."

Eric raises an eyebrow. "That's not what I've heard."

Grace makes a face and says, "Wait a second, what did Annie tell you?" Sometimes when Annie is watching a show or if a commercial comes on and there's a catchy song, Grace has been known to dance in short bursts.

The brothers glance at each other. "That you're a chaotic, spirited, and delightful dancer," Daniel says.

Grace snorts laughter. "I can't believe she told you guys that."

"She tells us a lot of things," Eric says. Then, "I know just the thing for you. Table thirteen!" Eric stands. "Time for group dancing."

Riley's eyes light up, and Will looks nothing short of terrified.

Grace's hair has fallen out, and she's heading to the pizza section of the late-night buffet with Daniel when Brooke stumbles out in front of them. "What the fuck, Grace. You didn't want to come say hi to us? It was just a bunch of people from high school. Like Jackson. Remember the huge crush you had on him? But he's gone to bed now. He's no fun anymore. Fucking moves out west and leaves us all." She starts to run a finger down Daniel's chest, but he steps away with a grimace. "Who is this? You're like a glimmering Greek god. A Greek god, you hear me, Greasy Grace? Do you remember we used to call you that in high school?" Brooke stumbles forward and back as if on a ship in high waves, unable to stand upright. "Grace used to wear the exact same sweater to school every single day."

Grace's whole body goes rigid, burning from the inside out, as she sinks back into herself with humiliation. The room tilts under her as her mind goes back to high school. To May's languid eyes, to the red PAST DUE and FINAL NOTICE stamps, to Alex's hockey bag ripping wide open at a practice and his equipment scattering across the floor. They missed the last bus and had to walk two hours home with his equipment stacked precariously in their arms. She takes a wobbly step back.

"W-w-ait, one more thing," Brooke says, catching Grace's arm.

"Do you regret it?" Grace just looks at her, unable to form words, a pull of nausea in her stomach. Brooke juts her chin out at her as if it's obvious. "Leaving Alex? Bet you were kicking yourself when he went pro."

Daniel's shoulders rise protectively. He's about to say something when Riley comes to stand between Grace and Brooke. "Back the fuck up, bitch," Riley says, her tone cold and even. Her face is dark and fierce in a way Grace has never seen before. In a way she didn't even know possible.

"I *love* your dress," Brooke says to Riley. "I meant to ask you earlier where—"

Riley punches Brooke square in the nose, and for a brief moment, everything in the room freezes. At least, that's how it is in Grace's mind, like everything has stopped. Then blood starts to drip over Brooke's mouth, and the world picks up again, like a paused video being resumed. Brooke teeters on the spot for a second, in total shock.

"I think you broke my nose," Brooke says, staggering backward. "I think you broke my nose." Her hand comes away from her face, smeared with blood. "I'm going to press charges."

Will joins their semicircle, facing Brooke. "I'm a cop, and from my angle it looked like you slipped and slammed your face on the table."

"As a lawyer," Daniel says, "I'd corroborate that statement."

"But I . . . I was just joking," Brooke says.

"Might want to work on your material," Riley says. "Sounded pretty weak to me."

Grace turns from the group, grabs her purse from their table, and goes out to the lobby. She finds a dark corner and, feeling woozy from the shame, lowers herself onto the bench, her fingers fumbling for her phone.

"Grace," Daniel says, sitting beside her, but she angles away from him. She starts to search for the number of the cab company. "Grace." He puts his hand gently on hers as a tear rolls down her cheek. "That woman is a nothing. Her words mean nothing."

"All those . . . ," she starts, her voice breaking. "All those things she said are true. I'm embarrassing."

"Absolutely not."

"You only say that because you know my past. You know what I come from. You feel sorry for me." She puts her hand to her cheek as another tear falls. Her face is on fire.

"You are amazing," he says. His voice is soft, and he leans into her. "You are an amazing human being. Your past is a part of you, but it's not who you are now, not if you don't want it to be."

She shakes her head. "When I left him, he was only a kid."

"So were you," he says.

She turns to face him. She had never thought of it that way. That she was just a kid too.

She had always wondered what she could have done better. How, if she had been mentally stronger, she could have just powered through. Found a job near Sarah's and stayed in Alex's life. But deep down she knew that that hadn't been an option for her. She'd needed to leave. To get ahold of her mind, which was so breakable at the time.

Riley kneels in front of Grace. "People like her. Something went wrong in her life, or maybe she was just born with a screw loose. She's a miserable son of a bitch. Forget her. Let's go back in there and welcome the New Year."

"Thanks, Riley, but—"

"You are not alone in this," Riley says, holding out her hand to Grace. After a moment Grace takes it, and Riley kisses the back of it.

They return to the room as people start to yell, counting down. When the clock switches to midnight, there's a burst of confetti and streamers. Riley presses her forehead to Grace's and then she turns and kisses Will.

Grace gives Daniel's hand a small squeeze. "Thank you for tonight," she says. "I had—it was really nice."

He turns to face Grace. "Are you leaving?" She can hear it in his voice. He doesn't want her to go.

She nods.

"I'll walk you out."

"No, please," she says, not wanting to make this harder than it already is. "I'll see you."

She slips back through the people in their suits and beautiful dresses. Getting her coat, she pushes against the revolving door and out into the night.

The street is full of couples and friends with their arms linked. Groups parting around her yell, "Happy New Year!" She walks and walks on pellets of salt sprinkled over the sidewalk and through small mounds of slush until the noise fades and she is alone. On a street, in the dark. She thinks of Daniel sitting on the bench beside her, the kindness in his words, his body angled toward hers. Not pressing. Just there. Comforting her with his presence.

She knows now, for the first time in years, that she was about to have a panic attack. And he had brought her back from the brink. From that uncontrollable emotion erupting within her. Her heart galloping, the heat rising within her. With him next to her, it had settled.

The more she has gotten to know him, the less she is intimidated by his calm intensity. Why did it paralyze her so? Just looking into those vibrant blue eyes. She has feared interacting with people before but not like this. Not with someone who she actually wanted to interact with.

She has stopped without realizing it, and her mind drifts back to parts of the evening. Daniel's eyes widening when he first spotted her. Eric cracking open his lobster tail and accidentally splattering Riley with it. How she stared at him for a moment before bursting out laughing. Oh, how Grace had laughed as Beth leaned over to wipe Riley's hair with her napkin. The round of shots they had all done. And then another. Beth telling stories about the brothers in South Africa, and Daniel glancing at Grace throughout. Dancing with them all. She had never danced like that in her life. She could feel it in her feet now.

And then, after the incident with Brooke, he didn't look at her with pity. Daniel, Beth, and Eric all had the same blue eyes. The exact same shape. But Daniel's could sharpen in an instant and then go totally unreadable. A flash of intensity and then still.

The scariest was when they emanated concern. It would fill his whole face and unwrap her with his kindness, causing her breath to stop. She had to fight the urge to leave or turn away from him. When the look was fleeting, she could guard herself against it, but if it settled on her for too long, that's when she felt her body open, emotions coming over her that she hadn't allowed herself to feel in years.

As he spoke to her, his voice was steady, his hand on hers, letting her know that he was there, that nothing could hurt her, and he had meant it. Brooke was a nothing. Her words meant nothing. And he didn't care what she had said. None of them did.

With that thought buoying her, Grace turns around.

TEN

She has run the whole way back to the hotel, but when she reaches the lobby, she forces herself into a walk. She stops in the entrance of the ballroom, scanning the people who are left. It's half past midnight, and everyone from her group is gone.

In the elevator she presses the same floor as the night of the fire and hopes that he's in the same room. A lightness has come over her, and she takes her shoes off. The door dings, sliding open, and she runs down the length of the hall, her feet pattering against the scratchy carpet.

She stops outside the room and knocks lightly.

Nothing.

She knocks again, a bit louder.

After a minute she turns to leave when the metal handle clunks down. "Oh, thank God it's you," she says as the door opens. She can barely conceal her smile. Daniel stares at her, unable to hide his surprise. "Did I wake you?"

"No, I was just heading to bed. I thought you'd left."

"I did but then I came back."

He's wearing a gray hoodie and black shorts, revealing muscular legs. She feels a sudden and intense attraction to him. A current rippling through her. She steps into him slowly, and as she raises her mouth to his, his blue eyes search hers. He hesitates, as if uncertain, but then he presses his lips softly to hers, placing his hand lightly on her hip. She smiles and pushes him back into the room. He moves smoothly at her touch, and the door clicks shut behind them. Shielded by the dim room, she is bolder. She grabs his hoodie into her fist and pulls him closer. He is easy to kiss, and the more she does it, the more she wants to.

"I've never had sex," she blurts out suddenly.

His face is inches from hers, and he wraps his hands around the small of her back. He clears his throat. "Do you want to?"

"Only if . . . if you do."

He goes still. Totally still. Like he's considering what she's just said. Shit. She shouldn't have told him it was her first time. He's probably freaked out and doesn't want to do it with a virgin but is too polite to say so. Her body tenses and she draws back, but he doesn't release his grip on her.

"Yeah, no, we can definitely do this." He says it matter-of-factly, nodding slowly, like he's going over the logistics in his head.

"But do you *want* to?" Grace asks, needing to clarify.

"Yeah, Grace. I do."

"Do you have a condom?"

"Yeah." He lets her go and disappears into the adjoining bedroom. There's the crackling of a package, and Grace turns away. Nervous. Excited.

But then she wonders, *What if it doesn't go well, and I can never face him again?* She could call in sick every time he came to visit. She could . . . His hands are light on her shoulders as he comes up behind her. His nose gently burrows into the side of her neck. Oh God, was he already naked? She has seen dozens of men unclothed before, but they were all octogenarians. Not toned and fit. She turns to face him, half cringing, and is relieved to see he's still dressed.

"Are you sure about this?" he says. She loves him for asking, but it's the patience in his voice that draws her toward him. His unhurriedness.

She nods. She has always wanted to have sex. She just never thought it would be with Daniel Hurley. In the Forester of all places.

"Because we can stop at any time. You just say the word if it's uncomfortable for you."

"Okay." She takes him by the arm and leads him to the couch. "Do . . . do you want to take your shorts off?"

"We can ease into this a bit if you want."

"How do you mean?"

He leans in and says softly against the curve of her ear, "Like this." He starts to pull the material of her dress up, watching her closely as he does it. She can feel the heat emanating off his body. Slowly he curls his finger around the seam of her underwear and pulls it to the side. The tip of his finger slides over her, circling. The tiniest motion. And yet she has to grab the columns of his biceps, afraid that her knees might give. "Is that all right?" he asks.

"Yeah." A sudden urge to touch him comes over her, and she slips her hand inside his shorts.

He lets out a groan from deep within his chest as her hand wraps around his erection. She presses her lips to his, and he does his best to kiss her back, but his lips part as his breath shudders. She grins into his mouth.

Easing him back onto the couch, she kneels and slips his shorts down to the floor. She lifts the bottom of his sweatshirt and rubs her nose against the taut ridges of his stomach. His cock twitches. Such a small movement, but this is what makes her wet. To be the cause of this rising pleasure that Daniel is experiencing, no longer in control of his limbs. She opens his legs wider and presses her lips to the inner part of his thigh.

"Fuck," he grits out.

Grinning up at him, she starts to open her mouth, but he puts his hands on her shoulders and gently pushes her back.

"Wait," he says, his voice reedy and his chest heaving. She can just make out his eyes in the dim light. They're fully dilated. All pupil and glazed over.

She loves this effect she has on him. The hunger in his eyes. She runs the blade of her thumb just under his belly button and feels him swell at her touch. Like she's doing something special. She leans forward again, but he pushes her away, this time with a bit more force.

"Grace, stop." He grunts, and she can hear the desperation and slight pain in his voice.

Confused, she sits back on her heels. She really thought he was enjoying this. "Am I doing something wrong?" she asks, her voice small.

"No. Come here." He reaches for her and pulls her to him. She settles in so that she's straddling him on the couch. "You are perfect." He leans forward and kisses her slowly, letting his lips linger on hers.

She reaches between his legs and starts to rub him.

He moans and turns his face away. "Grace, please." He puts his hand on hers and lifts it off.

She goes still. This time seriously concerned that she *is* doing something wrong. She tries to move off him, but he wraps his arm around her waist like he wants to tether her to him.

He's not breathing normally.

With her head bowed, she says weakly, "I don't understand what you want, Daniel."

He takes a long moment, as if trying to collect himself. Then he swallows and says, "I want this to be for you. An experience for you." He nods at his fist, and it trembles slightly as he opens it. "Take it."

She lifts the condom from his palm and slides it over him, allowing her fingers to graze along the shaft of his cock. "I don't think I'll be very good at this," she says apologetically. She's nervous now.

"It's okay. No one is their first time." He reaches behind her, unzipping her dress, and pulls it down just enough so that her breasts are exposed.

"I bet you were."

"You'd lose."

"Hmm?" She's distracted because his tongue is circling her nipple and then he bites down on it ever so gently.

"You'd lose that bet."

She holds on to his thick shoulders as she eases onto him, shutting her eyes to the pain.

"Grace," he whispers. "I've wanted you for so long."

"What?" She opens her eyes as she starts to rise and fall, a sensation gathering within her. She grips his shoulders, and his hand shifts from the couch where he's bracing himself to her thigh. "What do you mean?"

"You said you spent years trying to avoid me. I've spent years wanting to meet you."

This startles her. "But I was just a voice on the other end of the phone."

"I love your voice."

Her breath shudders. She clutches the couch on either side of him, her head dropping as a low, involuntary moan lifts in his throat. He adjusts her hips, angling her slightly, and that's when he hits a spot in her that has her unravelling.

"Jesus," Grace mutters. The fabric of his hoodie grows damp beneath her chest and she can feel him straining not to go over the edge. Not unless she comes with him. His hand slips between them to create more friction, to give her what she needs and God she loves him for it. They reach the tipping point together—their breath erratic in the dim light. She lets her chin rest on his shoulder and he wraps his arms around her, holding her close for a long moment. Then she lifts herself from him and slides the condom off. Picking up her underwear, she goes into the bathroom to clean herself and tosses the condom in the garbage.

When she's done, she comes back into the room where Daniel is sitting on the couch in his shorts and a white T-shirt. "Was that . . . was that all right?" she asks, holding the material of her dress over her chest.

"It was lovely, Grace," he says.

"Would you mind doing me back up?"

"Sure." He stands but then hesitates. "You can sleep here if you want." He's only a silhouette in the darkness, but she can hear the longing in his words.

She lifts the hair from the nape of her neck and turns.

He comes to stand behind her and, leaning into her, says, "Up or down?"

"Down," she breathes.

He kisses her neck before slowly unzipping the rest of her dress, running his finger down her back. "Just out of curiosity, how would you have gotten out of this?"

"Scissors? Though there's a chance I could've dislocated something in the process," she says. "I almost did getting into it."

He laughs softly. "Well, we don't want that."

She shimmies the dress down and lays it over the back of the armchair. He pulls his gaze away from her body and roots around in his bag. "Here." He passes her a soft white undershirt, and she breathes in the faint scent of pine and aftershave as she pulls it over her head.

"Thank you."

The core of her is still chilled from her brisk walk, so she sinks into the bed and pulls the sheets up to her chin. Daniel curls in toward her, cupping her face in his hand. The weight of it on her cheek is comforting. Soothing and calming. Strangely, it feels more intimate than the act they've just shared. She takes his hand in hers, kisses his palm, and then tucks it back toward him. Though it's a small gesture, he understands. He straightens out and in doing so moves farther from her. She lets out a breath and falls asleep.

She wakes in the early hours of the morning. The air in the room is stifling and heavy. The thick duvet that had warmed her a couple of hours ago now agitates her, weighing down on her skin. She slips from the covers and, in the dim light that seeps through the crack in the curtains, finds a robe and a pair of hotel slippers.

The adjoining room is cooler but not much. She opens the sliding door to the balcony and is hit by cold air. A welcome relief on her clammy skin.

She leans against the railing and it dawns on her that Jackson is staying in this very hotel right now. The same one as her, all these years later. With fleeting nostalgia, she remembers him lying next to her in a lounge chair by the pool, late-night Ping-Pong games, showing her how to slice a backhand on the tennis court, arguing with her about who the worst character in Harry Potter was. And then them both realizing at the same time Dolores Umbridge, of course.

"Hey," Daniel says, giving her a start. "Sorry. Didn't mean to scare you." He comes to stand at the railing, a few feet down from her. The city lights cast a soft glow on his face. "I thought you'd left."

"No, just wanted to cool down a bit," she says, her breath rising above her as she talks.

"There are outdoor lights," he says, nodding at them.

"I was never one of those kids who was afraid of the dark," she says.

"Neither was I." He glances at her. "What was it like living with May? Alex said she was good to you guys."

Grace grimaces and nods. "She was in the beginning."

"And then?"

"She was a good cook, bought us nice clothes. She took pride in being complimented on our appearance, but her friends didn't have any interest in hockey, so she never cared much for it. I arrived when I was ten, and Alex joined me shortly after when he was two. He had long curly hair... a broken arm and bruises on his back." A heaviness takes hold of her.

Daniel's eyes sharpen with concern. "Were you ever . . ."

"Abused? No. Not physically, at least. Just moved from home to home until I landed at May's. It's a strange feeling floating from one place to the next. New houses, new personalities to navigate. Then the sense of relief and dread at being told May's house would be permanent. Making the best of it because it was the only way through. And yeah, I never really felt comfortable there. Her gambling started to affect our lives when I was fifteen, and I tried my best to keep that from him."

After a moment Daniel says, "Are you comfortable with me?"

She turns and rests her back against the railing. "I feel differently with you than I do with anyone else," she says by way of answer. Then, "I must be. Or I wouldn't be here now."

He nods slowly. "What were you thinking about when I came out here?"

"Jackson."

"The boy you had a crush on?"

"I didn't have a crush on Jackson. He was my first real friend. His family was really good to us," she says. "I'm the one who gave him the nudge to go out west, and like Brooke said, he didn't come back."

"You missed him?"

"Quite a bit."

Daniel grips the railing and leans back, lifting his head to the sky. "We lived on this farm in South Africa for a couple of years. On clear nights you could see so many stars, it was like a white blanket above you. Eric, Beth, and I would sneak out and sleep on this big old trampoline in the backyard."

"What were your parents like? You don't talk about them much."

"There's not much to say."

She crosses her arms, annoyed. That wasn't fair. "So you can ask all these questions about my life, things I've never spoken about to other people, and you won't discuss yours?"

"I have to pry those things from you."

"It's not easy for me to talk about," she says, hurt by his words. She strides back toward the slider and into the sitting room.

As she reaches for her dress, he shuts the door behind him. "They enjoy each other's company much more than they enjoy ours." His deep voice cuts through the darkness. She stops and, letting her dress go, turns to face him. "They're teachers at the best international schools in the world. As part of their contracts, they were each able to send one child to school for free. They sent me and then Beth, but they wouldn't pay for Eric. So he was enrolled in some shit school and came home on the first day without any shoes. I pleaded with my parents to pay for him, but they said it would make him stronger, give him character. He was this scrawny little four-year-old. So I'm eight and I go into the school office and ask to be unenrolled so that Eric can take my spot. They try to send me back to class, but I refuse. My parents can't come down to the office because they're both teaching, so they call my nan, thinking she'll talk some sense into me. I explain the situation to her, and she doesn't say anything. That night when my parents come home, they tear a strip off me for how much the phone call is going to cost them." His gaze rests on something in the distance. "The next morning, the school calls—Eric's tuition has been paid in full."

"Annie."

He nods. "Our nan. She drained most of her savings putting him through school. She's always been there for us in a way our parents never were, and none of us are particularly close with them."

"If she drained most of her savings, how does she . . ." Oakwood was expensive, not to mention the years-long waiting list to get in.

"I graduated from university, then law school, and worked my ass off. Beth used to check in on her, bringing her food and driving her around. But when Annie couldn't look after herself any longer, I put her in the best home I could find."

And then it dawned on Grace. Shortly after she started at Oakwood, some of the nurses were in the lunchroom talking about new blood pressure machines they'd just received. One for each floor. It had been around the same time that Annie was admitted. From an anonymous donor.

This story explains so much. By the guarded pain in his voice, she knows that it's not easy for him to share this with her.

"Does Eric know?"

"No, he does not. And although Annie's not great at keeping things to herself, this one she'll take to the grave."

The fact that Daniel has opened up to her with something so personal and private, that he has trusted her with it, scares her a bit.

This connection she's building with him is unlike any she has ever had before.

"When you answered the door, wearing that hoodie, I was so drawn to you."

"This hoodie?" He puts his hands in the pockets. "I felt the same when I saw your pink nose, the wisps of hair framing your face, your eyes on mine."

"I've never dated or been with anyone—not that we are dating—but I don't know the nuances, what I'm supposed to do. It doesn't come naturally to me." She can't meet his eyes as she makes this confession. She's too embarrassed. If he comes closer now, her body will repel, like two magnets being pushed away.

"Grace, I work with people who bullshit for a living. I've always appreciated how straight you've been with me. There's no right or wrong in all this."

"Do you remember the night at the pie café?" she asks, forcing herself to look at him.

"I remember it well."

"I wanted to hit you," she says.

"Why?"

"Because I was angry. All these emotions I hadn't allowed myself to acknowledge and you just laid them out there so plainly. Sitting there so calmly. I wanted you to retaliate so that I could hate you because I was afraid."

"Afraid of what?"

"Of you. And all the sense you spoke. You were right about everything. I'm just a coward."

"You are not a coward, Grace." He lifts his arms and starts to wrap them around her, but she pushes him away.

"Don't," she says thickly.

"Hey," he whispers. He eases closer, and she shakes her head but doesn't push him away as he pulls her in close.

When she wakes again, Daniel is turned away from her, heavy with sleep. She goes into the bathroom and finds a mini tooth brush in the extras bin. She has a shower, pulls on a robe, and comes out of the bathroom drying her hair with a towel.

Daniel's awake and wearing black shorts, his chest bare. "This place does a great buffet," he says, heading toward the bathroom.

"Yeah, I wouldn't stick out at all." She gestures toward her lilac dress.

"Is that what's stopping you?" He reaches for his phone and after a moment says, "Morning. Would you mind if Grace borrowed some clothes to wear to breakfast?"

"What? No," Grace says, whipping around. She whisper-yells, "Daniel!"

"Perfect, thanks." He hangs up. "Beth will be here in a minute."

"Was she wondering why I was here?"

"No," he says and shuts the bathroom door behind him.

Grace cuts across the dining room, wearing a loose white knit sweater, dark jeans, and her square heels from the night before. A super chic outfit that does not make her stand out in this room of well-dressed people. She's deciding between the eggs benedict and some sushi when a voice she would know anywhere says, "Grace."

Her face breaks into a smile as she turns. Jackson is standing before her, his eyes crinkling slightly as he smiles back at her. He's in beige pants and a blue collared shirt, one side of it sticking up, and his brown hair is a bit ruffled.

"Jackson." She hugs him, holding his lean body close for a long moment. It's all so familiar. One of the few things from her past that she still clings to.

When she pulls away, he says, "How are you?" But not in the casual, offhanded way people ask. He truly wants to know how she is.

"I'm good," she says.

"Yeah?" He tilts his head down.

"Yeah."

"Good. I'm really glad to hear that."

"I hear you're still living out west," she says.

"I am. Someone gave me some good advice when I was in a dark place, and I've never looked back. But I did think about you," he says. "I called your house a few times, but the woman never seemed to pass on the messages."

"You did?" Grace hardens, thinking of May.

Jackson waves someone over. A woman with chestnut hair and a toddler on her hip approaches. "Marina, this is Grace, a friend of mine from—"

"I remember," Marina says with a warm smile. "He's told me about you. It's so nice to meet you, Grace."

"You as well," Grace says. "And who's this little guy?"

"Cole," Marina says. "This is a good friend of your papa's. And that's our other son." She points to a little boy reaching for a waffle. "I'm gonna go help him."

"You're a dad," Grace says in disbelief.

"Crazy, isn't it?" he says. Then, "I've been to a few of Alex's games. The arena's not too far from our house. He's something else, Grace. I mean, Marina doesn't know the forwards from the defense, and even she could tell."

Grace can feel someone over her shoulder, so she opens her body. "Daniel, this is a friend of mine from high school, Jackson," she says.

"It's nice to meet you," Daniel says, and he holds Jackson's eye as he shakes his hand.

"Did you know you're standing next to the best Ping-Pong player in our high school?" Jackson says, nodding at Grace.

Grace smiles. "Second best."

"You play Ping-Pong?" Daniel says.

"I did. I haven't in a long time."

"Listen, you gotta come visit us out west. Marina and I would love to have you, and you too, Daniel," he says. Grace almost says that they're not together, that Daniel is just a friend, but then she stops herself. She notices that Daniel doesn't say anything either. Jackson reaches into his back pocket for his phone. "I'm serious."

"I know you are," Grace says.

"Here, give me your number."

As she types it in, Daniel nods politely at Jackson and carries on, leaving them to it. "How's Lettie?" Grace asks as she returns his phone.

"She's good. She's studying to become a physiotherapist."

"She'd be great at that."

"You know, when we used to hang out, she had a bit of a crush on Alex."

"Did she?" Grace says. "She played it very cool."

"She swore me to secrecy," he says, putting his hands up. "She ran into him at a bar recently. Said she really enjoyed hanging out with him."

"Oh, that's so nice to hear."

"Wouldn't it be awesome to get the four of us back together again?"

"It would."

"Have you talked to him at all? Since . . . since all that stuff's gone down."

She shakes her head. He doesn't press her, and she loves him for it. "I'm glad we ran into each other," she says, hugging him once more.

"Me too. I've always been a big fan of yours, Grace." He pauses. "You know that day in English when I sat down next to you?"

"Yeah." She would never forget it.

"When they posted our classes on the cafeteria wall, I saw that we had the same homeroom. I came in late that day, hoping that seat would be open."

She snorts a laugh. "'Cause no one ever wanted to sit next to me."

"I wanted to sit next to you," Jackson says and shakes his phone at her. "You stay in touch, you hear?"

At home, Grace changes out of Beth's clothes, neatly folding them and placing them in a bag. She comes down the stairs and feels for the first time like her house is lacking. The white walls, the simple furniture. She needs a plant or some artwork. Something to liven the space up. She puts on some light coffeehouse-type music and does a twirl as she comes into the kitchen and opens the fridge. It took her years to realize she enjoyed cooking, the stress of coupon cutting and budgeting behind her.

Riley had invited her to a cooking class at the last minute after her friend bailed. Grace said that she would try to make it but didn't confirm. She arrived half an hour early, paced every aisle in the grocery store, and then trudged up the stairs to the class just as it was starting. Riley beamed as she came in and moved her purse from the seat next to her. Grace ended up loving it. They signed up for eight more classes that night and decided to put their new skills to the test. Every Monday they took turns bringing in lunches from the recipes they had learned. Although the classes had long ended, they still carried on with the tradition, every Monday taking turns bringing in a lunch for the other.

Grace shuts the fridge door as a sudden urge to talk to someone comes over her. She calls Riley, who doesn't answer, so she fills the kettle with water and throws a pile of clothes into the washing machine. She's adding a bit of milk to her tea when she notices her phone is lit up.

"Hey." Riley is panting. "Is everything all right?"

"Yeah." Grace realizes that she's never called Riley before. Just texted. "I was just calling to chat. Is this a bad time?"

"No, I was . . . out for a jog," Riley says, catching her breath. "I'm walking now."

"Oh, sorry. I didn't mean to bother you."

"No, no. You said you wanted to chat. I love chatting."

"I, um, slept with Daniel last night." In the silence that follows, Grace wonders if she shouldn't have told Riley this. Has she just broken some unspoken code that was universally known by more experienced people? She usually just launched into topics with Riley and then Riley hurled things back at her. Now she's standing at her counter, gripping the handle of her tea mug. "Are you still there?"

"Yeah, I'm still here." Riley's smiling. Grace can feel it through the phone. "It's just . . . that's big." Grace picks up her tea and takes it with her to the couch. "I've never heard you this happy before. I've always like Daniel."

"There's more. I also ran into a friend from high school who I haven't seen in ages." Now Grace is the one smiling.

"Okay," Riley says. "I just got home. I'm putting on the tea. Start from the beginning. I want to hear everything."

ELEVEN

Six Years Earlier

When Grace receives her first paycheck, she pays off her Visa bill. With her second she has just enough money to rent a studio apartment she's found in a nice, safe area. It's a short walk to the bus stop and the grocery store and ten minutes from work. She spends the first two weeks sleeping on the light wood floor. The neighborhood is quiet, and the cricks in her back will be temporary. Piece by piece she buys the essentials she needs to live. Making lists, doing the calculations, combing the flyers for deals. A bed, sheets, pots and pans, utensils, and a decent, reliable car that she pays for with manageable monthly installments. Finally, some breathing room.

Four months in she sends an envelope with $500 in cash and no return address to Alex, stacking and wrapping the bills carefully so that they won't bulge or show through. *To spend as you want. I love you.* That's all she writes inside. She had put so much time and energy into counting every penny, never being able to justify buying new clothes, scouring the stores for every deal. She knows that Sarah will provide for him, but she wants him to have the freedom and flexibility she craved.

To be able to go to the movies, to dinner, on field trips without having to feel beholden to someone else's generosity, without having to ask.

She sends $500 every few months until the day he is drafted into the NHL.

She's at the nursing home when it happens, going over arm exercises with Tony Senior. His son, Tony Junior, is sitting a few feet away, taking notes for his father, and the TV is on low volume in the background.

Grace is holding a can of black beans in each hand, and Tony has the three-pound weights his son has just bought him. She brings her hands up to her chest, her elbows sticking out. "Good," she says as Tony mirrors her. "And three more times, nice and slow to engage the muscles."

That's when she hears "Alex Saint" and "picked first overall" in the same sentence. She lowers her arms as Alex's face fills the screen, his dark curly hair tamed a bit with some gel. He's smiling, but it's not the smile she knows. It's more guarded and reserved. The camera pans out to show Sarah sitting next to him, in a navy blue dress and a black blazer. She gives him a small nod. A nod that says *you've done it*, and Grace is filled with relief and gratitude. She picked the right woman. It's clear in that moment that she didn't push Alex to do this. This is what he wanted, this is what he worked for, and she's there in quiet support.

They don't hug. Alex stands and puts his hand on Sarah's shoulder, a small gesture that Grace knows will mean a lot to Sarah. This acknowledgment for the world to see. Grace's face warms with emotion as he walks down the aisle toward the stage. He has grown tall, broad and muscular, into the hockey player he has always wanted to be.

That night she sends him a note only.

I am proud of you. I love you.

Grace knows that he won't be living with Sarah any longer but that she will forward the note to him because that's just the kind of woman Sarah is.

Grace had parked on Riley's parents' street almost an hour ago with the intention of getting out of the car. She had hesitated, the briefest blip, and now she's sitting with the engine off, her breath a light mist rising above her. She runs her hands down the corduroy skirt she had bought earlier that day. The figs she'd stuffed with gorgonzola and wrapped in prosciutto are sitting on the passenger seat beside her.

Grace and Riley had been laughing in the lunchroom when Riley asked her, out of nowhere, if Grace wanted to come to her parents' Christmas Eve party. It had caught her completely off guard and she said yes without even thinking. What an idiot.

For the past hour, she's watched people park and get out of their cars with gift bags, bottles of wine, and platters of food. Through the bay window, she sees that they are greeted warmly, undoing their coats to reveal shimmering dresses, long skirts, collared shirts, and vests. The large table in the window is covered with food and wineglasses. People are laughing. Talking with their hands. Telling stories.

She can't do it. Feeling sick to her stomach and full of shame, she starts the car and turns around.

"Chicken's almost done." Ramon, the head cook for their building, puts Annie's salad on Grace's tray while the chicken sizzles in a cast-iron skillet behind him. "It's a new recipe I'm trying out. I've wrapped it around some brie and cranberries, but it's taking a bit longer than I thought."

"She's going to love it." Grace has been trying to convince Annie to eat in the dining room, but some days are just easier than others. There's a new resident Grace thinks Annie would like, an Italian man named Tony, but so far they have only exchanged pleasantries in the hall.

Riley sets up a tray next to Grace's, and Ramon passes her a plate with two cabbage rolls, some perogies, and a heap of sauerkraut. Must be for Carl. It's the first time Grace has seen Riley since her skiing holiday in Vail with her family over the holidays.

"Nice trip?" Grace asks.

"Yeah," Riley says curtly. She's waiting for the sour cream.

"Was the skiing good?"

"Look, if you didn't want to come or something, you can just tell me."

Ramon glances from one woman to the other and then lowers his head and busies himself. It's the first time Riley has ever shown annoyance toward Grace, and she's surprised by how much it affects her.

"I did want to go," Grace says.

"Honestly, I won't be offended. I'd prefer it."

"It wasn't that. I just . . ." Grace peters off, trying to shut out the memory of sitting in the cold car, her breath rising above her. The thought of it now brings blood rushing to her face. Angry with herself and embarrassed, she angles away from Riley, not wanting her friend to see her face redden. Ramon flicks a generous helping of sour cream into a side bowl, and Riley picks up the tray and takes it from the room.

Grace stands there, staring at the counter.

"You all right, Grace?" Ramon asks, placing the chicken next to the roast potatoes.

"Yeah." She swallows down her shame and takes the tray. "Thanks, Ramon."

She had wanted to go to that party, or she wouldn't have said yes. She'd met a few of Riley's friends at one of their cooking classes, and they had all been nice and easy to talk to. But she's spent so much time avoiding social get-togethers that these things seem so daunting, so overwhelming. This deep and intense fear has crept into her. Entrenching itself in her bones and holding her still, causing her breath to run shallow at the mere thought of these interactions. Whoever the fuck said visualizing was the first step to success clearly had never actually been through this.

But at the heart of it all, the main reason she couldn't enjoy herself at the party was this: How could she allow herself to connect with others, to enjoy companionship, when she had turned her back on the one person who mattered most to her in the world? As she drove away, she had been angry with herself and slightly nauseous, but she also realized that she deserved to spend Christmas alone.

Riley is also Grace's only real friend in this city and a great one at that. Grace needs to try to right this.

At the end of the workday, Grace goes into the lunchroom. There are a few other nurses, changing out their shifts, collecting their empty lunch containers or putting their snacks in the fridge for the evening.

Grace lifts her black coat from the rack at the same time that Riley reaches for her fitted beige trench coat. Usually in tandem with each other, today it feels awkward, their in-sync movements making them more distant. "Would you like to grab dinner with me?" Grace says, trying to make it sound casual, not like this is the first time she has ever said this.

Riley slides the strap of her mint-colored dome purse onto her shoulder without any indication that she's heard Grace. After a moment she says, "There's a Vietnamese place I think you'd like."

"Perfect. I'll follow you."

Riley orders without opening the menu. Grace, after perusing the menu, has no idea what to get.

"I'll take the same," Grace says. She passes her menu to the server as Riley pours jasmine tea into two small cups for each of them. "Thanks. Were . . . were many of the other nurses able to make the party?"

"I didn't ask any of the other nurses to come."

"Oh."

Riley sips her tea.

Grace stares down at the intricate place mat. On the drive over, she had made a decision. It's time she told Riley a bit more about herself. She'd been determined to keep her past a secret, not wanting it to be the lens through which people saw her. But if there was ever a person she was going to tell, it was Riley. She's organized her thoughts and knows exactly what she's going to say. "I grew up in a foster home," she says, cutting through the silence. She doesn't look at Riley as she talks.

"It was me and another foster kid, Alex. He was eight years younger, and we were quite close. Our foster mother developed a gambling addiction, and I knew if I reported her, we would be separated. I found a good woman who would take Alex, and I outed May—the foster parent we lived with. I left and I haven't been back since. Or spoken to him." Grace lifts her hand from where it's resting beside the place mat. There's a condensation mark where her palm was.

"You haven't spoken to him at all?"

"Hmm?" Grace didn't think there'd be follow-up questions. She moves around in her chair. She's going to need to get a grip or she might be too nervous to eat. "Well, I sent him these notes and some money from time to time, but he's all good now, so I don't anymore."

"What do you mean, he's all good now?"

"He's got a good job and can support himself," she says, starting to feel a bit nauseous.

Riley is quiet for a long moment, and all Grace can hear is the thudding of her heart.

"Grace, I can't even begin to imagine what it was you went through, but it sounds like he's quite important to you."

"He is," Grace says.

"Have you tried to reach out to him at all?"

"No, I haven't." A bowl with broth, noodles, meat, and vegetables is placed in front of her. "I'm sorry, Riley. I can't . . . I don't really want to talk much more about it. I'm not trying to make excuses for why I act the way I do, but I wanted to give you some context if I sometimes do things a bit differently. I have . . . it's not that I don't want to, but I, um . . ." Grace's voice trails off and she shrugs, as if to punctuate the sentence—to end it—the words she cannot drag from her mouth.

Riley stares at her for a minute. "Thank you for sharing that with me."

Grace nods, relieved they're done discussing it.

"Grace . . ."

Crap.

"I could get you the name of someone if you wanted. My dad

knows lots of people at the hospital."

"What do you mean, people at the hospital?"

"You know, like a therapist or a psychologist. Someone you could talk to."

That would be her worst nightmare. "Oh no, I'm good. Thank you, though."

"Lots of people talk to therapists," Riley says, circling her chopsticks through the noodles. "It's, you know . . . it's totally normal."

Yeah, nothing about Grace's life was normal.

"If you don't like it, you don't go back." Riley reaches into her purse for her phone, and Grace swallows and stares helplessly at her steaming noodles.

Grace takes the bus to the hospital, too nervous to drive. When she steps down off the platform, she doesn't allow her feet to stop, afraid that they might betray her if she does. She keeps moving, toward this massive complex of a hospital. Section E. That's where she needs to go.

The receptionist behind the desk checks over Grace's form. "You need to check one off." She taps the bottom of the sheet.

Grace glances again at the boxes labeled depression, anxiety, stress, emotionally disconnected, mood swings, and so on. "Why do I *need* to check one off?"

"Just to help the doctor diagnose whatever mental illness you may have."

Grace's chest tightens at the words *mental illness*. She doesn't like anything about this. Not the uncomfortable chair she has just risen from or the rickety coat stand beside her. "I'm not mentally ill."

"Right. I just mean to help guide us in the right direction."

Grace is sweating. "You know what, I don't think this is for me."

"You'll be charged in full if the cancellation is less than twenty-four hours. It's our policy." She points to the sign on the wall.

"No problem." Grace pulls out her wallet.

"Grace?" a voice from the hallway calls. It's firm yet not unkind.

Grace turns to see a woman in her early fifties. She's in jeans, a simple long-sleeved shirt, and running shoes. "Why don't you come into my office?" She doesn't smile, but her tone and body language are inviting.

"But I didn't check any of the boxes," Grace says.

"That's absolutely fine."

Grace hesitates. *You have nothing to lose*, she tells herself and then follows the woman down the hall.

The room is small. Uncomfortably small. With concrete walls.

"Why don't you sit?" The woman gestures at one of the chairs and, picking up a clipboard, sits across from Grace.

Grace's heart rate has quickened and that nauseous feeling is rising in her. She's also a bit light-headed. Fuck, that's new.

"So why are you here?"

"My friend told me I should talk to someone."

"Why is that?"

"Because I grew up in a foster home." The woman starts writing. "And, uh . . ." Grace pushes down on a pang coming through her ribs. The woman glances up from the clipboard, and Grace can see it in her eyes, the look of discomfort as she shifts. Grace wants to call the woman out for it. For not being able to play it cool while witnessing this physical response taking over Grace's body, but instead Grace lowers her head. "This is why I'm here. Because I can't have a conversation like this without dreading it. I almost turned around a dozen times on the way here. I feel like there's a boa constrictor tightening around me right now and like my heart might just burst through my chest because it's beating so intensely."

"Look out the window," the woman says.

"What?" Grace says.

"Look out the window. What do you see?"

Grace turns toward the window. "Um, leaves blowing in the breeze. A squirrel chasing another squirrel. A dog taking a dump."

"What do you smell right now?"

"Minty, like gum or Tic Tacs, and an industrial building smell with cement and old carpets."

"Good. Think of your stomach as a balloon. I want you to breathe in and fill that balloon." The woman sits back in her chair to demonstrate. Grace watches and then does the same. "Now hold in that air . . . and exhale. And again." She puts on some soft cinematic music. "We're going to do this for a few minutes. And let's keep our focus on some of these things. What we see, what we smell, and what we hear."

As Grace does this, the woman doesn't speak, and the boa constrictor loosens its grip on Grace. She breathes in the smells of the building and lets the music fill the space around her. She looks out the window to the sidewalk below and watches two women chatting. Slowly the pang subsides.

"Lovely," the woman says, observing Grace. "Who did you live with in the home?"

"Our foster mother and my foster brother."

"What was your relationship with them like?"

"Um, the woman, shit. Hated her. My brother, I . . . I loved him more than anything." Grace clutches her side as something pierces through her once more, and the woman puts the music on again.

"Let's fill that balloon. Turn your attention to your surroundings. When you have trouble focusing, let these things distract you from the tightness in your chest. Do you exercise?"

"I walk a lot."

"How do you feel when you walk?"

"Refreshed. Rejuvenated. Good. I feel good."

"It's a great way to get your mind off things—getting the body moving. Using tactics like these can help you manage intense emotions, especially when you're feeling low or nervous. If you're in a situation where you're experiencing some discomfort, tune in to what's going on around you." She glances at the clock. "Next time we can delve into your life at the home. Jot down some notes for us to use as a point of reference. About your relationship with the woman and the boy. It might be easier for you to talk about if you have a bit of a guide. In the meantime, I'm going to write you a script."

"A script?"

"Sorry, a prescription."

"No, I know was a script is. I just—I don't want meds."

"I think you might find them helpful for your situation. To relax you."

"Are you referring to a mental illness?"

"To your mental health in general."

Grace scoffs. "I'm not taking drugs, and I'm not mentally ill."

"It's not a bad thing, Grace. The stigma around it—"

"I'm not saying that it is bad. I'm just saying that I am not. And I don't want to be labeled as such." Grace stands. "It was nice to meet you, but I don't think I'll be coming back."

"Grace, we have a lot of things to talk about. Things we need to delve into and discuss."

"You want me to talk about my life? Which part? About growing up with a gambling addict who didn't give a shit about me? Or how I worked so hard, I started to develop the shakes? I know what I went through was fucked. I know I have issues because of it. Why would I want to relive that?" Grace reaches for the door handle but pauses. "Thank you for these strategies. I'll give them a shot."

On her way out, Grace passes her health insurance card to the receptionist, and she punches the information into the computer. "So we suggest that you make your next appointment in six weeks' time—"

"Oh no, I'm good. Thank you."

The woman blinks at her. "You don't want to make another appointment?"

"If I do, I'll call you." Grace takes her card back and makes her way down the sterile hall, her head down, her thoughts on the session she just had. The same rush of adrenaline that had come over her as she entered the hallway is leaving her just as quickly. Seeping from her bones and replaced by a wave of elation. Just as it does whenever she conquers something slightly terrifying. She is going over the techniques she has just learned in her head when a male voice causes her to stop.

"Who've you been assigned to next week?"

Looking up, Grace realizes that she's in a winding hallway she doesn't recognize. A young man and woman, both in scrubs, amble down the corridor toward Grace. It's the same way she and Riley walk when they have a busy day but want to catch up.

The woman side-eyes him, clearly savoring whatever she is about to say. "Carlsen."

"Fuck me." The man takes off his glasses and wipes them on the hem of his scrubs. "I've got Crimp."

The woman smirks at him. "At least you'll get to know each patient really, really well."

He puts his glasses back on. "Brutal. She's absolutely brutal. So slow and tedious at everything she does."

Grace reads the Neonatal sign above her and the one a bit farther down the hall that says Ultrasounds with an arrow. She realizes that she knows exactly who Carlsen is. She definitely did not come this way into the building. What section is she in?

"Excuse me," Grace says to the residents as they pass by her. "Do you know how to get out of the building?"

"Yeah, you follow the exit signs," the man says without glancing at Grace. "Carlsen's skit the other night was one of the greatest—"

A tall, lean man comes into the hall. He's fair with white blond hair and pale blue eyes. A man who Grace has met only once but who was very kind to her. He's studying an ultrasound on an iPad and rotates the picture by turning the whole screen. The picture moves again just as he seems to get it where he wants it. Frustrated, he clicks it off and holds the iPad in his hand, oblivious to those around him.

"Dr. Carlsen." The man with the glasses shakes his head in admiration. "You were an absolute legend the other night."

Dr. Carlsen gives the man a swift nod of acknowledgment and continues down the hallway, his mind on other things. Then he stops. "Grace?" He turns toward her.

"Hi, Dr. Carlsen." She had been introduced to him as Kristian, but she felt she should address him formally being in his place of work.

"Kristian," he says to her. "How are you?"

"I'm a bit lost, actually," Grace says. "Do you know which way the exit is?"

"I'll show you," he says, holding out his hand.

"Oh no, you're busy. I'll figure it out."

"I was just heading down to the atrium to grab a tea anyway."

"Earl gray?" Grace asks. It's the only kind Riley drinks.

"It's the best one."

Grace makes a face, and Kristian smiles. The same warm smile as Riley. And for the first time since Grace stepped foot into this labyrinth of a hospital, she feels her shoulders ease a bit. The man with the glasses gapes at them as they pass by him.

Once they're out of earshot, Grace holds out her hand. "May I show you something?" Kristian doesn't hesitate as he passes over his iPad. She slides her finger down the screen. "If you click here, the picture won't rotate when you move it. That way you can move the screen whichever way you want, and the picture will stay where it is. And if you click it again, it undoes it."

"Would you look at that? That's not something they teach you in med school."

She hands it back. "Too busy learning how to use a typewriter?"

"A typewriter!" he exclaims. "How old do you think I am?"

"I'm just joking with you."

He grins and shakes his head. "Riley told me you have a sense of humor. One of those ones that sneaks up on you."

"Did she?"

"You know, she was really annoyed with me after you two interviewed. Almost didn't take the job because I called in for her." He pushes the down button on the elevator. "I didn't want her to have to work the crazy shifts like I did when first starting out. Especially if she ever wanted to be a mother. I've known Judy for years, and Oakwood is well run. I convinced her to stick it out until the end of her probation, hoping it would grow on her." He follows Grace onto the elevator and presses "L." "But it's you I owe a big thank you to."

"Me?" Grace's taken aback.

"The stories she tells when she comes to the house for dinner—

you're in almost every one."

The doors open into a large atrium with a tree in the center of it, a food court, and an eating area where people are sitting in pairs or on their own. He steers her to a bank of doors that lead to the parking lot.

"Can I ask you something?" Grace says. "Confidential."

"Sure," he says and waits patiently.

She looks at the floor, at his chest, over his shoulder, anywhere but at him. "If there was something wrong with you, something that you had to manage every day and most days you could, would you take drugs to quell the bad ones? Or would you stay off them and ride it out, hoping it would get better."

"Why do you not want to take the drugs?"

"Because I . . . I don't know why this happens to me. I'm afraid that if I take them, then whatever is going on inside me wins. I want to feel everything. I don't want to dull my emotions. This is the first time in my life that I feel like I'm in control of what's going on, like I don't have to rely on others, and like maybe I can get ahold of it. Is that stupid?"

"No. That's not stupid. Not at all. We're all built differently. We react to and process things in our own ways. However you want to do that is up to you." Kristian puts his hand on her shoulder. The gentle weight of it steadies her. "There's such strength in you, Grace."

And in that moment Grace knows—Riley told him about her past—and she is surprised to find that she doesn't mind.

"Thanks, Kristian," she says offhandedly, trying to make light of what she's just said.

"You take care of yourself."

"I will."

She goes through the first set of doors and pauses in the vestibule to do up her jacket. She struggles with the wonky zipper, trying to coax it up, but after giving it a small yank, it comes off completely. Guess it's time to get a new one.

About to push through the second door, she notices Kristian getting back onto the elevator—without a tea in his hand.

TWELVE

A Few Months Earlier

Lettie Martin's date is fifteen minutes late, so when the hostess brings him to the table, she does not rise to greet him.

"Lettie, right?" He holds his hand out, and as she shakes it, he's not looking at her but at the phone he's pulling out of his breast pocket. He places it face up on the table. "Graham," he says, shuffling his seat forward. "Sorry I'm late." As his eyes settle on her, there's a shift in him, like he's appraised her and realizes that she's much more attractive than he thought she would be. He then compensates for his lateness by being overly enthusiastic, asking her question after question, about what schools she went to, which people she might know.

Should she tell him now that she's an introvert? That although she enjoys hanging out with people, she's not much of a mingler and the names he's hurling at her are just vague faces?

"What can I get for you?" the server asks.

Lettie glances down at the menu, which she's grateful she perused before he got there. "I'll have the Caesar salad . . ." She flips to the mains.

"I'll have the steak and fries." Graham passes his menu to the server, who then takes Lettie's menu from her hands. The woman whips around and is striding away before Lettie can say that she also wanted the steak and fries. She needs to take some control here or she's going to be bombarded with questions until this meal is done.

"Do you like to travel?" she blurts out.

Graham grips the edge of the table and leans back. "That is a great question, Lettie." *Dear God.* "This is the way I see it. We have mountains, the ocean, great restaurants, and a first-class arena where you can see any number of musical acts or catch a game. Why would I want to go somewhere else? If it's history you're seeking, you can read about it in a book. We have every single season. Something for everyone."

When her salad is placed in front of her, she takes a bite and watches as he cuts into his steak.

"What's that?" he says, pointing with his fork.

Lettie glances down at the clay on the back of her hand and thumbs it away. "I had a pottery class before this."

"Oh yeah? What'd you make?"

"I'm working on a couple of mugs and a little syrup pitcher."

He dips a few fries into his ketchup. "You know you can buy stuff like that from IKEA for dirt cheap, right? Wouldn't even know the difference. All those knickknacky things."

At least the service is quick.

When they stand after their meals—if she can call her salad a meal—his smile fades. It takes Lettie a beat too long to realize that it's because they're standing eye to eye. What seems to be an internal struggle comes over him. "Do you wear heels?"

"Not often, but from time to time I wear small ones."

"Well, if this thing has legs, that's not really going to work for me."

She lifts her light-pink coat from the back of her chair and puts her purse strap across her body. It most definitely does not have legs.

Out on the street, he places his hand on the small of her back and she stiffens, but he doesn't seem to notice. "You want to swing by my place?"

Swing by? Absolutely not. A group of women burst out of a side door into the alleyway, which is blocked off by a barrier beside them. They are laughing, and two of them exchange quick words in another language. Russian, by the sounds of it.

"I was actually going to meet up with some friends." She gestures at the bar beside them. The only people she knew in the city were the ones Jackson had introduced her to and a handful of people she had met in her program and went to coffee with.

Graham's eyes light up. "You're going to Opus?"

Oh shit. She'd heard about this place. It was members only and super exclusive. No one she knew had actually ever been inside, only talked about it.

"Yeah, but there's a strict one-only policy. So just me," she says.

"That's awesome. Listen, you shoot me a text when you're done here, and we can chill after, yeah?"

"Sure," she says, desperate to get out of this interaction. The credibility of the friend who set her up on this date is totally shot.

"Great. This has been a really nice evening, Lettie." He leans in for a kiss, but she weaves her head to the side. He turns in toward her like it was just bad timing, and she takes a step back.

"Okay, see you," she says airily.

He doesn't move.

Was he going to *watch* her go into this place? A group of people approach a man at the door, and he holds up a black tablet to check their names. There's no way she's going to be able to get in. Just then one of the women in the alley punches some numbers into the keypad on the door and holds it open while her friend flicks her butt into a metal canister.

Lettie hikes up her white minidress, plants her hand on the metal barrier, and, with her long legs and like her life depends on it, leaps over it. The women vanish through the door, and Lettie catches the heavy metal by her fingertips just as it's about to shut. There's a banging clatter behind her. Graham had tried to hop the barrier too, but his legs, which are shorter, did not clear it, and it collapsed to the ground with him splayed on top of it. As he's scrambling to stand, she makes a quick decision and shuts the door behind her just as the man with the tablet arrives.

The place is a maze. A literal maze. Hallway after hallway. She passes the same bathroom twice and then stops. She needs to get her wits about her. Follow the music. There will be people dancing somewhere.

She comes out into the mouth of the dance floor, and the music pulses through her. There's a large square bar where the closest bartender is wearing a black lace crop top and has doves tattooed up her chest. Her eyes are ringed with metallic eye shadow, and she's moving to the beat of the music as she mixes a drink in a metal canister.

Lettie will stay for a few minutes to give herself a buffer and make sure that Graham is gone. Becoming quite warm in this mass of bodies, she takes off her coat and stands on her tiptoes, trying to see over the heads. Through the darkness and blue-gray lights, she can't make out any markings for an exit.

"Lettie!" Her name is yelled, cutting across the people.

Dread fills her. Did they let Graham in here? *Fuck.* She starts to shoulder her way through the people, determined to find her way out. Why did she wear a white dress? In the strobe lights, she's glowing.

"Lettie!" She hears the voice again, strong and urgent, deep and gruff. Not Graham's higher-pitched voice.

She turns and there's a man in front of her. He has fought his way through the bodies to reach her, and he has no shame in it. His hair is dark tight curls. He's got to be six two, and the way his dark-green T-shirt sits on his shoulders, she can tell he's lean. She has seen him on TV countless times, but she's not prepared for this.

"Alex!" she exclaims. She doesn't know if it's the familiarity of his smile or the happiness that fills his face as she yells his name, but she is just delighted to see him. In a city full of strangers, finally a person she knows. She flings her arms around his neck and holds him tight. After such a shit night, this was what she needed.

"Hey," he says, hugging her back but not nearly with the same enthusiasm, his arms loose on her back. As she pulls away, she remembers the accusation and knows then that it has weighed on him. "How are you?" he asks a bit sheepishly.

"I'm good. I just went on a horrendous date." She makes a face, one she's pretty sure she's never made before in her life, but she's trying to lighten the mood. To put him at ease. And just as the bass drops, she asks, "Do *you* like to travel?"

He tilts his head down and places his hand on her back as people jostle by them. "What?" he yells.

"Do you . . ." She is yelling right into his face, but her words are swallowed by the force of the speakers. It's hopeless. She surrenders to the noise engulfing them.

He gestures for her to follow him, and she takes his hand for fear of being separated by the flailing bodies. She narrowly avoids being body-slammed by a woman who has let loose, throwing herself into the beat, only to step into a group of men who try to lift her over their heads.

"Yo, man, she's good." Alex bends and yells at the man who's just grabbed Lettie's ankles and then he waves off another guy.

Lettie places her hand on Alex's back, feeling the heat of him under her palm, and stays right behind him so that she doesn't lose him. They slide through a few more bodies and break out of the vortex of people. She follows him up a set of stairs into a much calmer area. The party of people below them is still loud, but comparatively, this is a quiet oasis. Alex leads her to a dark semicircle couch built into the wall with a table in front of it. As they sit he says, "What were you saying back there?"

It feels silly now, that being her first question after all these years. "It was nothing."

"Tell me."

"I asked if you were interested in traveling."

"I am, yeah. Are you?" He angles in toward her, his broad shoulders open, his knees inches from hers.

Lettie nods. "If you could go anywhere for two weeks, where would you go?"

He glances away, thinking. "Italy. You got pizza, pasta, gelato, nice beaches, historical sites that would be really neat to see. If you'd given me three weeks, I'd've said Australia. Surfing and snorkeling the Great Barrier, chilling on beaches along the coast. What about you?"

"Those both sound amazing," Lettie says. "I studied in London for a year and explored every chance I could get. I did Venice, but I'd love to see more of Italy."

"You studied in London? That's so cool. When was that?"

"Can I get you something?" a woman in a short black skirt and toned legs asks them.

"Um, I'll have a Coke," Lettie says. She's already drunk half a bottle of wine and knows that she won't do well with more alcohol on an empty stomach.

"I'll have a Coke too," Alex says and then turns back to Lettie. "You don't drink?" It's not judgmental, just a question.

"I do, but I ordered a Caesar salad at the restaurant and then the server took the menu before I could say a main. I should've said something, but I didn't and now I'm starving."

"Was this on the horrendous date?"

"The very same."

"Why was it horrendous?"

"Every single time his phone lit up, he'd glance at it and totally lose his train of thought. When the server brought the wine, he swished it around, stuck his face *into* the glass, and sniffed it like he was doing a line of coke. Does it all over again and says to her, 'That's fine.' I wanted to die."

"How old was this guy?"

"He was . . . I don't know, a couple of years older than us."

"He sounds ancient."

"Oh! And I'm too tall."

"How tall are you?" Alex asks.

"Five ten."

"You're a giant!" he exclaims, smiling at her. That smile she remembers from childhood.

She laughs and can't help but stare at him. His filled-out face, his muscular arms and thick thighs. His powerful hands. When they were younger, she thought he was cute, but his features have sharpened, becoming rugged and handsome.

"Do I look different?" she asks.

"Nah, you look the exact same," he says.

"Oh."

The server sets their Cokes on the table in front of them.

"Thank you," Alex says. "Could we also get a pizza?"

"What would you like on it?"

Lettie says pineapple and ham at the same time that Alex says bacon and mushrooms.

"Pineapple, ham, bacon, and mushrooms," Alex says, raising his eyebrows in question to Lettie.

"Sounds perfect," Lettie says.

Alex Saint was Lettie's first kiss. And to think it might never have happened. When Jackson asked Lettie to play tennis with a girl from his English class, she'd said no.

Lettie tried to avoid Jackson's friends like the plague. They drove her nuts. *Oh my God, Jackson, your sister's adorable. How do you get your hair that shiny? Does your brother have a crush on someone? Don't worry, you can totally tell me.*

"Please, Lettie." There was a glimmer of desperation in Jackson's face that she'd never seen before.

"Just this once, Jackson," she said. "But you owe me."

"You're the best."

She and Jackson walked the short distance from their house to the tennis courts, Jackson carrying their parents' bag of rackets and balls,

Lettie wearing her brand-new running shoes. As they got closer, Lettie couldn't believe it. Alex Saint, the cutest boy in her grade with his tight dark curls and the same Nike shorts he wore to school every single day, was standing on the court. He was smiling and saying something to a pretty girl who was tying her wavy brown hair back into a ponytail. He was teasing her, and the girl was just eying him. It was clear from the moment Lettie set eyes on them that they were close.

As Jackson made the introductions, Lettie noticed the missing strings and hockey tape around the handles of their racquets. Their balls were so old, her parents wouldn't have used them as chew toys for their dog.

"Hey, you guys want to try these rackets?" Jackson said, pulling two more from their tennis bag.

"Oh no, it's okay," Grace said. "Those look really nice."

There was a hiss as Jackson cracked a new canister of balls. "They are nice," Jackson said. "My mom won them at a charity auction. She never uses them." He passed one to Grace and one to Alex.

Lettie was self-conscious at first. She had once loved to run and play, but over the past year, her friends became more interested in other things, and her body wasn't used to moving the way it once had.

She was paired with Alex and half-heartedly went for the ball, not getting to it on time. "Yo, Lettie." Alex nodded at her new shoes. "Get those runners running."

Get those runners running. She needed to move her feet and get back into what she had once loved. She went for the next ball and hit it cleanly, but it was just out.

"Nice one, Lettie," Grace called from the baseline. "It was close."

Jackson was different with Grace than he was with his other friends. He smiled easily and made lighthearted jokes. He was fun to be around.

Lettie was nothing short of disappointed when their last game ended.

Alex passed her the racket he was using. "Thanks for that," he said.

"You're really good," she said.

"So are you." And he didn't add *for a girl*.

As she zipped up their tennis bag, Jackson knelt next to her. "Is it cool if I invite them back for a swim?" There's an unspoken communication that can happen between siblings, in the flash of an instant, with no words uttered. "Awesome," he said and swung around. "You guys bring your swimsuits?"

One of the things that Lettie grew to love about Grace was that she always spoke to her like a fellow human being. Not like she was eight years younger or like she wanted something from Lettie.

Lettie liked to wear shift dresses, skirts, and colorful tops. She had a nice smile, half-moon eyes, and sleek honey-colored hair. A natural beauty, she had been told by many people. Grace and Alex never commented on her looks like Jackson's other friends.

"Dude, your sister's going to be a babe one day," she'd heard one of his volleyball friends say. When they came over, she stayed in her room.

Alex was fun to hang out with, and she loved playing with him in the pool. He pushed her but never made her feel uncomfortable. He was easy to talk to. He would ask her how she had done on the presentation she was nervous about, how her violin exams went, and how her dance classes were going. Alex, Grace, and Jackson let her practice her biology presentation three times—three whole times—giving her pointers and encouraging her.

By the next summer, the four of them hung out regularly, and Lettie loved it. After another great day at the beach, Lettie and Alex ran up the dune one last time—just as the sun was setting. Lettie was wearing a purple dress that rippled in the breeze coming off the lake.

Girls in her class had started talking about boys they'd had their first kiss with. After a couple of near misses during spin the bottle, she wanted to know what all the fuss was about. And more importantly, she didn't want her first time to be in front of a group of people. Feeling playful and confident and mostly just curious about what it would be like to have someone else's lips pressed against her own, she said to Alex, "Will you kiss me?"

"Sure," he said so nonchalantly that it annoyed her.

"If Krista Vain asked you to kiss her, would you?" Lettie asked. Krista was the most popular girl in their class. She wanted to know if Alex would've said yes to any girl. But then, all of a sudden, Alex kissed her in one swift movement, and she was totally unprepared for it. His lips on hers and his hands at his sides. It lasted an eternity and was over in a flash.

"No, I wouldn't kiss Krista," he said, pulling away.

"Don't tell anyone, okay?" Lettie said. The thought of her friends at school, the teasing they would do if they found out she had asked Alex Saint to kiss her, put her into a panic.

"Why would I tell anyone?" he said.

"Not even Grace."

"Lettie, I won't."

They crested the dune. A moment ago they were excited to run down it one last time, but now they walked side by side, their feet cutting through the soft sand.

Down below Grace was rolling the beach towels and shaking the sand from their picnic blanket while Jackson collapsed the chairs. Alex took the other end of the blanket and folded it with Grace. There was such ease to their movements. They never bickered or fought. Not that Lettie and Jackson did much, but they definitely argued over which radio station to listen to or who's turn it was to unload the dishwasher. There was something about Grace and Alex. How they relied and depended on each other, looked out for each other, and genuinely enjoyed being together.

It was because of these hangouts that Jackson and Lettie had grown closer. Seeing how naturally it came to them. It was a good, positive vibe. The four of them together. It was Lettie's favorite summer of her childhood.

Then, on the first day of grade seven, Alex wasn't in her class, so she assumed he was in the other class across the hall. But at lunchtime she didn't see him, so she went to the principal's office.

"Alex Saint," said the school secretary, punching away at the archaic keyboard. "He was unenrolled this summer."

"Unenrolled? Why?"

"Must have moved districts."

Moved districts? She went through the rest of the day unable to focus, the words of her teachers and peers washing over her. She needed to talk to Grace and find out where he'd gone.

She rode her bike to their house right after school. The grass was patchy, and there were massive weeds taking over the front yard, the big spiky ones you had to be careful of. She walked around the rusted beige car in the driveway and leaned her bike against the porch. She rang the doorbell, then knocked and took a step back.

A woman with short feathery hair opened the door. Her clothes hung off her like she'd just lost a bunch of weight.

"I'm not interested," the woman snarled.

"I'm not selling anything," Lettie said. "May I speak to Grace?"

The woman pursed her lips like she had just sucked on a slice of lemon. This couldn't be the woman Grace and Alex lived with. She was so unwelcoming, so unkind.

"Is she here?"

"No," the woman said and slammed the door in Lettie's face.

That night she called her brother. "Hey, Lettie," he said, sounding happier than he had in a while, the old vibrancy in his voice back.

"They're gone."

"Who?"

"Grace and Alex."

"What do you mean, they're gone? Where'd they go?"

"I don't know."

After Lettie finished grade twelve, she flew out west to visit Jackson and Marina. They drove into the mountains to go on a hike and found a sports bar for dinner with flat-screen televisions mounted to the walls.

Partway through their wings and pizza, Jackson's eyes widened. "Holy shit," he said, staring up at the screen behind Lettie.

She looked over her shoulder, and it took her a second to realize what she was seeing. Alex Saint was walking toward the stage. The first player picked overall in the NHL draft.

The camera panned to a smartly dressed woman who was clapping and watching him proudly. A woman they had never seen before. In her midfifties, with glossy blonde hair and a touch of makeup. Grace was nowhere in sight. What caught Lettie's attention was Alex's smile. It was different from the one she had known.

"Do you come here often?" Lettie asks, tossing the last pizza crust onto the platter. She's so completely comfortable with Alex, unguarded in a way she's never been with any man who hasn't been related to her. She's staring again, at the sharpness of his cheekbones, his strong jaw. She feels a closeness to him, like she could talk to him about anything and he wouldn't judge her. Like he would actually be interested in what she had to say. Just being with him, she is light and happy.

"No," he says. "This is my second time here, actually. I'm not a member. A buddy invited me."

"Jackson and I came to see one of your playoff games last year. You were amazing. I mean, I knew when we were kids that you played a lot of hockey, but I didn't realize how good you were."

"You guys came to one of my games?" he says.

She nods.

"I wish I'd known."

"Well, I wasn't sure, you know, with you being a big hockey star now, how all that worked, like if you'd want us reaching out to you," she says.

"I would've loved to have seen you guys," he says. "I really enjoyed spending time with your family when we were kids."

Lettie deflates, a sinking pit through her stomach. That's why he had been so excited to see her. He felt kinship to her because of her family, because of the nostalgia, not because of her. It's their shared history. She can't help but be disappointed.

"Yeah, those were good times," she says, pulling her knees away from his and in doing so turning her whole body. "I'm really glad I ran into you."

His brow furrows. "Wait, what's going on?"

"I should get back. I've got a pile of readings to get through tomorrow, and I don't want to stay out too late."

"I've said something wrong."

"No, you're lovely, Alex. You've always been lovely." She stands. "Good luck this season, not that you guys need it. Seems like you've got a powerhouse team." He moves so that she can get her purse and jacket and looks up at her with confusion on his face. "And for what it's worth, I want you to know that I never believed the accusation. Not for one second."

On her way down the stairs, she slips past some surly-looking people.

As Alex watches her from the railing, her white dress shimmering purple and pink under the strobe lights, he wishes he'd gotten her number. What had caused such a change to come over her? He could see it in her face. Disappointment and hurt. He replays the conversation in his head. What was it he'd said? It was right after he'd mentioned her family. He was trying to show his gratitude and appreciation, how much they'd meant to him, but it had caused her to tense up.

Sergei comes to stand next to him at the railing. "You all right?" he says.

Alex nods. "I think I'm gonna head out."

"I'll let my driver know." Sergei pulls out his phone.

"No, it's all right, thanks. I want to take the bus," Alex says.

"The bus? You sure?"

"Yeah. I'll see you tomorrow."

Alex's mind is on other things as he walks toward the bus stop, his hands in his jacket pockets, so it's not until the last second that he realizes Lettie is sitting on the bench. They make eye contact, and he glances down, embarrassed. "I swear I'm not stalking you," he says.

"I missed the bus. Next one's not for twenty minutes." She slides down, and he joins her but sits on the far edge. After a moment she says, "I didn't take you for a guy who rode the bus."

He nods. "From time to time."

"You don't have a driver?" she says.

"I do."

"Then why take the bus?"

He hasn't made eye contact with her throughout this whole interaction, but now he turns away from her completely. "Because it reminds me of Grace."

This statement hangs between them.

"Alex, I shouldn't have left so quickly back there. I was being selfish. I've been going on all these dates for months and none of them have amounted to anything. Then I saw you and things were so easy. I got my hopes up, but I wasn't thinking. You were just being nice and saying that you enjoyed being around my family. I should've been gracious. I'm sorry."

He's staring at her now. *That's why she left.* He couldn't even think about dating right now, not with everything going on with him, and even before that he had had trouble with it. He also found Lettie easy to talk to because she knew the part of his life that was missing. He would never have to navigate how he would explain it to her. That most important part of his history and the hole it had left in his heart. The one that kept him up at night wondering how she was doing. If she was okay. "This is the first time I've been out at all since the allegation," he says. "Other than practice and games."

"What's going on with all that?"

"Grace set me up with a lawyer, this guy Daniel. He broke everything down for me, and I told him exactly what happened, didn't sugarcoat anything, and he seemed pretty confident. So I guess we'll see," Alex says.

"You've spoken to Grace?"

He shakes his head. "Just the lawyer. He wouldn't take any money from me, said Grace did a lot for his family. She's his grandma's nurse."

"Grace would be a great nurse."

Alex nods. His broad shoulders have hunched, and there's an ache in his chest. "You say I'm this big hockey star now, and yeah, maybe that's true, but I'm still the same kid you knew, Lettie."

She slides toward him, and he settles into the softness of her gaze. She squeezes his hand, and the tension in his shoulders eases just a bit.

THIRTEEN

One Year Earlier

Sergei is late for dinner, but they would never start without him. His wife, two sisters, and mother wait patiently in the sitting room, chatting about their day. When he walks in the front door two hours later than expected, none of them mention that the meat is overcooked or that the vegetables are wilted. They greet him warmly and go about serving the borsch, sitting at the table without saying a thing about it. Ludmilla knows when his pale blue eyes won't meet hers that something big is on his mind in a way someone who has known you almost your entire life can.

On the ice Sergei glides effortlessly, skating along the blue line without ever having to look down at it. He can just feel it there beneath him. His hand-eye coordination is unparalleled. His legs are strong, his thighs as thick as tree trunks, his chest deep, and his arms big. It is a feat to get the puck off him and almost impossible to knock him off balance. But off the ice, without skates on his feet and a stick in his hands, he is not graceful but clunky and rough in his movements. The handle of his chair clips the table as he shuffles his seat forward, sloshing red over the side of his bowl.

His mother can't wait any longer. "What is it, Sergei?" she asks.

Sergei runs the tips of his fingers together, something he does when he's nervous, while the women brace for the worst. "I've been approached to play in the North American hockey league." The way he says it, they all know he has made his decision, if not on paper, then in his heart.

"But why, Sergei?" his mother asks.

"The North American league has the best players in the world, and I want to play the best. It will be for only a few years and then I will come back," he says.

"What do you mean, I?" Ludmilla says.

"I will not ask you to come with me and leave your life here behind."

"You are my life," she says simply. "You have always been my life." They had grown up on the same street, had sat next to each other in school and in the pews in church. His mother had taught her how to cook, his sisters were her closest friends, and when his father had died of alcohol poisoning, she had shared in the private relief of the family. "Besides, who will cook you proper meals if you go alone?"

"For how many years?" his sister Tanya asks.

"Four."

His mother's spoon clatters against her bowl. He has signed the contract, they all know then.

"When do you leave?" Tanya says.

"I fly out in two days. They want me to join the team as soon as possible." He reaches into his back pocket and slides a piece of paper across the table to his mother. "I bought you a house."

His mother opens the paper and gasps as she reads the address. "Sergei, no," she says. "It's too much."

"It's done," he says. "The deal's gone through."

"But you can't afford this. No, take it back," she says.

"I can, actually. It's for the three of you."

Tanya and Sofia usually stay to help Ludmilla clear away the dishes, but tonight they get up from the table and put their coats on, wanting to give the couple some space. Sergei walks them to the door. He hugs his mother first, then Sofia, but Tanya is in the corner wrapping her scarf around her neck, her back to Sergei. He and Sofia exchange a glance before Sofia gently leads their mother through the door.

"Tanya," he says, and she finally turns to look at him. "Don't fuck around with school this year."

Tanya rolls her eyes.

"If you want to party, party. Have a good time, sure. But you keep those marks up." He puts his finger to her temple. "You have a great mind. Don't be stupid. Don't throw it all away, okay? If you want something, get after it. If you need something, you let me know."

Her face scrunches as she tries to fight her threatening tears.

"It's okay," he says, pulling her into a hug. "You take care of Mama."

She nods into his shoulder and then wipes her eyes before whipping around and shutting the door behind her.

Ludmilla finishes washing the dishes and wipes down the table while Sergei paces the small kitchen behind her. She knows what he wants. For her to say something, to turn to him and tell him that everything will be fine. That she is fine with this. But she still needs time to process what he has told her and him pacing right behind her is not helping. Finally, he leaves to take a shower. She scrubs her hands, dries them, and sits on the couch.

She takes a moment to collect her thoughts, her mind starting to roll through the many things that have to be done without the time to do them. Then she looks around at their apartment. It isn't much, but it's the first place she has ever been truly happy. Safe and comfortable. With this man and his family.

Sergei comes out of the shower and changes into his pajama bottoms and a white T-shirt. He knows that if he talked to his family about this, they might have tried to change his mind, but his mind is made up. The opportunity too good to pass up. The money he will make in four years is more than anything he could ever make in his league. Ludmilla won't have to give up her life here. They can FaceTime, she can move in with his family if she wants, and he'll be back during the offseason. It will be for just four years. He needs to speak with her.

Ludmilla is sitting on the couch in their living room, her laptop on her knees and her phone on the table in front of her. He comes up behind her and puts his large hands on her shoulders. "What are you doing?"

"We're not the first ones to do this," she says midway through typing an email. "I have reached out to Pavel and Anna. They've given me a list of things to do, people to contact."

He leans down to see her screen. "I don't need an English tutor."

"You and I only know the basics."

"That's fine. I'm there to play hockey."

"Well, *I* am not."

"Ludmilla, what about your class, your kids?"

"There are other teachers. Someone who will take my place," she says offhandedly, but he knows her too well. Teaching brought her great joy, and watching her stand her ground in front of unruly parents brought him great joy. She didn't take any shit. Many thought that now that she was a hockey player's wife, she would settle in at home. But Ludmilla had always wanted to teach. To be all the good teachers she had experienced in her life all at once. She was warm, firm, and encouraging with her students. She sought ways to relate to each one, even the little shits, because Sergei had once been a little shit. He had been kicked out of school, only to be allowed back in because of his ability on the ice. His father had been a controlling, abusive alcoholic whose death was not mourned by the family. Publicly and especially at church, they played the part. But it was in the wake of his father's death that the family had been able to thrive. His sisters started doing well in school, his mother was promoted at the factory where she worked, and he was able to play hockey without the fear that his father would appear in the stands to accost people.

There was always a reason a child was disruptive. There were twenty-seven personalities in her class, and she worked hard to bring out the best in all of them.

"Ludmilla, please, stay here with Mama and the girls. I don't know what to expect in North America."

"I'm going with you, Sergei, unless you want to divorce me. Hmm? Is that what you want?"

"No, that is not what I want."

She reaches up, running her hand through his short sandy hair, feeling it bristle against her palm. He kisses her neck, and she swats him away. "I don't have time for this," she says.

He rests his chin on her head. "Thank you for this and for all that you are."

Pavel told Sergei that the NHL would be different, but he was not prepared for this. On his Russian team, they played as one, cycling the puck between the forwards and the defense, working together as a unit, collectively. Sergei could feel his teammates around him on the ice and anticipate their moves.

Here the play is much more physical, all elbows and high sticks—their style of play individualistic. There is no creativity, no rhythm or flow to it. Their pace is foreign to him, with no one setting anything up; they just skate through the middle and hope to score. For the first time in his life, he is off-balance, having to glance down at the puck, passing to a man who is not expecting it.

On his KHL team, he was the star player, the one people bought tickets to see. Here he finds no ease in his movements, no smoothness as he skates. He can see it in the eyes of his teammates and his coach. This was a mistake. He is too slow. Too unsure. His confidence in his ability wanes. He is worried, and his frustration brews.

And this little shit, the captain of their team who is only nineteen and five years younger than Sergei, is the most individualistic *look at me* player of them all. Sergei seethes, watching him from the bench. His hands, his ability to move around the ice, is unlike anything Sergei has ever seen, but he does not pass the puck or backcheck when he should.

After Sergei's second abysmal game, he comes out of the locker room to meet Ludmilla. She isn't standing with the other wives, and she's holding back tears. This is a woman he's seen cry only a handful of times in his life, but here in this foreign country, away from her language and culture and friends, she is alone. Isolated and excluded from these people. Their English lessons are no match for their conversations, their quick greetings and small talk. Sergei takes his wife's hand and leads her out. He knows he cannot leave. He has signed the contract and bought a house in addition to the one for his mother and sisters. But he can teach that little shit a lesson. He is going to send a message.

During the next practice, Alex is skating up the curve in the boards after another selfish play. Sergei skates backward, lining up his target. He unleashes the full weight of his body and sends his hip into Alex. Catching the movement out of the corner of his eye, Alex pulls up, faster than anything Sergei has ever witnessed, and Sergei slams his hip into the board.

It takes him a long moment to get up. Then Alex has the nerve to come over and offer him a hand. Sergei wants to punch him in the face.

That night he is fuming, pacing their large new kitchen, their empty living room, around suitcases and boxes. Ludmilla hasn't unpacked yet, and she hasn't ordered furniture. The only thing they have is a mattress and sheets.

Someone knocks on the door, and Ludmilla answers it. Sergei cringes at the voice.

"Hi. Ludmilla, right? I'm Alex. I realized yesterday that we're neighbors," Alex says. *The audacity.* Sergei comes to the door, ready to slam it shut, but Alex is holding a basket that fills the frame. "Hey, Sergei." Alex smiles at him. "I brought you guys some housewarming things." He speaks slowly and clearly, pointing as he goes. "My favorite barbecue spice, a succulent—these things are pretty great, and you don't have to water them much—some coffee from the shop on main street, and tickets to see Cirque de Soleil. Wicked show. Oh, and some maple syrup." Ludmilla doesn't understand all of it, but she gets the gist. This man is lovely, absolutely lovely. She's overcome with emotion at the kindness of his gesture. She takes the basket and shoves it into Sergei's arms.

"Come in," she says, waving him in. "Come."

"No, no, you guys have got a lot going on here." Alex nods at the boxes. "I'm having a dinner tomorrow night. Gus and Diana are coming—they live down the street. Nothing fancy, just a couple of steaks on the grill. You guys free?"

"Yes," Ludmilla says.

"That's my house there." He points to a dark-gray house a few doors down. "Come around five o'clock?" He holds up five fingers and says, "Tomorrow," with a hand motion.

Sergei shifts the basket so that he can clench the doorframe.

"Tomorrow, five o'clock." Ludmilla nods. "We bring what?"

Alex waves her off. "Nothing, don't worry about that. You guys just get settled in here."

Ludmilla shuts the door and goes into the kitchen. She takes the car keys from the island and cuts through the tape on one of the boxes.

"What are you doing?" Sergei asks.

Ludmilla just shoots him a look like *isn't it obvious*. "Unpacking."

Ludmilla has been listening to English tapes all day, walking through the house, repeating after the man. Sergei has been trying to tune them out. He doesn't need them. The interviewers always ask the same questions. He has the hockey lingo down and has no desire to speak to his teammates off the ice.

Ludmilla does her hair and puts on a dress and some heels. She is making an effort; she's looking forward to something. Not wanting to deflate his wife, Sergei goes out and buys a nice bottle of wine, showers, and puts on a dress shirt. For tonight, he will call a truce and be gracious—or, at the very least, polite.

Ludmilla has texted Anna to ask questions about the social etiquette here in North America. Apparently, it's polite to arrive a few minutes late, and so at ten after five, they walk down the street. When they knock on the door, Sergei is tense, and Ludmilla is nervously excited.

A tall woman with fair hair and freckles scattered across her nose answers the door. "Hello," she says warmly, shaking each of their hands. "I am Diana, Gus's wife. I don't think we've met, as I was back in Sweden for a wedding." She has long and slender limbs, which make her large baby bump seem even bigger.

"Hey, guys," Alex says from the kitchen. He's seasoning some thick steaks and turns to grab something from the fridge. Ludmilla notes the spinach, goat cheese, and strawberry salad, asparagus, corn, and garlic bread on the island. She's impressed. The table is set for five, with a booster seat in the corner for a little girl with white blonde hair on Gus's shoulders.

"This is Elin," Gus says, lifting her off his shoulders and setting her gently on the ground. She couldn't be much more than one. With her pudgy little legs, she runs between Alex's, and he playfully snaps the salad tongues at her.

After dinner, which Sergei has to admit is pretty good, Diana brings out a strawberry angel food cake and adds whipped cream to it. Both she and Ludmilla notice how Sergei's eyes close when he takes his first bite.

"I can give you the recipe," Diana says to Ludmilla.

When they finish dessert, Alex clears their plates, and Diana and Ludmilla move to the sectional with their wine, tucking their feet beneath them.

Sergei leans back in his chair, and Alex rejoins him and Gus. He slides a USB stick toward Sergei. "I've watched some footage of you playing back in Russia," Alex says. "Your style is quite different from what we do here. Maybe we could talk with Coach, incorporate some of your systems when you're on the ice."

"Ludmilla," Sergei says sharply in Russian. "What bullshit is this kid saying to me?"

Ludmilla turns over the back of the couch, her face set in a glare, and Sergei knows he's in trouble. He's embarrassing her. But he doesn't care. He has done his part.

"He wants to talk about your style of play," she says tightly. "Work it into their game."

Sergei scoffs. "Right, just learn the entire Russian system. Easy-peasy." He stands. "Let's go."

Back at their house, Ludmilla doesn't speak. She gets into bed and turns her back to him. The next morning, she makes only one cup of the delicious coffee Alex had brought them.

At the end of the week, Sergei and Ludmilla receive the news that Pavel has been traded. He is joining Sergei's team. While he and Anna wait for a home to come up on the market nearby, they are going to stay with them. They have more than enough room, and both Sergei and Ludmilla are delighted. A piece of home.

Diana takes Ludmilla through her house to show her how she has decorated. The cushions are soft pastels, floral and striped. There are bright vases, cozy blankets, colorful dishes, and plants placed around the rooms. The space is inviting and vibrant, simplistic yet warm, with lots of natural light. Ludmilla is surprised to find that almost every-thing—the cushions, side tables, furniture, and table set—are all from IKEA.

But then Diana shrugs. "We're Swedish."

The day that Pavel and Anna are to arrive, Ludmilla is still chilly toward Sergei. He tries to kiss her, but she turns away. He smiles at her, and she averts her eyes, busying herself in the kitchen or just leaving the room entirely.

That night at the dinner table, Ludmilla is light, laughing with Anna and Pavel. But when they go to bed, she turns away from Sergei.

Slowly, tentatively, he places his large hand on her back. "Ludmilla, please. How can I make this right?"

After a moment she turns to face him. "Stop being so angry all the time. We are here for four years, Sergei. Four years of our lives. You have to work harder at enjoying it. Making friends."

"But I—"

She puts her finger to his lips. "These people are trying. Why can't you?" She reaches for his arm and gives it a tender squeeze.

This woman. She has asked so little of him. Supported him her entire life. From their early school days when she would help him rush through his unfinished homework to their long walks home together, picking up his sisters along the way.

On days when his father drank away their lunch money, his mother would scrounge together just enough for his sisters, but Sergei had always been a big eater. His mother would tie her hair back in a tight bun, getting ready for her shift at the factory and glancing nervously at Sergei in the mirror.

"Don't worry, Mama. I'll be fine," he said.

It was Ludmilla who would share her meager meals with him. Always.

Sergei's father died when he was eleven. Alcohol poisoning. It was a relief. The excuses they'd had to make for him during his life, the dark cloud they'd lived under. With his passing they no longer had to navigate his moods. His temper.

They lived in the dingy basement flat of an old apartment building —the cheapest one in their district—but they made it their own. With cozy quilts and eclectic furniture collected over the years. Every month his mother had struggled to pay the rent, but with his father gone, she was able to manage the money he wasn't drinking away.

Ludmilla's foster mother lived in the basement apartment across the alley. The night after his father's passing, there was a quick rap on the windowpane of Sergei's room. A stone flicked up by someone biking by perhaps. But then it came again. More like a knock this time. Unlocking the window, he opened it an inch and then threw it wide. Ludmilla was squatting next to it, her thick hair covering her face. She was trying to hide it, but Sergei could tell that she had been crying. He helped her through the opening and into his room.

"What happened?" he asked.

"Nothing," she said, her voice small. Not at all like the Ludmilla he knew.

He rolled back on his heels, unsure of what to say but wanting to put her at ease. Wanting to help her. He would never forget the trepidation in her eyes right before she bowed her head and said, "Can I sleep here with you?"

The question startled him but not as much as the words that came out of his mouth. "Of course."

"Not just tonight," she said quietly. "But for a while maybe?"

"Yes."

"Even when I bother you?"

"Yes."

"Even when we fight at school and you are not happy with me?"

"Yes, Ludmilla. Always."

As they laid down side by side, their scrawny bodies next to each other, he heard her breath slow in the darkness, felt her body relax as she pulled the quilt around herself.

He never locked his window again, and he left a chair underneath it so that she could get in easily even when he was away at tournaments. For years they slept side by side in his single bed. Even on days when they bickered or went through a whole day when they didn't speak at all. The nights were an unspoken truce, Ludmilla's safe space. It lasted into their awkward early teen years, but when Sergei got a girlfriend, Ludmilla knocked on the windowpane. She never knocked.

She was kneeling down next to the opening.

"What are you doing? It's freezing out there." Sergei's fingertips were going numb just from holding the window open.

Ludmilla wouldn't look at him. "Now that you have a girlfriend, maybe we shouldn't do this anymore."

"No. Don't be silly." He offered her a hand.

"But what if you want to bring her here?"

"She lives on the other side of town."

"But what if you did?"

"I would let you know."

"Are you sure?"

"Yes. Of course I am sure." He offered his hand again, and this time Ludmilla took it.

Her body next to his was even more natural to him than skating. There was nothing more consistent in Sergei's life than his mother's and sisters' love and admiration for him and Ludmilla sleeping next to him at night.

At eighteen, he and his girlfriend broke up before he went away to hockey camp. That summer, Sergei filled out. His chest became wide, his shoulders broad, his body long, and his arms and legs thick.

He came home at the end of August to a feast prepared by his mother and his sister Sofia. Tanya peppered him with questions, wanting to know all about where he had been and what he had been up to. Since their father's death, she had come out of her shell and was a curious, bright young thing.

His mother said, "Tanya, he did not travel for an entire day just to be pestered. Leave him be."

"It's okay, Mama," he said. He loved being in the warmth of his home again. Around the gentle touch of the women in his life.

His mother and Sofia had made all his favorites, shaslik, pirozhki, pelmeni. While he ate his dinner and then dessert, his mind was on Ludmilla, and he found himself wondering. Had she still come through the window during the summer while he was away? God, he hoped so.

He said good night to his family and went into his room, checking to make sure that the window was unlocked and that the chair was still there. But his bed was as neat as ever. There was no sign of Ludmilla. Disappointed, he curled into the wall and fell asleep. Then something woke him—a weight on the bed—at what time he didn't know.

"You came." He turned to face her.

In the darkness he could just make out a small, sad smile.

"What is it?" He sat up, concerned.

"You are much bigger now." She nodded at his body. "I won't fit."

He pressed his back up against the wall and lifted his arm. "You will always fit."

She laid down carefully, near the edge of the bed, but she was still right up against his body. He wrapped his arm around her, trying to get comfortable, and then they both felt it.

"Shit," he said, glancing down, embarrassed. "I'm sorry." He pulled his arm back, trying to push his body even farther into the wall, to put some space between them.

"It's okay, Sergei," she said. "It's okay."

She leaned forward slowly and rubbed her nose against his. Then she kissed him. Their first kiss. His lips pressed to hers but then he turned his head away, a pained expression on his face. "Ludmilla, don't." He cupped his hand over his cock. "You are not helping."

"We can, though, if you want?"

"No." He said it so aggressively that she recoiled. "I mean, I do want to. More than anything." She smiled. "But not like this."

After a moment she said, "Do you remember Miss Garin?"

"The school librarian? I try not to."

"Her unibrow. Leaning over us and telling us to be quiet. The smell of her rank—"

"Ludmilla, why are you talking about Miss Garin right now?"

She laughed quietly. "I'm trying to help you, Sergei."

"Oh, I missed you," he breathed.

Now he brushes her hair away from her face. The face he sees every night before he shuts his eyes, even when he is at away games and she is not with him.

"Okay," he says. "I will work harder at not being so angry."

"Thank you."

Sergei comes home to find Ludmilla, Diana, and Anna have taken over the kitchen and living room. IKEA catalogs, house and home magazines, paint swatches, and fabrics are splayed across the island and couches.

Pavel comes down the stairs. "You and I are going to Gus's," he says, which Sergei thinks is a fine idea. Give the women some space. Let them do their thing. "We're going to watch tapes and develop a new system of play that works for all of us."

Sergei stifles a grunt.

He is sitting between Alex and some guy named Mike, who plays defense on their team, his shoulders drawn up tight. He can't play dumb now that Pavel is here and can translate everything. For some reason he has taken it upon himself to become quite fluent in English.

"See, see here." Pavel pauses the TV and gets up to point at the players on the screen. "How we pass in our own zone, setting up the play, and if it doesn't work, we take it out and set it up again. Cycling the puck back and forth between the defense and the forwards."

Alex nods. "You guys have a slower style of play."

"Yeah, because we don't charge through the middle and get knocked on our ass," Sergei says in English.

Alex and Gus glance at each other. "You speak better English than you've been letting on," Alex says with a grin.

At their next practice, they ask to play together. Gus, Pavel, and Alex as forwards and Sergei and Mike as their defensemen. As they skate around one another, they have no flow and can't anticipate where the other will be. Sergei gets a whiteboard and a marker.

"Okay," he says. "Alex, Pav, and Gus, you move like this." He draws Xs to indicate the players and then arches with arrows. "Around and around. We"—he points at Mike—"cycle like this. Then there are many men open and many options available. The other team's defenders do not know who to defend."

"That seems like it will be pretty slow," Mike says. When Sergei glares at him, he adds, "But hey, I'm willing to try it, man."

They stay well after practice is done working on their movements, yelling at one another, trying to get their communication down verbally so that it can become nonverbal.

Sergei spent so much time disliking Alex that he missed the one thing about him that he is known for. It's in Alex's introduction during their skate with the underprivileged youth program that Sergei hears his story for the first time. A foster child who came up through the system with the help of a wonderfully supportive foster mother, Sarah. How, before her, he traveled on public buses to get to games and used secondhand equipment, his lifestyle dire. Sergei glances at his teammates in shock, but none of them bat an eye. They have heard this story so many times before that they are unaffected by it. It is when Sergei looks at Alex that he sees how the introduction affects him. Alex's eyes set in the same way that they do when he's disappointed in a play he has just made or a shot opportunity he has missed. He goes somewhere else in his mind. Frustrated and annoyed. Shut off.

But then the next moment, Alex is up, shaking the organizer's hand and greeting the kids with a warm smile. And the kids gravitate to him. His easygoing nature, his natural ability, and his encouraging words.

At the end of the day, Sergei approaches Alex as he's putting the pylons they used into a mesh bag. He puts his hand on Alex's shoulder. "Good job with those kids today," he says.

If Alex is surprised, he doesn't show it. "Thanks, man. You too."

Sergei struggles for a moment but then decides to tell Alex something he doesn't talk about. Ever. "My wife's childhood was a bit like yours," he says. "But she did not have the wonderful Sarah."

Alex stares at him and then just nods and hoists the mesh bag onto his shoulder.

Ludmilla liked Alex from the moment she met him. In all her years of reading youth and discovering the layers of their many personalities, she never showed favoritism, but there were some kids she just liked more than others. And she had a soft spot for him. It was his kindness and his reservedness but also his keenness to try to make others feel welcome.

She had never seen Alex all that interested in a particular girl. He was polite and nice, as he was with everyone, and easygoing in a nonthreatening way that made the girls gravitate to him.

It was his friendliness that got him into trouble. The incident in the limo. They all knew what the woman was after, and Ludmilla was happy to see him leave with someone. She wanted Alex to let loose, to have some fun. To get laid.

It had taken her a while to pick up on the way Alex's mind would wander, the way he would retreat into himself. Probably because she herself was so adrift in the beginning, in a foreign country without friendship or inclusion and having to attend all these events she just dreaded. But now she looked forward to them. With Anna and Diana, she had women to sit and laugh with. To tell stories to and share in private moments with. Becoming more comfortable and confident, she grew to know the other wives too, women who were much friendlier than they'd first appeared.

It was at a black-tie gala that she first noticed Alex's demeanor. She thought he was having an off night but then she saw it again at another event. On the ice and at press conferences, he was focused. Razor sharp. But having spent a fair amount of time with him, she started to pick up on the little things. The nuances of his personality. It was with a small lurch in her stomach that she realized there was something missing in his life. Or, more devastatingly, someone. A void in his heart that made it hard for him to truly connect with people.

She asked him how often he spoke to Sarah. Every few weeks he'd said, and she'd flown out to help him move into his new house. By the casual way he talked of Sarah, Ludmilla knew that it wasn't her. She googled the stories about Alex and read his Wikipedia page, but there was nothing. No trace of someone else in his life who she could peg down as the one.

She wanted him to be happy, to fill this void. But she should have known better. She should have gone with her instincts and warned him away from that woman. And now there was this mess.

She's in the middle of a yoga class when she sees it. On every TV in the gym, there's a montage of Alex at the Olympics, with his league team and skating with the underprivileged youth. In downward dog position, she raises her head to read the caption underneath and just catches the words. *Sexual assault.* It doesn't make sense. They had all been there. They had all seen that young woman all over Alex. She starts to stand, but Diana gives her a subtle headshake. It wouldn't look right. So Ludmilla waits until the class is over and then texts Sergei: Tell Alex to come for dinner. The last thing they need is for him to be alone.

They have just sat down to eat when Alex's phone lights up with no name attached. Ludmilla has seen Alex answer the phone before, not knowing who will be on the other end, and she wonders why. Why does he answer the phone when he does not know who is calling? She would never.

Alex doesn't usually have his phone out at the table, but with everything going on, they understand. A man's voice comes through the phone, and Alex lowers his head, disappointed. He is about to hang up but then his tone changes completely. "Grace told you to reach out to me?" he says all in one breath, with hope lining his voice. He stands in one swift movement, and Ludmilla and Sergei glance at each other. "Yeah, yeah, this is a good time." He starts to mouth *sorry*, but Ludmilla shoos him away. He goes down the hallway and out of earshot. She knows then that whoever this Grace is, she is the reason he answers the phone when there is no name attached, and she is the reason he never fully engages with people and goes to another place in his mind.

Fourteen

Alex is talking to Ludmilla with one eye on the door. It's the first time Ludmilla has seen him wearing a dress shirt and slacks in his house, and he's rubbed the back of his neck twice now. Lettie is twenty minutes late.

"Go," she says, trying to distract him. "Make the kebabs with Sergei and Pav."

Alex had come to their house earlier that week, standing on their front porch, but he wouldn't come in when Ludmilla invited him.

"No, I don't want to bug you guys," he said.

"What are you talking about?" Sergei yelled from the couch. "You're not bugging us."

Ludmilla waved her husband off. "What's going on?"

"I've invited someone to dinner on Friday, and I thought maybe you guys could come and meet her."

"The woman from Opus?"

"Yeah," he said, relaxing slightly. "That's the one."

"We're going to Baro on Friday," Sergei said gruffly.

The man had impeccable hearing and absolutely no tact. "We will cancel the reservation, Sergei," Ludmilla said over her shoulder. Then to Alex, "What time do you want us?"

"The usual?"

"Perfect."

Ludmilla had been inwardly beaming, happy to see him excited about something, someone like this. But now she is worried. Where is this woman?

A few weeks earlier, Lettie had just settled in for the night on her small balcony with a mug of earl gray tea, a slice of banana bread, and the latest novel by her favorite author. It was an unseasonably warm fall evening, and everything about it was cozy, quiet, and peaceful.

She propped her feet up on her footrest and was reaching for her flashlight when her phone lit up. She glanced at it, and a zing of adrenaline went through her. One whole week after Opus and giving Alex her number at the bus stop, he had texted her.

Hi, it's Alex.

She grabbed her phone.

Hi ▢

She cringed, having sent it without thinking. Oh God, she was way too keen. But then three dots appeared, and she lowered her feet from the footrest. This was Alex, she reminded herself, not her classmates, not the guys she went on a few dates with. Alex.

Just getting on the plane home. Do you want to go on a hike tomorrow, around ten?

She put her book on the table and paced the balcony as she typed.

I would love to.

She switched over to Jackson, about to ask him if she could borrow his car.

What's your address? I'll swing by and grab you.

She clutched her phone to her chest and then, smiling like a Cheshire cat, typed it in.

Three dots.

Great, see you then.

They went on a hike, a bike ride, a brewery tour, and now this latest time while at a local market eating pulled pork sandwiches, he asked her if she would like to come over for dinner on Friday night to meet some of his friends.

This caught her off guard.

She had explored more in the past three weeks than she had in the past three months. When she had first moved there, Jackson had invited her out with him and Marina dozens of times, but she'd made up excuses here and there, to seem like she was making friends of her own. Now she actually was going out and doing things, but she wasn't ready to tell anyone about it yet.

Not her parents who kept wanting her to go out on dates to find someone nice and financially stable to spend the rest of her life with and definitely not her friends who, after moving here, she realized she wasn't all that close to. This was for her. To get to know Alex again on her own terms, not the nudging of others. Admittedly, if she did tell someone, it would be Jackson, but she'd only told him she'd run into Alex.

So far they'd only gone out to places. She'd never been to his house, and he'd never been inside hers, only picked her up or dropped her off. He hadn't tried anything, just hugged her when he said good-bye. This left her wondering—was she just a friend meeting other friends?

Because of all these things, she hesitated.

"Or not?" Alex said, dragging a napkin across his chin to wipe away the pulled pork sauce.

"No, I'd love to, Alex."

Lettie changes three times, finally settling on a white and purple shift dress paired with a long navy blue blazer. She pulls her sleek golden hair into a side braid and as usual deliberates but then decides not to wear makeup.

Alex had offered to send his driver to pick her up, but she had politely declined. She calls an Uber, grabs the chilled bottle of white wine and her purse, and puts her hand on the vase but then decides to leave it.

The Uber driver pulls up to a house with a rotting front porch, a chewed-up driveway, and an overgrown front yard with plastic kids' toys scattered throughout the long grass. This doesn't feel right.

Lettie checks her messages again. "Shit," she mutters. She typed in Amelia Street but Alex sent her Amelia Avenue.

She apologizes and reorders the same Uber, this time with the right address. As the man turns into Alex's neighborhood, he slows down, taking in the houses. He glances at Lettie in the rearview mirror and says, "Who lives here?"

"A friend," Lettie says.

"And what does he do?"

He. Not they or she. She fights an eye roll.

When she doesn't answer, he says, "Hmm?"

She stares out the window, ignoring him. He stops somewhat abruptly in front of the house, and Lettie steps from the car without thanking the man.

Right after Lettie knocks, she realizes that she's sweating. A woman with thick blonde hair opens the door. The same woman Lettie had seen in the alleyway at Opus, not the one with the cigarette but the other one, and then passed on the stairs when she left. She smiles at Lettie, and in that moment her whole face is transformed.

"Hi there. I'm Lettie." She holds out her hand, but the woman ignores it, instead taking her by the arms and kissing both her cheeks.

"Of course you are. I am Ludmilla. Come." Ludmilla ushers Lettie into the house.

"I'm sorry I'm late," Lettie says. "I went to the wrong street in a totally different area."

"It's not a problem," Ludmilla says, taking Lettie's blazer from her.

As Ludmilla turns to hang it, Lettie wipes a light film of sweat from her brow. Ludmilla directs her into the house. "I will introduce you. This is Sergei." Ludmilla presses her fingertips to a man's huge chest. He is perched on the edge of the sofa and has cropped hair and massive arms. He nods at Lettie and then goes back to talking with the other man. "Pavel." The man speaking to Sergei nods at her with a warm smile. "Gus, making the salad." She points to the kitchen, and Gus holds his tongs up in greeting. "Anna." The woman setting the table waves at her. "And Diana is feeding the baby. Oh, and Elin." A little girl runs by them, and Sergei picks her up over his head. She squeals in delight before he gently sets her on the ground and she continues running down the hall.

Lettie goes over the names in her head. She is taken aback by how much their faces change when they greet her, the way they soften and welcome her into their group with their body language.

Another man walks up to Lettie. "And I'm Mike." He holds out his hand, and Lettie shakes it. "A defenseman. I play with Sergei over there."

"Right," Ludmilla says and leads Lettie briskly toward the kitchen.

Alex comes in through the slider with an empty tray. "Lettie," he says, coming over to her, his voice tinged with relief.

"Hi, sorry I'm late. I had some direction issues."

Alex reaches for his phone, worry creasing his brow. "Did I give you the wrong address?"

"No, it was my fault. I brought you some wine." She sets the bottle on the counter and moves so that Anna can grab the napkins. "You have such a lovely home."

"Thanks. Sarah set me up with an interior decorator, so they did everything. I just okayed the colors and vibe and stuff."

"Sarah's the one you lived with after . . . well, after—"

"Yep." He puts the platter in the dishwasher and opens the fridge. "Can I get you something to drink? I have wine, coolers, Coke."

She reaches across him and takes a gin smash from the fridge. Their chests are inches apart, the edges of their hips touching. "This is perfect," she says.

Neither of them move. "Great," he says.

"Alex," Mike says. "Might want to check on the 'cue."

Alex shuts the fridge door. Smoke is billowing out of the side of the barbecue. "Be right back." He puts his hand lightly on Lettie's shoulder.

"So, Lettie," Mike says, grabbing a beer off the island. "How'd you two meet?"

Sergei comes between them to open the oven and calls to Ludmilla, "How do I know when it's ready?"

"When it's golden," she calls back from the couch where she is talking to Anna.

"Ah." Sergei shuts the door.

Mike slips around Sergei so that he's next to Lettie again. He nods at her, as if trying to prompt her.

"We went to the same elementary school."

"So you knew him before he went to the bigs." Mike pops some nuts into his mouth. "Could you tell back then that he was going to go pro?"

"No. I knew he played a lot of hockey, but he and Grace never talked about how good he was."

"Who's Grace?" Mike asks, chomping on the nuts.

Lettie realizes then that she needs to be careful. This is Alex's private life, his story, and although the world might know aspects of it, it's not her place to fill in the gaps. "Um, a girl he lived with."

"Neato. So what's your story? What're you up to?"

"I'm in school to become a physiotherapist."

"No way! The team could use someone like you." He leans in and smiles at her, squeezing her forearm just a little too hard, and it leaves a white mark that vanishes instantly. "You should have Alex put in a good word for you."

"I'm not sure where I want to work yet. I'm considering a few options—at a clinic or a hospital or starting my own practice."

Sergei scratches his ear and then opens the oven door again. "What do you think?"

Lettie realizes that he's talking to her. "Is it an angel food cake?" Sergei holds up his hands like *it very well could be.* She opens a few cupboards until she finds toothpicks, pulls the cake out, and pierces the center of it. Holding it up, she shows Sergei. "Done."

Diana comes into the kitchen, carrying a small baby in a sling. "Thanks for keeping an eye on it, Sergei."

"Anytime, Diana." He winks at Lettie.

"So, Lettie," Mike says, squeezing Lettie's forearm again to redirect her attention.

She pulls her arm away this time and says, "I'm going to see if Alex needs any help."

As she heads out the door, Sergei places his hand on Mike's shoulder.

"Hey, man, what's up?" Mike pops a few more nuts into his mouth.

"You touch her arm again, and I will smash your face through that table." He points at the glass coffee table.

Mike stares at Sergei like he is an absolute lunatic. "I don't know what you're talking about."

Lettie and Alex come into the house, carrying trays of kebabs and lightly grilled naan bread. "Mike, are you staying for dinner?" Alex asks, setting the trays on the island.

"No, he was just leaving," Sergei says.

"Have a good night, Mike," Ludmilla calls as she stands from the couch.

Lettie joins the others gathering at the island. "This looks amazing," Lettie says, dishing a chicken kebab, Greek salad, and some naan bread onto her plate. She heads to the table and takes the open spot next to Alex.

During dinner Gus tells a story about a midsummer celebration back in Sweden. His execution and dry, direct humor, along with his lack of embellishment, has Lettie laughing so hard that she's gasping for air. Anna and Ludmilla wipe away tears while Diana cuts Elin's food with an amused look on her face.

Sergei stands. "Can I get anyone anything? Another beer?" He nods to Alex's empty glass.

"No, I'm good, thanks."

Diana brings the cake over, and Lettie helps her add the whipped cream and strawberries.

"Oh my God." Lettie shuts her eyes as she swallows her first bite and then promptly opens them, embarrassed. Sergei holds his hand out to Lettie like *finally, someone else understands.*

Around eleven, everyone starts to get up and say their goodbyes. Ludmilla takes both of Lettie's hands and kisses her cheeks. "It was so nice to meet you."

"And you," Lettie says.

As people grab their jackets, she opens her Uber app.

"Yo, I can drive you," Alex says, sliding his finger through his key ring.

"It's okay, Alex. You don't have to."

"Just to make sure you don't get lost," he says with a grin.

Alex pulls up beside the four-story Victorian house that's been divided into apartments.

"That was a great dinner party," Lettie says. "I really enjoyed it."

"I'm glad." He puts the car in park, and she unbuckles her seat belt.

She reaches for the door but then turns to him and says, "Will you kiss me?"

He holds her eyes for a moment before he places his hand on her cheek, gently running his thumb over the ridge of her cheekbone. He leans over the console, his seat belt pulling across his chest, and kisses her. This time it's not just lips on lips. As his kiss deepens, she knows then that she wasn't just a friend meeting other friends. She pulls away with a smile. "I really like you," she says, letting her forehead rest against his.

"I really like you too."

"I had a crush on you when we were kids."

"I had a crush on Krista Vain."

"What?" she exclaims, sitting up straight.

"Kidding." He grins.

She playfully swats the back of her hand against his chest, but she's delighted that he remembers that day on the dune because, for her, every moment of it is so vivid. The sand edging his ear, the setting sun a soft pink on the Great Lake's surface. Sitting side by side, the four of them, watching it dip below the horizon.

In the afterglow of such a happy, carefree day full of possibilities, she ached with sadness, knowing that this would be their last night together. With Jackson and Grace off to university the next day, and Alex starting hockey again soon, who knew when they would all be together again.

Lettie could see Grace vividly in her mind. She was in light jean shorts and a white sweater, her eyes shut to the fading light, her windswept hair pulled back in a high ponytail. The pink was vibrant against her glowing skin.

She was beautiful.

Jackson saw it too. He glanced at Grace and then down, his arms resting on his knees.

"I have something I was going to bring you tonight but didn't," Lettie says. "I wasn't sure if you'd want it, but I made it for you, so you can decide. Do you want to come up with me?"

"Sure."

He follows her up the stairs to the second floor.

"Don't worry about your shoes," she says, but he flicks them off anyway.

There's a circular kitchen to the left with a vintage fridge, an old stove, and a teapot on the element. A pine table nestled into the bay window. Down the short hallway is a living room with a gas fireplace and some artwork. Alex peers into her bedroom, where her queen bed is neatly made with a light-gray duvet. "This is a great place," he says. "Now I can picture where you are when you say you're at home."

"The other day when we were at the market, you said you liked flowers but didn't have a vase." She picks up a white vase with a blue abstract design. "I made this for you in my pottery class."

He takes it from her and holds it out in front of him, turning it slowly. "You made this for me?"

She nods and shrugs. "Just a little something."

"I love it." He looks at her. "Thank you, Lettie." He heads back to the door. "I'll see you."

"Bye." She shuts the door gently behind him and then leans against it and bites her bottom lip, totally and utterly happy.

Alex is driving down his street just after midnight with one hand on the wheel and one hand on the vase beside him. He notices someone sitting on Ludmilla and Sergei's front porch. He pulls over and is about to text Sergei, but as he ducks his head to peer out the passenger window, he realizes who it is. He turns the car off and cuts up the lawn.

"Ludmilla?" he says tentatively. Her hair is draped over her face, making her eyes seem sunken in. "Is everything okay?"

She brushes the hair and tears from her face. "Yes, of course."

He hesitates, then sits a few feet down from her. "Are you sure?"

"Mm-hmm," she says, nodding slowly. Then, "In school they tell you, don't have sex, don't have sex." She holds up her finger. "But if you do have sex, use a condom. Go on the pill. Protect yourself. Why? Because if you don't, you *will* get pregnant. One time. One mistake. And you *will* be pregnant. They put the fear of God in you." She shakes her head. "They don't tell you how *hard* it can be, how you can do everything right and . . . nothing. They don't tell you that."

Alex slides toward her and puts his arm around her. Her chest heaves and her breath rattles.

"Please don't tell Sergei," she says. "I don't want him to worry."

"Does he want kids?" Alex asks gently.

"He does not say it, but I know he does."

"Do you want kids?"

"I didn't when I was young, not until I married that man. The best man in the world. He would be such a wonderful papa."

"He told me that you grew up in a home. Kind of like mine."

"It was not like yours," she says darkly. "My woman was no Sarah. She would date these men from time to time, and some of them started to look at me as I got older. I didn't like what I saw in their eyes. One of them came into my room when I eleven while she was on the phone, and I called out to her. He told me to shut the fuck up, but I was small and I ran around him and out of the house. I saw the light through Sergei's window. It was right after his father died and I didn't want to bother him, but I knew she had heard me and did nothing. And that scared me more than anything. So I paced the alley for a bit. I was nervous. At school Sergei could be so defiant and stubborn. Just looked angry all the time. Picking fights. All this aggression. But we started walking home together, and I saw this other side of him." She smiles a bit. "He was timid. And gentle with his sisters. He let me in that night and every night after. Even when he was angry or annoyed with me. He was never good with words, but I felt so safe. His room was a refuge for me. He never locked his window again. Never. It's why I know now that even if I can't have children, to do the one thing that he wants more than anything, he will not say a thing. And I am crushed by that."

The muscles in Alex's arm have tensed, and he pulls away from her. "I'm sorry that you had to go through that. And I'm glad that you had Sergei. But just for the record, I had a Sergei too, and it wasn't Sarah."

Ludmilla gives him a long, scrutinizing stare and then shakes her head like it was so obvious all along. "Grace. It was Grace."

"How do you—"

"I could tell by the way you said her name on the phone when that man called. Why do you not say anything to the media when they tell your story over and over?"

"They never asked me my story in the first place, and Sarah did a lot for me." He looks out at the dim glow of the nearest streetlight. "But Grace, she was there in the beginning. Before I ever put on my first pair of skates. Before anyone gave a shit. I know her better than I've ever known anyone. She wouldn't want me to bring attention to her in any way."

"Why do you not speak to her?"

"It's complicated."

"I'm an intelligent woman. You can explain."

He shakes his head.

"Give it a shot," she presses.

He glances down at his thighs, to where his hands have become fists. "It's because . . ."

"Because?"

"Because she's the one who left me," he spits, his voice breaking. "She sacrificed everything for me. Hid things to protect me. Her world crumbled around her because she was trying to keep us together. It took me years to realize that. When I told Sarah I wanted to speak to her, that I needed to, she told me that Grace needed some space. It was the only thing Grace has ever asked of me—to give her space. So how could I not?"

"I think she's had enough space."

"How would I know?" He stands suddenly. "I'm sorry, but you don't—you just can't understand, okay?" He storms back across the lawn and gets into his car, slamming the door shut. He grips the steering wheel. "Fuck," he lets out, his chest heaving. When he looks back at the porch, Ludmilla is gone.

FIFTEEN

Grace slides the blood pressure cuff up Annie's arm and secures it in place. It's her grandchildren's last full day before Eric and Daniel fly out, and although she's content, it's with an undertone of melancholy. Grace is doing only the necessities for her today, wanting to give them time and space together without intrusion. Beth is showing her a few pictures from her trip to Spain on her iPhone. From the ones saved in her favorites folder.

"Is that Grace all dressed up?" Annie puts her finger on the screen. "Next to Daniel."

Grace glances at the phone. There's a photo of Grace and Daniel dancing at the gala, both smiling, their bodies midmotion, with Riley just off to the side. It's a great photo. Daniel makes a quick throat-clearing noise. Annie, a woman with many wonderful attributes, is not known for her ability to keep things to herself.

Beth puts the phone in her purse. "Show me that photo again, Elizabeth."

"Later, Nan."

"Annie, I'm going to turn this on now, so no talking, okay?" Grace says. She presses the button, and the machine's motor kicks in as Eric reaches for the remote and turns the TV up a couple of notches.

"And just ahead of the big game tonight, a rivalry as old as any, we have news that the allegations against Alex Saint have been retracted."

Grace's eyes flicker to Daniel and then back to the screen. The camera pans to the crowd holding up signs of support for Alex. They're waving banners and yelling. Men and women.

"We have Alex here for a quick chat before the game."

It cuts to Kate, a former hockey player turned broadcaster, standing next to the ice, leaning over the bench. Alex's cheeks are pink, his curls slicked back, his gloved hands resting on top of his stick. Grace can feel his nerves.

"Is it safe to say these are your biggest fans?" Kate says, gesturing to the people in the stands.

"Yeah, they're awesome," he says.

"But we all know that it's your foster mother, Sarah. What an inspirational story that is," Kate says. She has a great smile. It's kind and inviting.

"I couldn't have done it without her," Alex says. Then hesitates, "But my biggest fan has never been to a game here."

Kate's smile falters. "Well, maybe they'll make it out here one day." The way she looks at Alex, it's like she's talking just to him.

"Maybe. Thanks, Kate." He gives her a polite nod and skates away.

Grace stands suddenly, overcome with emotion, but knows that she needs to keep it together.

"Grace?" Annie says. "Are you all right?"

"Yeah," she says, realizing that the machine has already kicked off. "These numbers are great, Annie."

Annie eases back. "Wonderful."

She slides the cuff from Annie's arm. "I'll check back in later, but if you need me, just page me, okay?"

She can't look at Daniel for fear of her emotions betraying her. She wants to thank him and hug him and then thank him again. But she takes the blood pressure machine and rolls it out of the room without so much as glancing at him.

She goes into the staff bathroom, locks the door, and fights to hold back tears. She's brimming with relief and happiness and guilt. *My biggest fan has never been to a game here.* He wasn't even mad when he said it, just stated it as a matter of fact. Alex was being lovely, and she was being a coward and—

There's a knock at the door. The bathroom is large, and she's standing in the center of it, her arms crossed in front of her chest.

"Busy," Grace calls and realizes that her cheeks are wet.

There's a knock again. *For fuck's sake.* She drags the back of her hand across her cheeks.

"It's me." She hears his deep voice through the door.

She hesitates and then opens the door, sticking her head out a bit to check the hallway. It's empty. "Daniel—" she starts, but he pushes in. "Wait. What are you—"

He locks the door behind him and then turns to face her, something like worry in his eyes. "Are you all right?"

"Yes, of course," she says, but the words come out shaky. Then, "I appreciate everything you've done. Thank you."

"Do you want me to tell you what happened?"

"You mean with Alex and the woman? No."

"But don't you want to know that—"

"No, Daniel, please. I know that he didn't do it. That's good enough for me."

"I can spare you the details."

Her shoulders rise and fall as she takes a breath, wanting to guard herself against it, the way she's turned the channel every time there's a hockey game on, no matter who is playing, or avoided bars and restaurants with TVs just in case he comes on the screen. But Daniel's face is open, with understanding and compassion, and she knows then that he'll be gentle with her. "Okay, but just the barest facts."

"The woman's story was flimsy. She came from a religious family and was pressured by her mom to say she'd been assaulted when in fact she came on to him. It wasn't a difficult case. Just a lot of paperwork and the PR stuff to deal with."

Grace lowers her head. "It makes me sick, thinking of Alex having to go through that."

"Yeah, he was a wreck."

Her head snaps up. "You said he was stressed."

"What?" Daniel says.

"When you called me with the update early on, you said he was stressed."

"Yeah, it was a bit more than that."

"Why didn't you tell me?"

"Because you never wanted to talk about it. It made *you* stressed."

"It's hard for me to think about him at all." A tear falls down her cheek, and he cups the side of her face with his hand.

"Please don't," she says. "I'm fine."

"I know." He swipes his thumb across her cheek as another tear falls. It's warm and comforting on her face.

She leans forward slowly, and he wraps his arms around her, holding her close. She stays like that for a long moment. Then she squeezes her eyes shut, collecting herself. "Totally fine," she says more firmly this time and straightens. "Daniel, if we're seen together, just the two of us, I could get into a lot of trouble."

"With Janine, you mean?"

Grace's eyes widen. "Did Riley say something. She shouldn't have—"

"I'm glad she did. I had the receptionist, Donna, get me a copy of the code of conduct for this home, and I checked the laws in this province. Janine's off base. There's nothing that says we can't have a relationship." He tilts his head toward her. "That is, if we wanted to. What she said to you was inappropriate. If she didn't like the fact that you were a nepotism hire, she should've fired you ages ago, but she didn't. Why? Because you're brilliant at your job."

"She could still fire me now. Make me redundant. I enjoy working here, the people. I can't . . ."

He is staring at her calmly, intensely, in a way that makes her nervous.

"What did you do?"

"She won't be talking to you again. Or at least not about that."

"Daniel." Her breath shallows. "She could make my life very difficult."

"Trust me," he says evenly, holding her gaze. "She won't."

"But Janine can sometimes say something and then . . ."

There's something about Daniel, his decisiveness, his assuredness, that quiets her.

"I had a little chat with her," he says. "I know things about this place. Like how they claim to have nonbiased waiting lists but how they actually accept large donations to let certain people go to the top. How residents are admitted here who shouldn't be. This home isn't authorized or given the resources to deal with dementia patients. It causes unneeded stress on the staff. And if these things were made known, it could make *her* life very difficult."

Why was he being so nice to her? Why did he do these things for her? She could look after herself, as she always did. Caught up in the frustration of it all, she says, "Goddamnit, Daniel."

"What?" he says, startled by her response. "She treated you unfairly, and people like her shouldn't be allowed to get away with that. She's a bully."

"Why are you so . . ." She paces left and then right, searching for the words. "When I'm with you, my emotions just burst out of me. And with everyone else, I can control them. And contain myself."

"You shouldn't have to control and contain yourself. Not around me, at least."

"And now I'm indebted to you. Once again."

"What are you talking about, Grace?" He sounds so befuddled, so perplexed by what she's just said. He holds his hands up as if trying to clarify something that he believes to be quite straightforward. "I do these things because I *want* to. Just like the night when you helped me out with Doug. That's it. Simple as that."

"I—well, thank you," she says, but he cocks his head, skeptical. "I mean it. You're . . . you're a good friend." Then she glances down at her feet before asking, "Will you come find me before you take Annie to dinner? To say goodbye?"

"Absolutely."

At 4:30 p.m. Riley comes out of Carl's room, her face panicked and pale. She's holding Carl's boots and jacket.

"I'll help you find him," Grace says.

This is the first time that he's gone missing that they can't call the police for their assistance.

"I'm gonna let Judy know," Riley says, running down the hall.

Grace darts to the staff lunchroom while dialing the station number Will had left her. Holding her phone awkwardly between her ear and shoulder, she grabs their coats and sits, dragging her boots toward her.

"Will speaking," he says.

"Hey, Will, it's Grace. Carl's missing—"

"I'm sorry, Grace." His words come out pained. "My boss said—"

"I totally understand," Grace says, shoving her foot into her boot. "I'm not calling for that. Does he have any go-to spots where you usually found him?"

"Try the river or the convenience store on the northeast corner. But I'd start with the river."

"Okay."

"If those spots don't work, call me, okay? Actually, would you mind letting me know either way?"

"Of course. Thanks, Will." She grabs her hat and pockets her phone.

She and Riley almost collide in the hallway.

"The river." Grace passes Riley her coat. "That's where we'll go first," Grace says as they rapidly descend the stairs. Grace pushes through the lobby door to the outside and mutters, "Shit." The sun is setting, the light through the thick clouds dimming. She's about to ask Riley if they should split up, but Riley is a runner and she's too far ahead already, so Grace does her best not to lose sight of her. Grace gets to the ridge of the icy embankment and holds on to the skeletal trees as she makes her way down. It's started to snow, and the flakes are swirling around her.

"Riley?" she yells.

"Over here," Riley calls out to her. "I've got him."

Grace runs toward the voice, holding the stitch in her side. Thank goodness Riley had thought to bring Carl's coat and boots. His sinewy hands and lined face are pink. He's staring at the river, oblivious to the cold. Grace helps Riley take Carl's slippers off and carefully maneuvers his boots on.

"Fucking hell," Riley says, throwing her head to the side to get her hair out of her face. She holds up Carl's sensor bracelets. The batteries have died. "His family was supposed to order new ones, but they're all squabbling about how they should pay for them."

By the time they get back, it's after five and the Hurleys have gone to dinner. Grace's shift is over.

"I'm going to go call his son, Tom," Riley says.

"Is there anything I can do?" Grace asks.

"No. Thank you, though." Riley plops down in the chair and steels herself before dialing.

Grace opens the door to Annie's room and glances around, thinking there might be a note or something left behind, but there's nothing. She can't help but be disappointed.

Grace is draining spaghetti that evening when there's a knock at the door, giving her a start. She doesn't get visitors, though she has often wondered what it would be like to have a dinner party, host a book club, or invite some friends in just to chill for the night. All fleeting thoughts that she doesn't allow herself to linger on for too long. She glances down at her outfit. Lululemon pants and a purple T-shirt. Her hair is pulled back in a ponytail. Presentable.

She opens the door, bracing herself as she always does after too much time spent alone. "Daniel," she says, unable to conceal her surprise and happiness at the sight of him standing on her porch.

"Grace," he says with a tilt of his head. Ever stylish, he is wearing slacks, a black pea coat, and a light-blue scarf. He's holding a bouquet of flowers. Light pinks and whites.

"Those are beautiful."

"Riley told me where you live—I hope you don't mind. I did say I would find you to say goodbye."

"Well, this is above and beyond." She takes the flowers and rests them in the nook of her arm. Then she notices the suitcase behind him.

"So I was in my hotel room getting ready to head out for drinks with my siblings, thinking about how I'm flying out tomorrow and then it hit me. That's not where I wanted to be."

It takes her a moment to parse what he's saying, as it catches her off guard. "You wanted to be with me?"

"If you'll have me."

"Did you tell Beth and Eric?"

"The moment they saw my suitcase, they knew."

She steps back to let him in. While he takes his shoes off and hangs his coat, she adds the sauce and meatballs to the pasta.

"Smells good," he says.

"I made extra for my lunch tomorrow, so you're in luck if you want to try some. I know you ate already."

"Can I help you with anything?" He rolls the sleeves of his dress shirt back.

"No, I'm just about done."

She puts the flowers in a vase, and they sit side by side at the island. Daniel sprinkles some Parmesan on top of his small bowl of pasta and takes a bite out of a meatball.

"They're hot," Grace warns.

"They're delicious," he says, blowing steam from his mouth. "You make these?"

"Yeah. Tony's son gave me the family recipe. Supersecret and super simple once you get the hang of it."

"Tony, the one Nan likes to sit with at dinner?"

"The very one."

They eat for a bit in silence. Grace is pleasantly surprised by how comfortable she is and how nice it is to sit next to someone and share a quiet meal together. The casual domesticity of it.

When they finish she takes his bowl and puts it in the dishwasher. He places the pots in the sink, squeezes some soap over them, and turns on the tap. Daniel Hurley is in her kitchen, scrubbing pots, the sleeves of his dress shirt rolled up his forearms, and she has never been more attracted to him. As she dries the pots and puts them away, Daniel braces himself with his hands behind him, leaning back into the counter, watching her. He moves so that she can hang the tea towel.

"You want to watch a movie or something?" he asks.

"Sure," she says. But she doesn't want to watch a movie with him. Not tonight. She slips a finger through a gap in his button-down shirt and tugs on it.

He looks down at her. "That's not why I came over."

She pulls her finger out instantly and is nothing short of mortified. "Oh."

"No, I just mean," he says as he pushes himself off from the counter, "I hope you don't think that's why I'm here."

"No. I—forget it." She starts to turn, but he places his hands on her waist, holding her still.

"Hey," he says. "I do want to. It's just . . ."

"Just what?"

He's staring at her. Or, more specifically, her lips.

"Just what, Daniel?"

His eyes drop to the floor, and she realizes that he's not answering her because whatever she's prodding him to say will put a stop to this. And that terrifies her. So instead she kisses him, and it catches him off guard. There's a slight hitch to his breath as he adjusts to it. To her.

She reaches up to cup his jaw in her hand. To steady him. And he pushes her back into the fridge as if wanting something solid to press against and anchor himself to. His lips begin to angle as he deepens the kiss, and she is swallowed up in the intensity of it. Of him, touching her. Holding her firmly against the fridge door. He slides his hand under her T-shirt and up her stomach. Only then does he come up for air. "This okay?" he asks.

She nods, and he lifts her shirt over her head. Tossing it on the counter behind him, he kisses her collarbone and unclips her bra, sliding it from her shoulders. It's so effortless that she's about to comment on the ease with which he's done it but then his fingers are lightly circling her nipple. She inhales as warmth gathers between her legs and she lifts her chin, exposing the long line of her neck, which he starts kissing.

"Daniel."

"Yeah?" His teeth are on her, grazing her. Nibbling.

She pushes her palm against his chest.

"Do you want to stop?" He lowers his hands, drawing back to look at her. His brow creases as his eyes study her.

"No. I don't want a hickey." She doesn't want to have to explain this at work, and if they see it, they'll ask. They'll definitely ask because it's her.

"I wasn't going to give you one, but I'm glad you told me."

She blushes and her shoulders tense. She feels suddenly exposed standing in front of him without her shirt on while he's fully clothed.

He glances down. "I'm sorry, Grace. I'm moving too fast here."

"No, I like it. I do," she says. "I'm just a bit nervous." Daniel takes a step back. "But I'm also excited." She takes him by the arms. "I want this."

"You'll let me know if you want me to do something differently or if you don't like something?" he says.

She nods and starts unbuttoning his shirt. "Can I touch you this time? Now that I've had my *experience*?"

With a soft chuckle, he shakes his head. "I'll grab a condom."

They make their way to her room, to the bed she makes every morning. She shimmies her yoga pants off while Daniel undoes his leather belt. She lies back on the duvet and takes a deep breath, tingling with anticipation as she hears the clink of the metal, the crinkle of the condom package. The mattress dips as he climbs up beside her.

His hand travels up her stomach, and he cups her breast. "You're so soft," he murmurs. He settles in over her so that she's flat on her back beneath him. He watches her closely as he hooks his fingers around her underwear and pulls them down.

Although he's barely touched her, her breath has quickened and her heart is racing. She's about to ask him what he's going to do when he clutches her thigh and begins to open her. He slips a finger inside her and she squeezes his arm, squirming and tensing.

"Relax," he whispers in her ear. "Trust me."

Trust him? She had trouble trusting anyone.

But the gentle tone with which he says it reminds her—he is unlike anyone she has ever known.

He presses his lips to her shoulder, and her body loosens at the slight hook of his finger. The pain eases into pleasure as he slides another finger in, and he groans against her ear as she clenches around them.

He kisses her breast, her rib cage, her stomach, making his way down her body. She's embarrassed by how her breath catches, by how her back arcs, by how her body craves his touch. It feels so good, what he's doing to her, holding her down and starting to work her with his tongue, pushing her wider.

"Oh *fuck*," she lets out and raises her hips, gripping the duvet. "Don't stop."

He doesn't stop. He keeps winding her up until her head hits the pillow and her orgasm takes her.

Before she can fully regain herself or her pulse has time to slow, he starts to touch her again. With his finger circling that spot. Oh God.

"Wait . . . wait," she gasps.

She wants to take a second. To have his muscled and powerful body over her, caging her in. To be with him, present in this moment before she loses control again. "Daniel," she says, but her voice is barely a whisper, and he doesn't hear her. He's so intent on what he's doing, kissing her inner thigh as her stomach hollows. "Daniel," she says, this time louder and with a slight pleading in her voice. She's started to tremble.

"Hmm?" he says, raising his head to look at her.

"I want to take a moment, if that's all right," she says.

He stops touching her, and she is suddenly empty. "Of course."

"No, not . . ." She reaches for his shoulders. "Can you come up here for a sec?"

As he hovers over her, his cheeks are flushed, and she can feel him hard against her. His eyes search hers. "Like this?"

"Yeah," she says. Then, "I find you very attractive."

"I think you're beautiful." He says it like a confession. Like a secret he's been keeping to himself.

She runs her hand down his muscled arm, and her fingertips graze the taut ridges of his stomach. She loves the way his eyes close, his sharp intake of breath.

"Grace," he whispers. "I've wanted this for so long."

"You said that the first time. At the hotel."

"No. I said I wanted *you*. But this . . ." He stares down at her. "This is what I've wanted."

She swallows. "You have?"

"You have no idea."

His thumb grazes her nipple, and he comes into her slowly, letting her get used to his size.

She winces at the sear of pain, and he immediately pauses. He brushes a strand of hair from her face and kisses her like this is all he has ever thought about. Like there is nothing he would rather do. Then he slides in farther and starts to send a ripple over her again and again, slowly, listening for her breath to catch. Finding a rhythm. Spasms of pleasure pass in waves over her body, and her head lolls back against the pillow. She lifts her chin to the ceiling and wraps her legs around his waist. As she runs her fingers through his dark hair, he pumps harder. She lets out a low guttural moan. A noise she has never made before.

His breath quickens, and he's pushing her into the mattress. "Is this all right?" he asks.

At the same time, "Oh God, Daniel," escapes from her lips. She whimpers and clutches his back.

He lets out a strained groan.

His slick chest presses against her as he loses control of his limbs, shivering against her. Their breathing slows and he kisses her, gently bringing her back to earth. Then he lifts himself off her.

Once the fog of her orgasm clears, she rolls onto her side to face him. "Obviously, I'm not talking from experience, but the way you do those things with your fingers, your tongue—"

"Don't look at me like that, or I'll do it again." He leans in and their lips catch lightly.

She smiles and runs her fingers in a light pattern over his chest. "Can I ask you something?" She hesitates. "How many women have you been with?"

"I don't know. Maybe a dozen."

A dozen. She draws back from him. "So I'm just adding to a number."

"No, Grace." His gaze is intense. "You're not just adding to a number."

"It's okay. It's not like we're together." She pulls the sheet up to cover her breasts.

"But maybe we could be together."

"Right," she says, mostly to herself. They lived a plane ride away from each other. The only reason she had allowed herself to be so free with him tonight was *because* he was getting back on a plane. Leaving. Back to his life without her, except for the odd phone call. "That's not really a possibility for me."

"Why not?" he says, propping himself up.

"Because I'm . . . me."

"Meaning?"

"Meaning that you should go home and enjoy the company of whomever you want."

"I don't want to enjoy anyone else's company."

She sits up and edges away from him. "But you can," she says aggressively, hoping that he'll be aggressive back. Distancing her with his words.

Instead, his finger trails gently down her back. "I won't be." His voice is soft, and much to her dismay, the tension across her shoulders eases.

She turns and catches his wrist, pinning it to the bed. Then she slips his condom off and goes to use the bathroom.

When she comes out, she changes into a white silk pajama set. The room is dim except for the streetlights cutting through the blinds and the glow of Daniel's phone.

"Checking in for my flight," he says, setting the phone on the nightstand. He gets up, and as he walks by her, he takes in her spaghetti stringed tank top.

As the bathroom door clicks shut behind him, she sits on the edge of the bed, and a sensation tears through her. The realization that she both wants him to stay and wants him to go. With equal intensity. It scares her, this attachment she's developing toward him. Seeing him throughout the day while she worked filled her with bursts of happiness. A snippet of conversation or an interaction with him would leave her smiling, fighting to stifle it when she saw someone else in the hall. Unless that someone was Riley. She's lost in her thoughts when the bathroom door opens, and it gives her a start.

She looks up at him. "If we plan on doing something like this again, I could go on the pill," she says. "If it's easier for you."

"I don't mind using a condom. I'm used to it."

"From all the women you've been with?"

"Hey, I was being honest with you."

"You're right. I'm sorry." She lowers her gaze, embarrassed. Then, "I wish you didn't have to go." The words slip from her mouth, and she's shocked to have uttered them. She goes very still.

He sits down next to her and pulls the string of her tank top to the side, running a finger softly over her collarbone.

"Oh Daniel, don't," she says. She knows that it'll only make it harder. Three and a half months until he touches her again. And yet she doesn't deserve to be touched so tenderly.

He tilts his head toward her, rubbing his nose against her cheek.

"Please," she breathes. "It's too much."

"What is?" He runs his hand down her arm.

"What you're doing right now. These feelings I have for you. I can't . . ."

"Can't what?"

"Be this happy," she says, punctuating each word. She turns away from him.

"Yes, you can, Grace." He rests his chin on her shoulder. "You can."

She gets into bed. He follows her, putting his hand on her stomach and spreading his fingers. It's a nice feeling, the weight of it on her. He starts to curl in toward her, but she stiffens. "I'm not—I don't think I'm much of a cuddler."

"Oh." He straightens out.

She glances at him, but his expression is unreadable in the darkness as he puts space between them. "Sorry," she says, flustered.

"Hey." He kisses the soft tendrils of hair at her temple. "It's no problem at all."

The way he says it, the gentleness of his tone, makes her almost believe him. That it *is* no problem. Her lack of affection. The first two times she had shared a bed with him, she felt awkward. Always safe. But awkward. And now, with his body next to hers, there's a calm that comes over her. His presence is soothing, and the fact that he had sought her out, had chosen to spend his last night here with her, makes her happy. Content in a way that fills her up. That makes her feel whole. Almost normal. "I'm glad you came over," she says softly. "Good night."

"Night, Grace," he says, and his hand slips from her as she rolls away.

Grace's alarm goes off, waking her from a deep sleep. She stretches slowly, out of her slumber, elongating her spine and legs. She can feel in her body that she's slept well. She slides her hand across the sheets toward him, but it keeps going and she raises her head. Light seeps through the crack in the bathroom door.

Lifting her robe from the hook, she ties the sash around her waist and heads downstairs. In the kitchen she spoons the coffee into the filter as Daniel comes down, dressed and carrying his suitcase.

"You want coffee? Eggs?" she asks.

"I would, but I'll have to grab something at the airport. I just ordered an Uber."

"I had the strangest feeling when I woke up this morning," she says.

"What was that?"

"I wanted to run my hand over your chest and hold you close."

He gives her a small smile. "I would've liked that."

She turns to get a mug, and he wraps his arms around her, filling her with such comfort and sadness at the same time. She reaches up, gripping his forearm, and he squeezes her tight. They stay like that for a long moment, watching the car pull into the driveway. "I'll see you at Easter," he says but neither of them moves.

There's the quick tap of the horn. Daniel nuzzles his face against the side of her head and then goes to put on his coat and shoes. Grace doesn't turn around until she hears the front door shut.

She stares past the pink and white flowers and picks up her phone. *You can do this.*

It's on the fifth ring that she realizes the time change and mutters, "Shit," about to end the call, when a croaky voice says, "Hello."

His voice is deeper than on TV, and she freezes for a moment, holding her breath. She could just let it go. In a sleepy daze, he might not even remember the call he got in the early hours of the morning, but instead she says, "Al."

There's a pause. A beat of silence. Then, "Grace." He is no longer sleepy but awake. Alert.

"I'm sorry for waking you. I wasn't thinking," she says.

"No, no, it's fine," he says, and she pictures him pushing himself up in his bed.

"I've wanted to call you for a while, but I've . . . I've been too nervous." She cringes at the ridiculousness of what she's just said, but it's the truth.

"You don't ever need to be nervous, not of me."

"No, not of you. Never of you," she says. "There were so many things going on with me that I needed to get ahold of. When I left you, I was unable to keep things together, and I didn't want to bring you down with me. But I'm better now." She thinks of Daniel's words. "I'm stronger." He doesn't say anything, but she knows he's listening, holding on to her words. She needs to say these things to him, to get it out there and explain a bit where she's coming from. "I was thinking, maybe I could come visit you next time you had a couple of home games over a weekend."

"I would love that," he says, his voice a wisp, and it sends a twinge of emotion through her chest. She presses her palm against it.

"Okay. Why don't you send me your schedule, and I'll shift some things around at work. We can make a long weekend of it," she says, trying not to let her voice break.

"I'll do that," he says.

There's a long pause.

"I'll see you soon. I love you," Grace barely gets out before hanging up.

Sixteen

There's a man with a sign waiting for Grace at the airport, standing right at the railing so that she can't miss him. She raises her hand in greeting, and he takes her bag from her in one swift movement like he's done it a thousand times before.

Exiting off the freeway, they drive along the edge of town and turn into a suburb. There are two pillars and a PRIVATE: RESIDENTS ONLY sign placed in a hedge of neatly trimmed bushes. The street is wide with a big oval green space down the length of it. The large homes are set back on deep lots. They are white and boxy, rambling bungalows, dark-brown tutors, red Georgians, all unique. He pulls into the driveway of a dark-gray house with three garage doors. It's one of the more modern-looking homes on the street. The freshly plowed driveway is illuminated by the outdoor lights.

Grace thanks him and steps down onto the light dusting of snow. She puts the code Alex gave her into the closest of the garage doors, and it lifts quietly. She makes her way around a deep-purple SUV Mercedes to the door, which has been left unlocked.

In the laundry room, she takes off her mitts and boots and wheels her bag in behind her. She moves slowly, wanting to take it in. This house, the space that Alex lives in.

It's an open-concept floor plan with neutral colors and hardwood floors. The kitchen has white marble countertops, an island with barstools around it, modern appliances, and a farmhouse sink. The kitchen flows from the dining area to the family room. There's a huge sectional, a fireplace that runs along the length of the far wall, and a massive TV above it. The tea towels are crisply folded, and the pillows and blankets are neatly arranged on the couch, like someone has just been through to clean.

Still in her jacket, with her purse slung over her shoulder, she perches on a stool at the island. She sees a note next to a beautiful white and blue vase.

Left this ticket in case you wanted to come to my game. Lots of food in the fridge. A

Grace slides the ticket toward her. She swallows and guilt presses on her as she dials. He picks up after the second ring. There are voices all around him.

"Grace?" he says.

"I'm here at your house." He doesn't say anything. He's waiting. "I really appreciate you leaving me this ticket, but I don't think I'll come to the game if that's all right."

There's a pause. "Yeah, sure. Whatever works for you," he says. "I'll see you at home after."

"Okay, sounds good." She hangs up and places her phone next to the ticket. She thinks back to her numb bum, the parents yelling, trying to block them out to concentrate, constantly writing out lists of expenses and rewriting them, hoping to cut costs, to find more money somewhere. Anywhere. To give her just a bit of breathing room. The stress of it all.

And then there was Alex. Upbeat and positive. Never complaining. Helping her troubleshoot wherever he could. Studying the bus schedules. Quizzing her on the parts of the human body. Gently nudging her awake when she'd fallen asleep, her body slouched against the window of a bus. The puck a blur on the end of his stick, the flick of his wrist as he tossed it into the net. It was a thing of beauty to watch. No matter where she was sitting. On a metal bench, on a rise of bleachers, in the seat of a community center arena. He would step out onto that ice, and as he glided across the surface, he'd look for her. Only lowering his head once he'd spotted her.

Her being there meant something to him. And she had loved watching him. She scoops up the ticket and then orders an Uber.

Her heart is racing as she steps out of the car. Most of the crowd has filtered into the arena, and Grace glances at the clock on the wall. She quickens her stride.

She funnels into the short line and holds her ticket out to the woman scanning them. She beeps Grace's ticket and then studies her machine. "First time here?"

"Yeah." Grace wonders what she's done wrong.

"You've come in the wrong entrance."

The giant ENTRANCE sign isn't the entrance?

The woman leans her mouth down to a mini walkie-talkie clipped to her breast pocket. "Gabrielle, would you mind coming down here a minute?"

"Is this not"—Grace moves so that the person behind her can get scanned through—"where I'm supposed to be?" They don't have any issues, and Grace notices that their ticket is a different color and shape from Grace's.

"Don't worry about it. We'll get you sorted."

Gabrielle comes toward them, and the scanner shows her the machine, then tilts her head at Grace. "She's new."

"Right this way, miss," Gabrielle says.

Grace follows Gabrielle past the security check area. They stop at the elevators, and Gabrielle leans down to swipe her lanyard against a black sensor. In the elevator, Grace is about to ask where they're going, but Gabrielle starts typing into her phone. It pings, and the doors slide open. Gabrielle leads her down a hallway to a large room overlooking the ice.

"Enjoy the game," she says.

"Thank you," Grace says.

There are about thirty people in the room, mostly women and their young children. Along the back wall is a table with chicken nuggets, hamburger sliders, and nachos. Grace pauses just inside the door. She breathes in the smell of the food, filling her stomach like a balloon, trying to get her heart rate down. She takes a step farther in, pauses, and then another, walking toward the floor-to-ceiling windows and the chairs lined up along the glass.

"There's daddy," a woman says to the small girl on her lap.

The players are finishing their pregame warm up.

"Excuse me," Grace says to the woman. "Is this seat taken or . . . ?"

"No, no. You can sit wherever. Most of us move around," she says and nods at her daughter. "Especially with these guys. First time here?"

"Yeah."

"Who are you—"

"Ladies and gentlemen," says the announcer, "please rise for the singing of our national anthem."

Ten players glide out onto the ice to stand in two lines, facing the flag. Grace knows Alex the moment she sees him, not by the name on his back or the dark curls sticking out from under his helmet but by the way he moves. The players take their helmets off and hold them under their arms. Right before the lights dim, Alex looks over his shoulder, scanning the people in the box.

God she's glad she came, just for this one moment alone. Thinking of him turning around and her not being there. She raises her hand just as the arena goes dark and the singer steps down into the circle of light. She can tell by the way his head turns slowly back around that he's seen her.

Once the game gets underway, the announcer says, "Is it just me, or is Saint flying around that ice tonight?"

"It's not just you, Ed. He's *electric*."

The horn sounds, signaling the end of the game, and the room of people stand, gathering their coats and purses. The two women nearest Grace are speaking to each other in an Eastern European language—Russian, by the sounds of it.

"Excuse me," Grace says, following them out into the hall. They go quiet and turn toward her, their gazes seeming to scrutinize her. "Do you know where I could meet up with one of the players?" Grace's heartbeat has quickened, but she's trying to ignore it.

"Who're you here to see?" one woman asks, adjusting the clip in her thick blonde hair.

"Alex Saint."

The woman makes a tsk noise. "You leave him alone." Then she turns to her friend and says, "He would have told Sergei or me if he had a friend coming to watch." The other woman nods and goes to speak with one of the staff members in the hallway. "How did you get in here? What is it that you want?" The woman's eyes are daggers. "Ah, never mind. I don't care."

"N-nothing," Grace stammers. "I thought I'd . . ." She trails off and crosses her arms in front of her chest to keep her body contained, to stop her hands from shaking.

The man comes up to them, and Grace is prepared to be escorted out. "Ludmilla, Alex has given her full access. She has as much right to be here as you do."

Ludmilla stares at Grace and then gasps and claps her hands together in front of her chest. "Grace. You must be Grace. I see why he did not tell me. A complicated history, no?"

Alex had talked about her? About their *history*? Ludmilla's face softens into a smile, and her features become warm so alarmingly quickly that it takes Grace a moment to adjust to this sudden change.

"I am Ludmilla, and this is Anna." She weaves her arm through Grace's. "Come, we will take you." As Grace walks with them, Ludmilla says, "My husband, Sergei, and I live near Alex. He comes to us for dinner; we go to him. My husband tells me he has never seen someone move the puck like Alex." She stops, throwing up a finger. "And we are Russian." They enter the elevator, and Ludmilla presses the button. "He did not tell me you were so beautiful."

Grace's breath shallows as the doors open to loud male voices, deep and boisterous, celebratory after their win. Grace falters and then stops, untangling her arm from Ludmilla's. "I'm sorry. I haven't seen him in a while," she says.

"I know," Ludmilla says. She pulls a strand of Grace's hair away from her face and tucks it behind her ear. "You will be great." She kisses Grace's cheek, and if Grace wasn't so nervous, she'd be startled by the gesture.

Ludmilla goes over to a man with a beak-like nose, cropped hair, and thick arms. He kisses her and then nods at Grace, asking Ludmilla who she is.

Grace is getting warmer, and she can no longer contain the shaking that is taking over her body. She tries to fill her balloon but can't. She has never been this nervous. Never in her life. She can't do this. She is going to vomit. She turns, striding down the hall, needing to get outside, into fresh air. She shouldn't have come here to meet him publicly. This was a mistake. A huge mistake. She presses down on the piercing pang that comes through her ribs as she searches for the exit, her heart pounding into her throat.

She pushes open a door and emerges into a parking garage with huge buses. Shit. She has no idea where she is. God, why did she have to panic so much? Why couldn't she just be calm for once in her life?

"Grace," a voice says behind her. Soft and deep.

She stops, and a tear rolls down her cheek. She brushes it away before she turns. She barely has a chance to see him before he wraps his arms so tightly around her that he squeezes the air right out of her. She can't tell if it's her heart thudding against her chest or his. When he lets her go, he drags the back of his hand across his cheeks.

"Hey," he says.

"Hi," she says weakly. Then, "Oh Al, I'm sorry. I'm so, so sorry."

He shakes his head. "No," he says. "I knew you'd come, when it was the right time. I'm just happy you're here."

"Where are we?" Grace gestures at the nearest bus.

"These are the team buses."

"A bit fancier than what we used to travel on."

He lets out a choked laugh. "A bit, yeah." He's wearing black pants and a fitted athletic jacket. He's filled out and tall, with the same unruly curls. "Let's get outta here."

They make their way back down the hallway, and a man breaks away from the group.

"Hello, I'm Sergei." The man with the beak-like nose holds his hand out to Grace. It's massive and encloses Grace's hand as she shakes it. "Are you two coming to dinner?"

"Um . . ." Grace glances at Alex.

"No, Sergei, they are not coming to dinner," Ludmilla says.

They drive for the first little bit in silence, a comfortable silence. Easy in the presence of the other, a presence they've each craved for years. Then at the exact same moment, they both start to talk.

"No, you go," Alex says.

"I was just going to say that it was really nice to see you play again. And your teammates, they seem quite fond of you," she says.

"Yeah, they're good guys." He signals into his neighborhood. "What about you? How're things?"

"The truth?"

He nods. "Hit me."

"They're pretty great right now. I really enjoy the nursing home where I work and the people there. There's this one woman, Riley, another nurse who started the same day as me, who is pretty awesome. You'd really like her."

"Yeah? Maybe I'll meet her sometime." He pulls into the driveway. "I want to thank you for putting me in touch with Daniel."

"I knew the moment I heard the news that it wasn't true. I wanted to help you in whatever way I could."

"Well, he really went above and beyond, flying out here to meet with me and all."

"He flew out here?" she says.

"Yeah. I was kind of struggling before he came, like mentally and stuff, and he told me how to go about doing things. Not just from a legal standpoint but from a perception one. Who to talk to, how to lay low, and he also listened to me. We talked about things I hadn't really thought about in a long time. It really helped me to get my head wrapped around everything." The car is off, but neither of them has moved.

"Did you tell him about our lives, about how we grew up?"

"Yeah. I told him about the shit you went through—"

"*We* went through."

"Yeah, but you shielded me from so much of it. It wasn't until later that Sarah told me some of the things going on in the background, and I really had to grill her for that. I wanted some answers, you know?"

"Sometimes I wonder if I held on too long. Like if I should've left sooner but was being selfish because I wanted to stay with you."

"Grace, I feel sick thinking about what you went through, but I'm so glad for the time we had together."

She glances at him. "We did have some pretty good times."

"The best times. Just being with you, knowing you were there, that I could always count on you. That meant everything to me."

"Sarah was good to you?"

"Yeah, yeah, she was great. But it wasn't the same. Not even close."

Grace unbuckles her seat belt, and he does the same. She gets out of the car and follows him through the garage and into the laundry room.

"You're saving, right?" she asks. "The money you make."

"Yeah," he says. "This house is paid for, and I have a monthly budget. The rest goes into a retirement plan I've got set up, safe blue-chip stocks that pay out dividends, RRSPs. All that boring stuff. Sarah set me up with a financial planner."

"Good," she says. "Now what are we thinking for dinner?"

"There are a couple of options," he says, opening the fridge.

They have both fallen asleep on different parts of the sectional. Grace stirs and sits up, the butter-soft blanket falling from her. Alex's large body is tangled in his. She tiptoes to her purse and takes her phone with her down the hall.

She dials Daniel's number and waits until his voice mail picks up. Oh, his voice—she wants to melt into it. "Hi, it's me, Grace," she says softly. "I'm here with Alex. I watched him play tonight." She pauses. "Thank you for everything you did." She waits for a moment and then hangs up.

They have the whole next day to themselves. Just the two of them. They drive to a bakery to get some Danishes and cinnamon buns, then to a specialty grocery store to pick up ingredients so that they can make fish tacos for dinner.

On the way home, Alex says, "May came to one of my games."

"What?" Grace turns so suddenly, her seat belt jolts her back. She should have told Alex how evil and manipulative she was. She should have warned him.

"Yeah. She told the conveyor that she was my foster mom for over ten years. Showed them photos of me growing up and stuff."

Grace is gripping the door handle. "Alex, May's—"

"After the game I saw her shuffling down the hall toward me, and there was a camera stuffed up my face. She reached up to hug me, and I just kept walking like I didn't even see her."

"Are you serious?"

"Yeah, I'm serious."

Grace smiles from the relief of it. "How'd she look?"

"Terrible. Absolutely terrible."

Grace laughs. She laughs and laughs.

After they finish their tacos, Alex sits back in his chair. "Do you want to go to brunch tomorrow with a friend of mine?"

He doesn't look at her when he asks. This person must mean a great deal to him. "I would love to."

The next morning, they walk into a restaurant with industrial lights hanging from the ceiling, charmingly old-fashioned wooden tables, and herringbone floors. They arrive just as the place opens, and people are already trickling in. There's a woman waiting just off to the side. She's in a soft pink dress, a blazer, and black boots. Riley would love her outfit. She would love this whole place.

"Lettie?" Graces says, realizing who it is.

"Hi, Grace."

"It's so good to see you." Grace pulls her into a hug.

Alex checks in with the hostess and rejoins them. "Grace, remember that vase you said you liked? Lettie made it for me."

"You did? It's beautiful." The hostess signals them, and they follow her to a table by the window. "I did a pottery class once with my friend Riley, and I accidently shot the little bowl I was making into the wall. We almost got kicked out."

Lettie laughs. "That was me in my first class, but I did get kicked out. I shattered the woman's crab dish beside me, and I had to find a new studio."

"Crab dish?" Grace says, sitting down.

"Yeah, it was really good. Had little claws on it and everything."

As they settle in with their menus, Alex leans back in his chair.

"I have a class on Tuesday, if you want to join me," Lettie says. "They allow walk-ins."

"I'm flying out that morning," she says and then glances at Alex. "But I do have lots of vacation. I haven't really taken any in a while, so maybe I could come again."

"Yeah." Alex sits up straight. "Yeah, that'd be awesome."

"There are some cool hikes we could go on," Lettie says excitedly but then falters. "I mean, or you two could go on."

"I'd love for the three of us to go, and we could see if Jackson is free," Grace says.

They drop Lettie off after brunch. On their way into Alex's neighborhood, they pass Sergei, who is heading out for a jog.

"Can you pull over?" Grace says.

She gets out of the car and goes up Ludmilla's driveway. The doorbell echoes through the house as she presses down on it. There's a long pause and Grace knocks, not loudly but not softly either. Ludmilla opens the door wearing thick-rimmed glasses and a bathrobe. "Excuse my attire," she says, tightening her sash.

"Don't worry about it," Grace says. "I was wondering if I could talk to you for a few minutes, but I can come back later if you want?"

"No, no, if you don't mind this," she says, waving at her outfit, "then come in. What can I get for you?"

"Nothing. I'm good, thanks." Grace leaves her shoes in the entrance and comes into the kitchen. "Um." She holds the knob of a tall chair at the island.

"Please sit." Ludmilla pulls out the chair, and they sit next to each other.

"Alex mentioned to me that you might be having some trouble getting pregnant."

Ludmilla stares at Grace and shakes her head. "No, no, I am fine." Then her eyes sharpen. "Did he tell you about a very *private* conversation that we had?"

"He did, yeah."

Her shoulders tense. "He should not have done that. I told him those things in confidence."

"He told me because he cares. And also because I might be able to help."

"What? What are you saying?"

"I have a friend, the most wonderful, warmest person in the world. Her father is a fertility specialist. He's renowned for what he does. He has an opening on Wednesday, a last-minute cancellation, and I booked you in for it."

"No, I can't. Sergei . . . I don't want him—"

"I know." Grace pulls a piece of paper from her pocket. "I booked you a seat on my plane with my credit card. Fly out with me on Tuesday and then back in on Thursday morning. You can stay at my house, use my car. They have away games, so he'll never know, not if you don't want him to."

Ludmilla holds her hand over her mouth and then lowers it. "You did this for me?" She taps the piece of paper with the flight information.

"Yeah," Grace says. "Worth giving it a shot, don't you think?"

"You did this for me," Ludmilla says again, slower this time, more intense. Then, "I can't accept; it's too much."

"But it's all done. I can't get a refund, and the appointment is booked."

"Why would you do that? You don't even know me."

"You're right, I don't really. But Alex does, and I know that you had a childhood similar to mine. Well, similar and different, but equally fucked," Grace says. "If you're not comfortable with this, that's fine. I won't push it."

"Okay, okay," Ludmilla says, getting up. She walks around the island once and then again. "What time would we leave?"

Grace grins. "Just after ten. Alex's driver will take us to the airport."

Ludmilla squeezes Grace's hand. "Okay. Now we must get ready."

"Ready? For what?"

"The friends and family skate." She sees Grace's confusion. "Alex didn't tell you? I can see why," she says kindly but intensely.

"Because I don't skate?"

"None of us skate. Except Diana—and Anna. They're actually

quite good." Ludmilla picks up her phone, a totally different woman from the one who answered the door. "He doesn't want to push you. It's okay. I know when to push."

The next thing Grace knows, she and Alex are standing in a sports store staring at a rack of female skates. Or, to be fair, Grace is staring. Alex has gone to speak with a sale's associate. Now that she's thinking of it, it would make more sense for her to rent a pair. She opens the search browser on her phone to google nearby rental places. She's holding her phone above her head, trying to load Google Maps, when a man asks her to sit down and slides a pair of skates that have a strong resemblance to Rollerblades onto her feet. His fingers move quickly, lacing her up, and then he asks her to stand.

"How do they feel?" Alex asks.

She wiggles one foot and then the other, surprised by how comfortable they are. "Good."

"Great. We'll take them." Alex goes with the man to ring them up as Grace puts her boots back on. That's when her eyes lock on the display skates in front of her. The ones she's just picked are the most expensive. By a lot.

"Al." She follows him out of the store, and the car beeps twice as he unlocks it. "I'm not sure those are the right ones for me."

"No?" He glances at the box under his arm.

"I didn't realize how much they were. What if I can't even skate? I've never done it before. Ever."

"I know, Grace. I know."

"I just wouldn't want it to be a waste of money."

"Look, I don't care if you wear them once for five seconds or a dozen times. I want you to have them." His face is so open and sincere that she swallows her apprehension and gets into the car.

When they get to the rink, Grace sits between Anna and Ludmilla to do up her skates. Alex, Pavel, and Sergei have gone to the locker room to grab theirs.

Anna glides out onto the rink in such a fluid, effortless movement that Grace is inspired. She makes it look so easy, the sound of her blades slicing through the fresh, untouched surface.

Grace steps down onto the ice, holding the ledge, then pushes off. Now she's three feet from being able to reach anything. "Oh God." She shuffles back toward the board but catches an edge and starts to fall. A hand grabs hold of her forearm, steadying her, keeping her upright.

"I've got you," Alex says.

Where did he come from?

He turns so that he's in front of her, skating backward, taking each of her hands in his. "Do you what I do. Left." He pushes out. "Right." He pushes out again, pulling her along with him.

"I'm not—" she's squeezing his hands so hard that she's probably hurting him, and she's hunched right over, her whole body tense.

"I've got you, Grace. I've got you." She looks up at him, and he's watching her so calmly. Relaxed and unhurried. Of course he does.

She nods and straightens, loosening her vise grip. She can do this. Left foot, right foot. Left foot, right foot.

"Push out more. Use those legs. Match mine."

"You've done this before."

"In the youth programs, some of the kids haven't skated much or at all."

"I find it helps," Ludmilla says, skate-walking beside them in choppy movements, "if you let go of the fear of death."

That makes Grace smile.

"Alex." A middle-aged man approaches them. "Would you mind? There are a few reporters here. They have a couple of questions about the friends and family skate—the experience. You know, the usual."

Now it's Alex's grip on Grace's hands that tightens.

"You go. I'm fine. Left foot. Right foot," she says, raising her eyes over Alex's shoulder to check how far from the boards she is.

"Could you ask Pav or Gus?"

The man is taken aback, seemingly not used to Alex saying no. "They've already spoken to them. They just want one more before they go." He lowers his voice and leans in a bit. "Another one of our top guys to round it out."

There's a sudden *shh!* and a massive body stops right beside them, sending a light dusting of ice over the man's pants.

"I'll go," Sergei says.

"You'll go?" the man says, unable to conceal his shock.

"Of course. It would be my pleasure." Sergei winks at Grace and skates away.

They stop for food on the way home, and as Alex starts putting it out, Grace goes into the guest room. She carefully lifts the world map from its mount on the wall and brings it out to the island.

"I was thinking." She reaches for the plates and utensils. "What if, over your summer break, we travel somewhere?" She turns to face him, and a smile pulls at her lips. "Anywhere. Is there somewhere you want to go?"

"So many places."

"Me too. I have twenty days of vacation saved up." She dishes out chicken fajitas, guacamole, and salsa onto her plate. "We could invite people to join us for parts of it too."

"Like Riley?" he asks.

"Or Lettie?"

"Or maybe it could just be us—for this trip."

"That would be nice too."

Grace hasn't told him about Daniel yet. Not that there's much to tell, but she's not sure what she would say. She was just about to say his name, then caught herself. She loves being around Daniel but can't really picture traveling with him. Riley and Lettie were so easygoing while Daniel lived to work. *Even when the rest of the world isn't.* When he was with her, he rarely glanced at his phone, but every time she came into Annie's room, he'd be reading something on his laptop or typing into his phone.

There's no way he'd break away from it all to go on a trip with them, and even if he did, he wouldn't settle into it. He stayed at hotels like the Forester. Grace wants to find places like the ones she's seen in Riley's photos. Boutique budget hotels and bed-and-breakfast houses with character. Comfortable and homey. Not luxury, high-end amenities at your fingertips. Manicured nails with voices that go up an octave if you look like you don't belong.

"Okay," Alex says, sitting down next to her. "Where are we thinking?" He pulls the map toward him.

Grace and Alex wake up early and have their coffee while Grace makes a spinach and feta frittata.

"You're a natural in the kitchen," Alex says.

"That is the highest compliment anyone has ever given me," she says. "I'm going to bask in it for the rest of the day." She is light. Happier than she's been in a long time. In . . . ever.

"I've always thought that," he says. "Even back when you'd make us mac and cheese with hot dogs."

When they say goodbye this time, it's not goodbye but *see you soon*, their upcoming adventures on their minds.

"Text me when you get home?"

"I will."

"Text me, just whenever?"

"I will. Absolutely." She smiles and hugs him.

Ludmilla is standing on her porch, ready right at ten. She's wearing large sunglasses with jewels on the sides and takes them off only once they get to the airport. Her eyes are quite red, and her body movements are deliberate, slow. She did not sleep well.

As they are boarding the plane, the man sitting next to Grace notices them talking and offers Ludmilla his seat. She rests her head on Grace's shoulder, dozes off, and then twitches awake ten minutes later.

She squeezes Grace's shoulder like she can mold it into something more comfortable. "So scrawny," she says. "I'm used to Sergei's." Giving up, she sits back in her chair and puts her sunglasses on again.

"I switched my shift around tomorrow so that I'm going in at seven. I can meet you at the hospital just after four if you want," Grace says.

"No, no, you don't need to," Ludmilla says. "But if you wanted to, that would be fine."

Grace smiles. "Okay, I'll come straight from work."

"How will you get there if I have your car?"

"I'll take the bus."

Grace opens the front door to her house, and Ludmilla follows her in. She places her huge purse on the kitchen table and lowers her sunglasses, scrutinizing the plain kitchen and bare walls of the living room.

"Oh Grace," she says, shaking her head. "This is not a home. There is no warmth, no life here."

Grace is affronted, about to defend herself or make something up. Some excuse for why her house is like this. Instead, she lowers her head. "I've never really felt at home anywhere."

"I will help." She starts digging into her purse and pulls out her laptop. "We must do something about this."

"I thought you wanted to nap."

"No, there is no time to nap." She waves her hand around the house. "We will start with the IKEA catalog. But first, what colors, what patterns bring you joy? Hmm? Grace, what brings you joy?"

"Um." Grace thinks of all the homes she's been in recently and what she likes about them. What brings her joy. But all she can picture is people. Alex and Riley and Daniel. Ludmilla is adamant, though, so four hours later, with empty containers of Lebanese food scattered across the counter, Grace has ordered an assortment of cushions, blankets, rugs, tea and bath towels, artwork, and paint swatches.

"Okay," Ludmilla says, standing. "We will go for a walk now."

"Don't you want to rest?"

"I rest better once I get my blood moving."

"So do I." Grace gets her jacket from the hook.

Later that night, after Ludmilla goes to bed, Grace opens her laptop and cancels all the orders.

She holds her phone in her palm. Daniel hasn't called her back or messaged her since her voice mail, and it's been five whole days.

SEVENTEEN

Oakwood is being decorated for the upcoming Easter weekend. Grace wheels Annie toward the dining room slowly, knowing that she likes to take it all in.

"Is that Ramon's lasagna?" Annie asks.

The smell of his signature tomato sauce wafts over them as they approach the dining room. Annie herself enjoys it fine, but it's Tony's favorite dish from the many excellent meals Ramon makes, and so she's excited. Grace parks Annie at her table just as Carmen comes into the doorway of the dining room. She waves her hand at Grace, signaling at her hastily. Annie's frail hand catches Grace's arm. The clipped wave and the alarmed look on Carmen's face can only mean one thing. Someone has died.

Grace leans over Annie. "I'll be right back," she says as the kitchen help places Annie's plate in front of her. When the woman asks what Annie wants to drink, she waves her off.

Grace goes to meet Carmen in the hallway. "Who?"

"Carl."

"Is he here?" Grace asks.

"Yeah, where else would he be?"

A relief. On so many levels.

"He has eight children, Grace. Eight! And no point of contact, and Riley's shift hasn't started yet and I don't know who to call."

This is Carmen's first death. "It's Sue and Tom she usually talks to."

"I just want to make sure I do everything right," Carmen says.

"Ladies." Judy's short legs pump down the hallway. "Have you called the family physician?"

"No," Carmen says. "But he's dead."

"We still have to call. And Grace—"

"I'll let the family know," Grace says.

"In this case, because there's no point of contact, we have to tell each child."

"Okay," Grace says. "Just give me a minute." She whips into Tony's room. His bar is down and he's ready to go.

"Annie is waiting, Grace."

"I know. I'm sorry," she says, helping him into the chair.

"It's okay. I just don't like to keep her," he says.

She wheels him briskly down the hall and into the dining room. Upon seeing them, Annie clutches her heart. She hasn't touched her food.

"Who?" Annie asks as they draw nearer.

"Carl," Grace says.

"Carl's dead?" Tony asks.

Grace nods.

"How tragic," Annie says, perking up in her seat. She signals to the kitchen staff. "I'll take my juice now, thank you."

The woman puts a plate of lasagna and a Caesar salad in front of Tony. "Ah." He breathes it in. "Ramon's done it again."

"It looks lovely tonight, doesn't it?" Annie says to Tony. "Now tell me, when is Tony Junior arriving for Easter?"

Grace is making the rounds of the fourth floor, taking everyone's orders for Easter dinner. "Annie, would you like the ham or the turkey?" Grace asks, holding her clipboard.

"I'll have a bit of both," Annie says, glancing up from her morning crossword. She has the excitement in her voice that comes with the impending arrival of her grandchildren. Grace has mixed feelings. Of suspense and dread. Daniel had gotten back to her a week later with a text: No problem.

No problem? Her stomach dropped when she saw that. Over the past few weeks, she'd come into Annie's room and hear his voice on the other end of the phone, but he never asked to speak with Grace. Even after Annie would say hi to her. Was he being purposefully elusive? Or his usual busy self? Had she misinterpreted their last evening together? "Can you help me order a cake for Beth's birthday?"

Grace flips to a new page. "Strawberry shortcake?" She writes it down.

"Yes. We'll have that on Friday. And then on Saturday a milk chocolate cake with a Swiss flag on it."

Milk chocolate was Daniel's favorite flavor. "A Swiss flag?"

"To celebrate Daniel's new job in Switzerland."

"Daniel's . . . going to Switzerland?"

"Oh Grace, I'm not sure he wanted me to say anything. You won't tell him that I did, will you?" There's real concern in her eyes, and Grace knows in that moment that Daniel must've been quite adamant about her keeping it to herself.

"No, of course not. Did he tell you when he's leaving?"

Annie points to her calendar.

It was on her *calendar?* How did Grace miss that? But then she sees why. It says *D going to S* on the last Friday in April.

"I'm so glad you've gotten to know him better, Grace," Annie says.

That made one of them.

Grace puts her clipboard in the cart and goes into the stairwell to sit. She puts her elbows on her knees and her face in her hands.

Daniel. The man had been at four firms in the time she'd known Annie. Each in a different city. He was a nomad. Transient. Working his way up.

"You're such an idiot," she says softly. Thinking he had cared more for her than he did his job.

She squeezes her head to block out the thoughts, the nausea and ickiness coming into her throat. *You can't cry.* Not at work. She needs to get a grip. She still has the whole day to get through. She reaches up to the cool metal railing above her, willing herself to stand.

The door swings open, giving her a start. "Hey," Riley says. "So the meeting with Will's mom went super well last night. Loveliest woman —what's wrong?"

"Can I stay at your house this weekend?" Grace asks.

She doesn't want to see him. Not at the nursing home. Not at her house. She doesn't want the remotest possibility of running into him or him coming to find her.

Riley sits next to her. "Of course."

"I'm going to ask Carmen if she can take my shift on Friday."

Riley nudges her with her shoulder. "What's going on?"

"Nothing—I just found out from Annie that Daniel's starting a new job in Switzerland at the end of April."

"He didn't tell you?"

Grace shakes her head.

"That's strange. He seemed like the type of guy who would've told you or said *something*."

"I think he might've been about to," Grace says. "But I didn't want to hear it."

After a moment Riley says, "I've got Friday off for Carl's funeral in the morning. Would you mind going with me? I hate funerals."

"Yeah, absolutely."

Riley pulls into Grace's driveway. She's waiting on her porch with a navy duffel bag and her work bag for Monday morning. They're both wearing black dresses and have their hair pulled back.

The family is in clusters—factions, Grace realizes, their presence large in the church foyer.

Riley and Grace make their way to each of the eight children, offering their condolences. There are a few they've never met before, and one of the sons introduces them. More to show that *he* knows who his father's nurse is, it seems. Middle-aged men and women. One of them is crying, being consoled by her redheaded daughter. Grace does not recognize either of them.

In the sanctuary, musk and incense hover in the air. There are massive bouquets at the front of the church and a large photo of Carl in his youth on a stand. The pews are full of mourners, and Riley and Grace squeeze into one at the back.

Riley can't stop fidgeting. For once, Grace is the calm one, and she puts her hand on Riley's to still it.

"It's weird, isn't it?" Riley says quietly, leaning into Grace. "All these people who never visited him in life."

Everyone stands as the family walks down the center aisle with the priest as the coffin is wheeled in.

From behind the pulpit, Tom starts his eulogy. "My father was a great man."

Grace looks around at the people dabbing tissues to their faces. Riley stares at her feet.

When they exit the church, Grace glances at her phone to check the time. She has three missed calls from Daniel and a voice mail. She holds her phone in her hand for a moment and then slips it back into her purse.

"You'll be joining us for refreshments?" Tom says, coming over to them.

"We'd love to, but we have Easter plans," Riley says.

"Well, that's a shame," Tom says. "A real shame you won't be coming."

As he walks away, Riley just stands there, a smile pulling at her lips. She whips around so that no one else sees.

"What?" Grace says.

"The relief." She's beaming now as they make their way to her car. "Never having to deal with those assholes again. Hallelujah," she says to the sky.

Riley had asked Grace if she wanted to join her family for Easter dinner, but Grace politely declined. She's got a movie lined up for the evening and a frozen pizza she can pop in the oven.

Her phone lights up, and she leans forward on the couch to pick it up. "Hello." It's silent. "Ludmilla?"

"Grace."

"Yeah?" Grace hasn't spoken to her since her visit.

"Grace." She draws out Grace's name like she's in awe. "I'm at the hospital. Well, in the car now."

"Is everything all right?"

"I'm pregnant."

"What?"

"They just told me, but Sergei's at an event and he's not answering his phone, and I wanted—I needed—to tell someone."

"I'm so happy for you."

"I don't have Riley's number—"

"She's here with me. Do you want me to get her?"

"Yes, Grace!" Ludmilla yells through the phone.

Grace laughs and goes to Riley's room. She's sitting on the floor, partway through curling her hair. Grace points at the phone and mouths *Ludmilla*, then kneels next to Riley. "Okay," Grace says. "You're on speaker with both of us."

"I'm pregnant!"

Her enthusiasm makes them both laugh with joy. Grace is delighted for her. Absolutely delighted.

"Oh Ludmilla, that's wonderful," Riley says.

"I want you both at my baby shower. I will have one here and a small one back home in the summer."

"I would be honored," Riley says. "Just send us the date."

"Okay, okay, I have to go," Ludmilla says and hangs up.

The doorbell rings. "I'll grab it," Grace says.

Will is on the stoop holding a bouquet of flowers, a bottle of wine, and a brown bag with a large loaf of bread sticking out the end of it.

"Wow, look at you." Grace nods at all the items he's holding and stands back so that he can come in.

"I got the flowers and the wine on the way home from work. And then my mom told me she made the bread to take. It's too much, isn't it?"

"No, not at all. They'll love it."

"Are you coming to the dinner?" he asks, hope in his voice. This is his first time meeting Riley's family.

"No. But you're going to be great."

"It's just sometimes I get a bit tongue-tied when I'm nervous."

"Tell some stories about being a police officer. I'm sure you'd have a tale or two—like the one where you saved someone's life."

"That's not a story I would ever tell. I had dreams about that morning for years."

"Until you saw me again?"

"Yeah."

"Sorry about that."

"Not blaming you." He shifts the bread so that it's resting in the nook of his arm. "I wanted to thank you, by the way, for inviting me to that New Year's bash."

Grace is taken aback. "That was months ago."

"I know. I've just never done something fun like that for New Year's before, getting all dressed up and stuff. Kind of felt like I was in a movie or something. It was actually the best New Year's Eve I've ever had. Except for that one woman. She was kinda whacked—"

Grace laughs. "She was kinda whacked. I had a great time too."

"And Daniel was cool. A really nice guy."

"Hey, Will," Riley says, coming down the hall.

Grace realizes the last thing she wants right now is to be alone with her thoughts. "If it's not too late, I think I'll come to your parents' house for dinner. I'll run home, grab something to wear, and then swing by—"

"Oh my God, Grace. Don't be ridiculous." Riley buttons up her fitted wool coat and strides back down the hall to her room. "I've got something that would be perfect for you."

"You can bring these flowers," Will says.

"I can't take your flowers," Grace says.

"I would really appreciate it if you did, actually. I was a bit embarrassed with all this stuff."

Riley comes back holding a black T-shirt and a purple wrap skirt.

"I don't think I can pull that off," Grace says.

"I'll be the judge of that." Grace takes the clothes into Riley's room, changing quickly. After a few moments, Riley knocks and opens the door. "Bohemian chic. My work here is done." She waves her hand over her head.

On Saturday, they make crepes and sausages, and Riley takes Grace to her Pilates studio. For dinner they order in Thai food and watch a movie. On Sunday, they sign up for the last two spots in an archery class, which is way more fun than either of them anticipated. Considering the circumstances, it's a very enjoyable weekend, and by Sunday night Grace notices how nice it is to have a companion to do simple tasks with as well as to try new things.

She sits on the couch sipping her tea with her feet in warm wool socks trying to read a book Riley gave her, but her thoughts keep drifting. Tomorrow she will ask Carmen if she can be the point of contact for the Hurleys and explain all the nuances that that job entails. Avoiding Daniel will be much simpler now that he's moving continents, and she's had years of practice. Eric and Beth have always been easy to be around, and she can maintain a surface-level relationship with them.

There. That's it. And then she can cut all ties with him.

But as she lay in bed that night, next to Riley, a wave of sadness comes over her. She had always enjoyed talking to Daniel on the phone, and she would miss that. But not nearly as much as she would miss the real-life, in-person Daniel. Standing there before her. Looking at her. *Seeing* her and accepting her for who she was. Who she is.

To say that she had been looking forward to his visit at Easter would be an understatement. She had thought about him every day. His touch, his voice, the feeling she had when he was near her. Oh, how her heart ached.

It was her own fault. For allowing herself to be so open with him. To be lulled into believing she was special. In all her awkwardness, she never felt judged by him, even at her most vulnerable. And worse, because of all this, she had allowed herself to want more. To want him.

The one thing she knew for certain was that she would not dwell on this. She would not dwell on Daniel Hurley or how, in a roomful of people, she would glance at him, and wherever he was, his eyes would meet hers. Or how his fingers lightly touched her waist when he leaned in to kiss her or how she had urges to run her hand down his arm. *In public.* Of him lying next to her in bed and the comfort his body brought just being beside hers. She would not think of how Beth and Eric had opened their trio, their triangle, to include her. Making her feel so welcome.

On Monday morning Grace drives to work with Riley and puts the pasta salad she made for them in the fridge. The Hurleys are gone. And everything can go back to normal.

"Did you have a nice Easter?" Grace asks Annie.

"I did. But Daniel wasn't himself," she says. "He seemed so happy when he first told me about going to Switzerland, but now I don't know."

"When did he first tell you?"

"It must've been before Christmas."

Before Christmas. "I'm sure he'll be fine, and if he's not, he'll come back. He does what he wants."

Annie looks at her. "You always put me at ease, Grace."

At the end of the day, Grace grabs her work bag and her navy duffel bag, wanting to clear her head by walking home. Twenty minutes later her shoulder is sore under the pull of her strap, and she trudges across her lawn with her head down. Out of the corner of her eye, a figure in dark clothing rises from her porch, and she jumps, startled.

"Sorry," Daniel says as her bag slips from her shoulder to the ground. "I didn't mean to scare you."

He moves to pick it up. "I'm good," she says, not wanting him to come any closer. "I thought you'd left."

"That's what I told Annie." He knew her too well. "Can I talk to you?"

"It's okay. You don't need to explain anything to me. I wish you the best of luck in Switzerland." She forces a tight, closed-mouth smile.

"Did you listen to my message?"

"No." She had deleted it. "I did not."

"Right. Okay. Give me ten minutes. Ten minutes to explain myself. And afterward, if you want me to leave, I will. You have my word."

"If I *want* you to leave? I don't think there will be any doubt about that."

"Is everything all right?" Grace's neighbor comes out of her garage, brandishing her hose like it's a flaming fire torch. Probably would've been more useful the night she accidentally lit her kitchen on fire.

"Yes, thank you, Mary," Grace says.

"It's Mrs. White," Mary says.

"Right. Sorry. Mrs. White."

"Are you sure?"

"I'm sure."

Daniel nods politely at Mrs. White, and she scowls back at him.

"Please, Grace," he says.

Grace wasn't going to invite Daniel into her house, but now that Mrs. White is standing sentinel, she has no choice. She doesn't want to argue with him in front of a neighbor. She will politely respond to his apology or whatever guilt is weighing down on him so that he can get it off his chest. Then he will leave, and they can put this all behind them. "You can come in." Grace digs into her purse for her keys. "But don't get comfortable." She nods at his wheelie suitcase.

"Wouldn't dare." She unlocks her front door, and Daniel follows her in, leaving his suitcase in the entrance. "You want to sit down?" he asks.

"No." She drops her bags and goes to stand on the other side of the kitchen counter so that there's a buffer between them.

"I know you're mad at me—"

She cuts him off right there. "I'm not mad at you, Daniel. You don't owe me anything. You have no obligation whatsoever . . ." She peters off. An expression she has never seen has taken hold of his face. Of confusion and hurt.

"See, that's a problem. That you think these things." He plants his hands on the counter, like a lawyer ready to make his case. "When I came home at Christmas, I had been approached for a job, but things were still under negotiation. I didn't know how they were going to pan out, so I didn't say anything." Pan out with the job or pan out with her? "You said you felt differently with me than you do with anyone else. It's the same for me." She lowers her gaze because it was true and it still is. "Come to Switzerland with me."

Switzerland. *Switzerland.* What?

That didn't make any sense.

She raises her eyes to his, about to question his sanity, but he's staring at her so intensely that she falters. Is he *serious*? He couldn't be. She was expecting him to say *it was nice getting to know you better* or *we'll continue to chat about Annie's medical needs* or *have a good life.*

Now she's annoyed and extremely confused. "Daniel, please don't be ridiculous."

"Ridiculous? I'm not trying to be ridiculous. I want you to come to Switzerland with me."

This was not something that she had steeled herself for. All the air leaves her lungs as she deflates, and she says the only thing she can think of: "I'm not normal." Her voice is quiet.

"Who is?"

"You deserve someone who can give you more of themselves, who doesn't fear such basic interactions." A rush of heat spreads through her, and her body grows warm. Saying these words out in the open and not in a dimly lit bedroom is terrifying.

"I know what I want out of life. I know who I want to spend it with. And it's you," he says simply. "I want you."

She shakes her head. "Disappointment has crushed me. Over and over. I can't allow myself to want things. To hope."

"But you have desires? You want more. Let that fill you up and drive you. You and I get each other. We don't seek out friendships, but we care deeply for those close to us. I can't stop thinking about you, Grace. Why not allow that drift, that pull? See where it takes us."

"To Switzerland?"

"To Switzerland," he says with a nod.

"There are so many things I need to figure out. For starters, this." She pulls out her phone. "*No problem?* You're absolute shit at communication. And you and I are different on so many levels."

"You're right, I could be better at it, but so could you. Don't rule out companionship, someone to do things with or come home to. Take this chance with me. Go through life with me, and you'll never have to face it alone again. Not if you don't want to."

"I've just reconnected with Alex. I can't leave him again."

"I'm not asking you to leave him. Switzerland isn't the moon. I have a gazillion points; you could fly back whenever you wanted."

"Daniel, this all seems so lovely, but you work all the time. I would just be a distraction."

"No, I'm planning to scale way back on work," he says. "No more weekends, no more evenings."

"No more strip clubs?" Grace asks. The thought of Daniel having to work for men like Doug makes her squirm.

"No. No more strip clubs. This line of work is a completely

different clientele. And I have five weeks of vacation."

Daniel lived and breathed work. "I don't want you to change for me."

"Not for you. For me. For us."

Us.

"Our place would have spare bedrooms for guests. Alex, Riley. Whoever you wanted."

Our place.

"If I did go, I could rent out my house," she says. Then, "I'm planning on traveling with Alex this summer."

"Yeah? Where are you guys going?"

"We're still deciding, but it's looking like New Zealand and Australia. I've only ever been to the Caribbean and Mexico on cruises. It's where our foster mother discovered her love for gambling and turned into a monster."

"So cruises are off the table?"

"Absolutely not."

"What do you say, Grace?"

"Would you mind giving me a bit to think about it?"

He nods slowly. "Of course." Then, "Is it your life here that you don't want to leave behind?"

"My life here?" The only thing tethering her to a world here was Riley. Everything else was peripheral.

"Because if that's the case, I could look for a job here."

Was this town even big enough to house the sort of office Daniel would want to work in? "No, Switzerland sounds like a good choice for you." She remembers Annie's words. *He seemed so happy.* "Something obviously drew you to it."

"That's just it, though. When it comes to choosing things in life, I'd take you over everything. Hands down."

She crosses her arms over her chest to guard herself against the intimacy of what he's just said. Annoyance fills her. Anger too. The way he's talking reminds her of the night at the Forester when he opened his room to her. Tossing it out there like a sensible option, like it was no big deal. But this isn't just for a night. This is her life. Her heart. And as it beats against her chest, she realizes just how fragile it is. "Daniel—" she starts, but he cuts her off abruptly as if reading her mind.

"Don't tell me not to say these things, Grace. It's how I feel, and I would regret it if I didn't. I wasn't being totally open with you before, and maybe a bit of that is because of the way I was raised. I've always just taken care of shit, and sometimes I don't communicate properly what my intentions are, but I'm being open with you now." He takes a step around the island and she tenses, so he stops. "I've been so restless my whole life, always moving, because I had this fear that if I stopped, for just a second even, that things would catch up to me. That I wouldn't be able to take care of those I love. But Annie, Eric, and Beth are good now. They're settled. And for the first time, I have breathing room. I feel like *I* can settle into something. And I want to do that with you."

He's looking at her so tenderly, so hopefully. It breaks her heart a little.

She has so many things she wants to say to him, but she doesn't know if she'll have the time to say them, so she asks, "When's your flight?"

He lowers his eyes.

"What?"

"I booked a one-way ticket here. I'm done at my other job. That's why I was so busy . . . well, busier than usual. I was tying up loose ends, and I had an assistant I wanted to make sure I didn't leave hanging. I set her up with a buddy of mine from school. A good guy."

"You booked a one-way?"

He nods. "Yeah. I'm here until the end of April."

Grace does the one thing she has wanted to do from the moment he rose from the porch. She closes the gap between them and wraps her arms around him. He hesitates, whether in surprise or relief she doesn't know, before lifting his arms and holding her close. She feels his hands on her back and melts into him, letting her cheek rest against his chest.

Eighteen

Fourteen Months Later

Grace hands in her green binder with the spring session's curriculum. Eight weeks' worth of English classes. When she got her TESL certificate, she never thought she'd enjoy teaching so much.

"You'll let me know the moment you want to come back?" Nadia says, taking the binder from her.

"I will."

"You're a great teacher, Grace."

"Thanks. You're a great boss."

On her way down the hall, she smiles at the people she passes, promising she'll be back soon, though she's not sure she will be.

It's a warm day in June, and after stopping at the outdoor market, she takes a moment to rest her feet, gazing up at the mountains as she sits on a bench. She lowers her eyes to the lake and picks up her basket, continuing the short walk home, her long skirt rippling against her legs in the breeze.

She unlocks the door to her house, puts the basket on a chair, and carefully bends to unclip her sandals. She puts the fresh fruit, cheese, and baguette away and arranges the flowers from her favorite vendor into a vase. Placing them on a deep wooden windowsill that overlooks the lake, she pauses and picks up the photo from the night at the gala. The one of her and Daniel dancing with Riley just off to the side. She sets it back down, next to the photo of her and Alex in New Zealand. Every time she sees them, it makes her smile. Then she checks the cushions and blankets.

"It's perfect," Daniel says, coming up behind her. "Everything is perfect. The housekeeper was in this morning and spruced up the whole place." He wraps his arms around her and holds the very large bump that is her stomach.

She leans back against him, the feel of him so familiar to her now, and puts her hand on his. "I can't wait to meet her," she says. "I never thought I'd be a mother." She turns to face him. "When I was in grade twelve, Jackson sat down next to me in English. He invited Alex and me to his house for a swim, so casually. That's the type of parent I want to be. The one whose kid can invite their friends over without even thinking about it."

He holds her gaze and nods. "Okay," he says.

"I love you so much," she says.

He presses a kiss to her forehead and says, "I adore you."

There's a quick knock, and the door opens.

Riley and Lettie come in first, each carrying a duffel bag. Riley's bump is just starting to show through her blue jumpsuit. Grace hugs them both and goes to show them to their rooms.

"Riley, you and Will are in here." Grace opens the door to Riley's room. "And, Lettie, I wasn't sure if you and Alex were sharing? So I can either put you in here and have him on the pullout or—"

"Oh. Um." Lettie glances down shyly. "We're sharing, if that's all right?"

"Yeah, that's perfect. Then you're both in here."

Will wheels a large suitcase into the entrance but leaves it to use the bathroom. Alex's bag is by far the biggest, as he's staying for most of the summer. He notices Daniel standing by the window with his hands resting on his hips.

"Hey, Daniel," Alex says, approaching him.

Daniel turns. "Alex." He holds out his hand. "How are you?"

"I'm good," he says, taking it. Then, "I hope it's all right that Grace invited me to stay until I go back for preseason training, what with the baby coming and all. I don't want to get in your way."

Daniel shakes his head. "You're not in the way at all. She's been looking forward to this for months, and I'm happy you're here. You're always welcome wherever we are. I hope you know that."

"I appreciate that."

"Al," Grace says, coming back down the hall toward him.

"Grace."

She hugs him, holding him close for a long moment. Pulling away, she says, "How was the flight?"

"Not nearly as comfortable as taking the bus."

She smiles.

www.ingramcontent.com/pod-product-compliance
Lightning Source LLC
Chambersburg PA
CBHW032158190726
48289CB00007BA/2289